"Howalt brings humanity back to the world of science fiction, substituting the glamour of traditional space-age machinery for the intricately developed individuals who inhabit this fantastic, surreal world. Howalt's provocative and visual prose exposes the multifaceted layers of the human—and non-human—mind with Luca, Teo, Renn, and Mender, four protagonists with whom we empathize and champion. Ladies and gentlemen, like King's *The Dark Tower* before it, this is sci-fi done right!"

- Dean Moses, author of *A Stalled Ox*

"Carefully paced and breathtakingly beautiful, *We Lost the Sky* is a post-apocalyptic tale which defies expectation in all the right places and will leave you feeling changed in ways you can't explain. Howalt is not afraid to delve into deep and meaningful issues such as inequality, poverty, and the willful ignorance to scientific fact – issues which many can no doubt relate to. Yet, Howalt unpacks these issues with delicate subtlety. The characters, world, themes and morals will stay with you long after you've finished reading."

- Kathy Joy, author of *Last One to the Bridge*

"*We Lost the Sky* is an engaging story of post-collapse rebuilding. Howalt explores future Italy with a variety of characters, finding societal faults and moments of human connection that even an exploding moon couldn't shift."

- Zach Bartlett, author of *To Another Abyss!*

"Marie Howalt offers a light at the end of the dystopian tunnel with *We Lost the Sky*. The world as we know it has ended and the city of Florence is domed, though not under the grandeur of cathedrals. Think FEMA camps. As in Tarkovsky's film *Stalker* and McCarthy's novel *The Road*, folks scrounge and divide. But Howalt brings hope through the intertwining stories of androids, cryogenics survivors, nomads, and the first fledglings of a resistance."

- Pam Jones, author of *Andermatt County*, *The Biggest Little Bird*, and *Ivy Day*

"*We Lost the Sky* asks the question of our values when stripped of all amenities and facing the end of worlds. It's a fascinating read and a great story to have fun while stopping to think after each event. From questioning the sentiency of artificial intelligence to chilling mirrors of the modern economic divide. We get glimpses of how the rich aren't always competent, and the skilled and smart aren't always wealthy. At the worst of times, the story is adventurous, fun, and poignant. At the best, Howalt's writing can fight off even the apocalypse. In this case, it does."

- Aden Ng, author of *The Chronicles of Tearha Series*, reviewer at AdenNg.com

WE LOST THE SKY

Marie Howalt

WE LOST THE SKY

MARIE HOWALT

SPACEBOY BOOKS

Denver, Colorado

Published in the United States by:
Spaceboy Books LLC
1627 Vine Street
Denver, CO 80206
www.readspaceboy.com

First printed February 2019

ISBN: 978-0-9997862-6-0

For Karen
who believed from the beginning

Prologue:
Luca

Something was wrong. Very, very wrong.

He was suffocating.

A thick, clear liquid enveloped him completely. It was in his ears and nose and mouth trying to gasp in nonexistent air. It was in his eyes and pressed against him, making his movements lethargic as he attempted to propel himself to the surface. His hands hit a solid barrier. He pushed. Pounded. Nothing happened.

Bubbles escaped his nostrils and mouth, and the liquid constrained him as he found himself enclosed on all sides. His heart was trying to escape his ribcage. He needed to breathe. He needed to breathe *now*.

The light changed. Something moved. Close to him. In slow-motion, he smashed his fists against the barrier, hoping to attract attention.

Then there was no more energy. Every muscle in his body convulsed, refused to take orders, and everything around him began to fade rapidly to darkness.

The world exploded. Sound and light crashed into him, a

thousand needles penetrated every bit of his body as he sucked in air. He was on his hands and knees, retching and shaking so violently that he slipped and crashed to the floor, biting his tongue, landing with his face in the sticky substance pooling around him

A voice shouted next to him. He couldn't understand it. He didn't care. His veins were on fire and he was trembling and sweating and freezing and retching again, throwing up transparent slime with specks of red. The vomit began to float away from him, and a thinner liquid crept over his whitish-blue fingers. Water?

More shouting. Then something, someone, got hold of his shoulders. "You will be all right."

He recognized the words and the voice. He blinked and attempted to wipe his eyes, struggling to make sense of everything. Of anything.

Another voice called out in the distance.

"Not any of them?" asked the voice close to him. Though he wasn't sure it was talking to him. Then, "We need to leave, Luca."

That was him. He was Luca. With that realization came an onslaught of memories. They marched in an assault on his mind until he understood their meaning. "Mom..." he rasped. "Dad... Where..."

"Not now," said the voice. "Put your arms around my neck. I'll carry you upstairs."

"Nanny," he whispered, "where is Leo and..."

His arms were draped uselessly around Nanny's neck and flopped back down. She scooped him up instead, water cascading off his naked skin.

"The water is rising rapidly," said the other voice, approaching.

"Can we take their bodies..." began Nanny.

"I'll try. Get him to safety."

Luca's head lolled to the side. He tried to focus on the other figure, but the movement as Nanny turned created a blur around them. "Wait," he croaked. "What..."

She pressed him tighter against her body. "Shh. You will be all right," she said again.

"Stop!" he managed. This wasn't the way it was supposed to be, was it? Yes, they had told him he would feel disoriented, that it would take a few minutes for him to recall everything. That he would have no sense of the time that elapsed and would feel uncomfortable at first. But uncomfortable did not even begin to cover how wet and cold and gooey his body felt, how much breathing stung his lungs, how weak and useless he was. Yet, he was beginning to realize that his own condition wasn't the worst part.

The floor was flooded. There had only been a little water a moment before, but it was rising rapidly. Luca's eyes darted around the room, searching... Part of the ceiling was gone, leaving a gaping hole above, and a mound of debris and rubble below. Over there was the pod. It hadn't opened like it was supposed to. Instead, one side had been crushed and shards were floating in the water around it. The other pods were... "No," he moaned.

"We need to..." began Nanny.

Luca twisted out of her grip. He landed on his side in the water, rolled and stumbled to his feet. He took one step towards the tall figure hunched over a shape in the water that looked as pale as Luca. A cloud of dark hair spread out from the head. Two more shapes floated next to it, like strange islands of frozen flesh, unmoving, undisturbed by the sound of gushing water and the moaning of the walls. Luca's legs gave out. His face broke the surface of the water. Part of his mind screamed for him to get up. The other part was begging him not to.

Nanny pulled him up once more.

"...before it collapses!" shouted the other voice.

"Yes," replied Nanny and picked up Luca, gently, but with no room for negotiation. Like she had done when he was a kid and didn't want to go to bed or when he was insisting on fighting with Leo although he knew Leo was older and stronger.

"No..." Luca repeated, but he didn't struggle anymore.

This was not how it was supposed to go.

Not at all.

1:
Renn

Moon's Road was laid out across the sky with its thousands of pinprick lights. It was a clear night, and Renn climbed to the highest point he could find to get a better view. Below the platform under his feet, the dead city lay sprawled like a fallen, shattered rock giant. The toughest of plants managed to find a home and spread out in green splotches of vines and leaves, but jagged shapes revealed the crumbled buildings underneath. To his right, a trail cut straight through the city, worn by years of usage. Animals and people would wander it in endless search of food and shelter.

Renn's gaze followed the trail out of the city where it almost disappeared; first into an oasis of richer vegetation shielded from storms by the ruins and bearing the blessing of a small lake. Beyond that stretch of green was a vast wasteland of barren ground where the trail had been dissolved in its losing battle against the elements. In the far distance rose mountains that would provide another sanctuary of plants and water.

He studied the expanse for any sign of humans. And there, so far away that he had to squint to be certain, was a flicker of light. A fire. He smiled. The Covey followed the path as he expected, and he should be able to catch up over the next few days. He was young and despite the danger of traveling alone, the speed was greater. They had a child, a pregnant woman, and an old man with them and a cart to pull along unless it had been lost to the dust storm.

Renn retreated from the platform through a paneless window to the shelter of the building. He moved carefully to keep his cloak and his long hair from catching on the rusty spikes framing the opening. It was too dark to risk climbing down the treacherous stairs, so he settled for the night in the corner furthest from the window, using his backpack to shield him from cold air blowing in. The lower floors smelled of animals, but up here, there was only the scent of dust and mold.

He lay for a while, not fully awake, but in a state he had trained himself to enter whenever it was his turn to stay vigilant for the Covey. He did not think. He merely was. All senses were keen, observing as well as one could in the darkness. Sounds, smells, movements... He was alert to everything and ready to act if necessary. Tonight there was nothing. He was alone in the tower. Every night sound was coming from outside and far below, save the quiet wail of the wind. He allowed himself to go to sleep.

The morning was already turning grey when Renn woke up. He rummaged in his bag for his flask and drank. Then he unwrapped a piece of meat from a bundle of leaves. It was dry and salty, but that was preferable to alive with maggots. Still, he would need more water and more food soon. Regardless of the hurry he was in to catch up to his eight travel companions, he wouldn't last long on an empty stomach.

As he descended the stairs, the world around Renn grew brighter. And smellier. On the lower floors, something had lived and possibly died. Rats maybe. Probably. Wolves and scarvhes didn't nest inside houses like that.

For a moment, Renn stood outside the building, getting his bearings back. Then he started north.

The space between the towering giants was so big here that it was hard to imagine a world with such an amount of people in it that roads of this magnitude were necessary. More than ten adults would be able to hold hands, stretch out their arms and stroll through this part of the city. It didn't matter how many times he traversed this or other long-dead cities. Renn still marveled; tried to imagine that world as if he could conjure up images of a time when people lived here by looking at the relics scattered around him. But it was nearly impossible. And, he reminded himself, irrelevant. A long-gone past he had never known would not help him now and was of no consequence to the future stretching out ahead of him.

His ancestors were only relevant when he was scavenging their cities. Then it made sense to guess where the forgotten people would hide items that could still be used. He had heard stories of wanderers finding food in sealed containers that could still be eaten, but the tales were handed down through generations and no one still believed they could find such bounty. The most useful thing Renn had ever discovered was a knife hidden inside a scabbard. The scabbard fell apart the moment he touched it, but the handle was undamaged and the blade not rusty at all. It didn't look like metal, but a hard, white material with an edge that could be whetted to the same sharpness as metal. He still had it, tucked away safely in his bag.

The only other treasure he had found was a box full of beads. They weren't as immediately useful as the knife, but they were decorative. He wore a few in his hair, interwoven in long pleats that were now tucked back with a piece of string. The rest of them hung on a necklace under his tunic. Or rather, what was left of them. The real benefit was that beads were usually in high demand when he bargained with the stagnants who never ventured far away from whatever ruin they had chosen as their home. As nicely crafted and beautiful as the beads were, Renn was more than happy to trade them for food and sometimes shelter, or even water during dry periods.

The broad road was intersected by another, almost identical in size and straightness and the derelict buildings were spaced out by the crossroads giving Renn a good view of his surroundings. Even without a map or a wayfinder, it should not be hard to figure out which direction his Covey had chosen. He shifted the weight of his bag on his shoulders and made his way to the corner of the closest building. As he searched for a message from his own Covey or someone else, he found two horizontal, parallel lines carved into the wall. At the end of them were arrows in opposite directions. They looked too old to have been made by his Covey, but they confirmed Renn's conviction that this was the trail of wanderers and that it went through the city and into the wasteland in both directions.

A sudden gust of wind whistled as it weaved between the buildings and sang in their hollow eyes and gaping mouths. Perhaps the wind heralded a storm, but it may as well be an empty threat or days away. As dangerous as it would be to get caught in the middle of a storm with no shelter in sight, Renn knew he could not stay here and wait for a thunderstorm or a dust storm that may or may not be headed his way.

He carried on, taking measured strides and using his staff as a walking stick to preserve his energy. Like this, he could go on for hours without a break. He did not make it more than a hundred paces, however, before he stopped once more. His hands gripped tighter around the staff. In a crevice between two half-collapsed walls with no buildings attached to them, there was something... Something man-shaped.

Renn narrowed his eyes and waited. The figure was still. Too still to be alive? He crept closer. "Hello?"

No reply. The shape appeared to be crushed beneath a

slab of one of the walls. What Renn could make out looked like legs and a lower torso sticking out from under the debris, but as he cautiously stepped closer, he discovered that it was not a human being after all. What he had taken for limbs was a weird mass of bones that looked like metal and a tangle of strings sprawled out like a parody of intestines.

Renn studied the shape. No, definitely not human. But not an animal, either, and not part of the buildings around it. Could it be an Other? He had never seen one before, had never really understood why they were called that. Animals had names, given to them by humans to define what kind they were. Rats, cockroaches, wolves, scarvhes, lizards, snakes. Even birds had names although they were few and far between. But Others were just Others. A long time ago Renn's mother explained that once there had been as many of them as humans. They were as different as an ant and a man, but they all served a purpose. When Renn asked where they were now, his mother told him that most of them were dead, but some still wandered the world, aimless and mad with grief because they had been servants of Moon.

Renn shook himself. This one certainly wasn't wandering anywhere. Its head probably lay squashed beneath the rubble, and no living thing could survive without a head. He considered prodding the figure with his staff, but it seemed disrespectful. Instead he bent down to examine it closer, curiosity triumphing over caution. One hand, because it definitely was a hand, stuck out at a strange angle. There was no skin or muscle. Just those odd strings of various sizes and the dusty, grey skeleton. Would stagnants pay for one of those little finger bones? Could the string be used as a cord for a necklace? Renn was reaching out, but stopped himself. He would not do that to a human skeleton. He would tear the hide off an animal or pry out its teeth if they could be of any use or value. But this... Renn had no idea how to categorize an Other and therefore no idea what respect its

9

remains demanded.

He tore his gaze away from the motionless figure, turned around and continued towards the trail.

2:
Renn

Renn had not expected the Covey to still be here, but there was something off-putting about the abandoned campsite with its charred remains. He had been certain that it was his Covey as he stared at the flickering light from the tower in the dead city and aimed for this spot for the past two days. Now that he was here, he would have to find a new point of orientation to go by. If they expected him to follow, they may have left him a sign. But it was growing dark, and he decided to stay for the night. The few rocks and trees provided little shelter, but would have to do. It had for them.

Renn put down his backpack and stretched, then dug out his knife from the bag and went to the nearby trees. There were a few dry twigs and leaves on the ground, but they would only work as kindling. Gathering his findings in his arms, he went a little further. He did not want to kill any of the precious trees, but they could spare a branch or two for his fire.

A shape on the other side of the trees caught his eye. It was a rock. But there was something unnatural about it, as if it had been placed there purposefully. When he approached, he could see a mound of fresh soil around it, roughly the length and width of a person. He kneeled. It was new. Too new to be anyone but one of the members of his Covey lying here.

"May Moon guide you," he muttered and touched the tombstone. Who was it? Not the child, judging from the size. A reasonable guess was the elderly man, but there were plenty of deaths to be had for anyone in this world. Renn wouldn't know until he found the remaining seven. He stayed a moment out of respect, but it was hard to grieve when he didn't know for whom.

He stood up again. Good thing they had put a stone on the tomb. He would have done it otherwise, but he may not have noticed the grave without one, and he would rather not be haunted by a spiritless body.

When he could carry no more, Renn returned to the darkened patch of ground and built a fire of his own. It was nearly dark now, and he welcomed the glow of the flames as wood began to crackle.

The next morning, Renn examined the site more thoroughly and found a sign scratched into the ground by a wanderer's staff. This one was new enough to have been left for him. It was another set of parallel lines, but there was only an arrow at one end. It pointed to the northeast. Surveying the expanse in that direction, he thought he could make out the traces of a path leading towards a rough silhouette of another fallen bastion of the past.

After a few hours of walking, Renn could not deny the fact that the wind was picking up. He pulled the hood of his cloak low over his eyes, and it immediately flapped back. He caught it and held it with one hand as he awkwardly covered his nose and mouth with his scarf with the other, effectively using it to keep the hood in place. He had fervently hoped that the storm would change direction, wait until he was out of the wasteland or abate before it really started, but now he knew neither would happen.

According to the legends, there were trees and flowers and vegetables growing everywhere once. There was no sand. But when Moon dropped her lantern, the elements became so distressed that they fought each other. That's why the sand blew in. Renn always felt there was a wrongness to the stories. Not lies, necessarily, but an uncanny wrongness. Why had Moon abandoned them so all humans had to struggle?

Right now, he certainly was struggling. The wind whipped every tiny bit of exposed skin and Renn dug his staff into the ground with each step, anchoring himself for a moment before moving on.

He needed to keep calm. Yes, the storm could kill him or at the very least give him stone lungs, but panic would lighten its task considerably. This was not the first time he would be caught outside during a storm. But it was the first time he was alone. Once, his Covey managed to get to an outcrop of rocky hills to shield them. On another occasion they were forced to lie flat on the ground, pinning down the canvas of a tent around them with their hands and feet and bags, staying inside the small space for hours with so little air and so much dust that Renn would almost rather have been outside. Almost.

Renn quickly weighed the time it would take him to get his blankets unrolled and get under them against the distance to the ruins of the city nearby. He weighed the holes of the threadbare fabric against the dangers of unknown ruins.

The ruins won. Renn strode on and stumbled against the hissing of the sand and the tearing of the wind. His eyes watered, his heart pounded, but he could not allow himself to breathe in more than strictly necessary. The air became so dense with sand and dirt that he couldn't tell if he were still going the right way. He clenched his teeth. No use doubting his decision. If he had made the wrong one, he would die. It was as simple as that.

A shape suddenly loomed in front of him, massive enough to block some of the wind. Renn reached out and felt a solid wall. He pressed himself against it. But he needed more shelter than this. He groped along the wall for an opening. Sweat trickled down between his shoulder blades and mixed with dirt in his face. Cracks and jagged edges scraped his hand. And then there was nothing. His hand thrust into open space.

Renn stopped. It was not a doorway. It was a window. He tossed his staff into the hole and heard it land, barely audible over the screaming wind. A moment later, he followed, pushed himself and the backpack through and landed heavily. His knees buckled under him. But the air he sucked in was clear here. He was safe.

He lay on the floor, awkwardly sprawled on top of the staff and the backpack, his chest rising and falling as he gulped in hungry mouthfuls of air. Air that smelled and tasted like dust and mold, but not sand.

The storm was raging, howling for his life outside, whirling sand through the window above him. He would have to move away from the opening soon. The sweat on his back began to grow cold. The palm of one of his hands was bloody from running over the rough wall, but it was already drying. He needed water... No, he would drink after he moved. He did not want to risk sand blowing into the flask.

So he got to his feet, trembling, picked up the staff and began to walk away from the window and into an empty, grey room. The far corner would do for now. He made it halfway before a noise as angry and intense as the wind escaped the ground beneath his feet. It was a dry, cracking sound, like branches snapping or stones violently scraping against each other.

Renn stopped. Cracks were spreading out in the surface of the floor around his feet. His breath caught in his throat. The muscles of his legs tensed, but he could not run from this. Pushing off from the floor may cause it to break entirely. So he slowly got on his knees first, then all the way down to lie flat on his stomach. This way, his weight would be spread out.

The floor groaned. Renn began to claw across the rough surface. He needed to get to the other wall. The principles of buildings must be similar to the principles of weight distribution in backpacks. The closer to the back heavy objects were placed, the less weight to pull at the body. He hoped he was right.

Boots scraped across the floor, the staff dragged through the sand and dust. Bloody hand prints on the grey surface. A cough stuck in his throat because who knew what a sudden movement would do to the floor. He pushed himself forward painstakingly slowly.

Only a little further. A line appeared just before his eyes, preceding terrible sound, a thunderclap all around him. The floor gave in. Renn thrust himself forward, managed to get a hold of an edge of the floor as parts of it broke off and hurtled downwards in a dark cloud. His feet found only empty air. How far down? Probably a story or more. He'd survive the fall if it were only one, unless he was crushed by falling chunks of floor. For a moment, he hung, still, but he could not hold on forever. He made one last effort to heave himself back up.

The rest of the floor gave out. Renn fell into the darkness below.

3:
Teo

Teo forced her gaze to stay steady on the horizon above the ridge of the hills. The posture made her spine straight and her chin held high. Her borrowed uniform was tight across her chest and hips. The cap, bulging awkwardly because of the bundle of hair under it, was drawn so far down that it grazed her eyebrows.

Behind her, one of the spotters was calling out to the assembled group of hopeful laymen, singling out the lucky ones.

"All good?" Arsenio murmured in her ear.

Teo checked herself before she jumped. Although he was a large man with heavy boots, she had not heard him walk up to the truck and stand beside her. "All good," she managed to reply, not looking at him. It *was* all good. She had made it past the first hurdle. They were outside the domes and outside the wall. If she lowered her eyes a little, she could see the shacks clinging to the hillside and the derelict buildings with boarded-up windows, mysteries in their elaborate construction to their occupants.

Arsenio nodded once. He was nervous too. Teo could

hear it. Not in his voice, but it hid in his breath as he exhaled. Not quite trembling, but almost. She couldn't blame him. Bringing her with them was a risk. Not the sort of risk that caused this kind of trip to be forbidden. It had nothing to do with what was out there. No, they were taking the risk of doing this without permission.

Arsenio began to circle the vehicle once more, his hand resting lightly on the gun. As if he needed the emphasis to radiate authority.

"No more. We only have room for three. Thank you!" Vanni called out.

The truck dipped slightly as the rear gate opened and the three laymen climbed in along with Arsenio and Vanni. The two spotters sat down on the bench on each side of Teo and the three slummers stepped over the equipment on the floor and scuttled to the bench opposite.

Behind them, someone yelled.

"Watch it!" Arsenio shouted, gruffly.

Vanni slapped the side of the driver's cabin with the palm of his hand. The truck barked to life and began to move.

Teo shifted her gaze to the people around her. Surely that was all right now. Vanni was leaning back with his eyes half closed against the sharp sun overhead. A faint stubble was visible on his chin in this light, and the curly locks on his forehead seemed almost auburn. Vanni's goggles were dangling on their leather strap around his neck, and his hands were resting on his thighs. He looked like he had done this a thousand times before. Obviously he hadn't. But probably fifty or a hundred. This was what he'd always wanted. Teo almost smiled. They'd played arbiters and sentries and technies, the two of them, and Alberta and Leonardo. It had been fun. Until Leonardo observed that Teo should be playing the part of a lady who needed saving a lot. She'd told him he could play the part of the gentleman who needed saving a lot. They all wanted to be the hero, at least until Alberta became more interested in playing games that had to do with dresses and makeup. In the end, only the bright and amiable Vanni Alesi earned a sentry uniform, and one with the surveyor unit's recognizable spyglass embroidered on the breast pocket, at that.

The truck lurched and shook. Teo grabbed hold of the railing behind her to keep herself steady. Vanni and Arsenio just followed the movements of the vehicle and seemed oblivious to the discomfort. Teo caught Arsenio glancing at her again. She smiled.

One of the laymen cried out in surprise and frantically tried to find something to hold on to. The others attempted to brace themselves, but one of them slipped from his seat and had to clamber back up. From where she was sitting, Teo could smell a potently acrid mixture of dirt and sweat and bad breath, due to either rotten teeth or health problems caused by dust storms. A familiar frustration began to gnaw at her, but she willed it away. Now was hardly the time for politics or charity.

The truck climbed and climbed, at one point veering to avoid a huge boulder on the road. Once this path had been one of the city's main arteries, Teo knew from studying ancient maps, supplying the people in it with fresh goods, visitors from other cities, and people who lived outside and worked in the city, a bit like the laymen. Now, despite being used frequently by the spotters, the road was covered with dust and debris in places and in dire need of repairs that no one was likely to undertake.

"How far are we going?" one of the laymen, the one who stayed calm during the rough trip, asked.

"Depends on what we find," Vanni replied, almost as if he were speaking to an equal. "Once we get out of the valley, we'll all look out for potential sites. The storm might have uncovered something we haven't noticed before."

Teo looked back the way they had come. Florence was

sprawled below, a strange sanctuary of domes behind the wall encircling the inner city. Both were for protection, but Teo rather suspected only the domes were efficient against the weather. The wall was efficient against the people clinging to the city, for protection, for work, for any scraps the city dwellers saw fit to hand out. She wanted to ask why they were there, but she knew the answer. It was better than the alternative.

Teo caught a glimpse of the cathedral's curved roof inside the biggest of the translucent domes, a dome within a dome, before she tore her gaze away from the city and looked ahead instead. The truck was coming up on flat ground now and she had her first real glimpse of the world outside.

"Close your mouth," Arsenio whispered.

Teo complied. She knew she was supposed to act like a seasoned sentry, but how? How, when the scattered clouds were drifting across the sky so far up and when sunlight sifted through the air, particles from the recent storm dancing and sparkling? How, when the earth stretched out as a flat expanse with a jagged line of mountains like a reading on a seismograph on the horizon and trees and bushes struggled against all odds to keep hold of the soil; and everything looked so pure that they may be the first humans to happen upon this place?

This was what she was really out here for. Searching for tech, seeing the city from a distance, those were interesting side effects. But it was the horizon she wanted to see. The world she had only heard of. And now that she was here, it felt weird that she had waited until she was more than a quarter of a century old to see this.

Florence was a sanctuary. An oasis. Legend had it there were once more of its kind, but they had been lost long ago and were so far away that no one had ever even caught a glimpse of their carcasses. Florence was the ark. It was a place for the survivors, the purest and the best of humanity, to live when everything and everyone else were destroyed by the fall. There was nothing to be gained by venturing outside. Apart from salvaged goods, of course, that were meant to be found. Only spotters, officers of the surveyor unit with proper training and equipment to brave the elements, ever left the safety of the domed city in the valley.

Teo squinted against the sun. This wasn't at all the grey expanse of nothingness that she had been made to believe. It was stunning. It was, in its own way, breathtakingly beautiful. It was... She searched for the right word and landed on 'raw'. Yes, that was it. Untouched by human hands for hundreds of years.

Vanni pulled the map out from its tube and unrolled it. Teo leaned over to better see. It consisted of two layers. The base layer was the map itself. It showed Florence in the center, roads that may be taken out of it and onward into the surrounding area. It showed mountains, bodies of water, woodland and even ruins of other cities and something labeled 'primitive settlements'. The layer on top of the map was transparent and had notes scribbled on it, a lot of them in Vanni's handwriting. They indicated sites of findings and were added to the map as the spotters found new resources, obstacles to the truck and landmarks to navigate by. Some notes had been crossed out again, possibly because dust storms have covered the locations or because they held no more value.

"Anything?" Vanni asked.

Arsenio had turned around to kneel on the bench and was using a set of binoculars to scout for potentially interesting sites. "Not... yet," he replied, too focused on keeping his balance in the truck and looking through the magnifying lenses to say much else.

Teo turned around to gaze in the same direction. The road stretched on ahead, obscured in places by dirt and rubble. On their left was a group of abandoned buildings, a ghost town of metal and concrete skeletons overgrown with vines crawling up the walls and weeds stubbornly spreading out from every little crack they could find. Teo turned back to look over the heads of the laymen and to the left of the vehicle. A long stretch of flat, empty landscape lay between them and the mountains. A glance at the map told her that the range was called the Apennines.

"We are around here," Vanni said and pointed to the map.

They were going in the direction of an abandoned city called Pistoia. On the way, another road intersected the one they were currently on. "What's Capello?" she asked, tracing the road.

Vanni made a non-committal sort of sound. "It's just a name," he said.

Well, obviously. Teo opened her mouth to ask what that was supposed to mean when Arsenio called out, "There!"

They all squinted and shaded their eyes with their hands to make out what he had found. There was a lump on the horizon, but it could be anything from this distance.

Arsenio banged the palm of his hand on the truck's cabin. "Right as soon as you can!" he shouted over the roar of the engine.

Without warning, the driver turned off the road. Teo was almost thrown across Vanni's lap, and the laymen were jolted mercilessly.

"What are we looking at?" Vanni asked, nonplussed.

"It looks like a hangar. If we're lucky, it'll have fuel and more vehicles," Arsenio replied.

It was still a lump to the rest of them, but they didn't have the advantage of Arsenio's binoculars or the ridiculously good eyesight that made him one of the best spotters. Teo sometimes teased him by saying that he could only see so far because he was tall. On these occasions, he would make a comment about her being short, although Teo was inclined to believe she was a fairly average person when it came to looks.

After a few hundred meters, the truck stopped, and the engine died. "You're on your own from here," the driver told them as he leaned out of the side window. "I'll be waiting."

"All right, you heard the man," Arsenio said and clapped his hands. "Get a move on."

Vanni instructed the laymen to take the heavy bags of digging equipment on the floor, rolled up the map and jumped from the truck.

As she landed on the ground in a cloud of dust, Teo saw why they had not been able to continue by truck. It wasn't only that the landscape was getting increasingly rocky. They had stopped a few paces away from a ravine cutting across the landscape in a zigzag line. It was too wide for them to jump across and so deep that they would break their necks if they tried and failed.

"It's not on the map," Vanni said. "Must have happened in the quake a few weeks back."

"Get the board out from under the seats," Arsenio told the laymen, and they dutifully pulled out a long sheet of metal and dragged it to the edge of the gorge.

"A bridge?" Teo asked. She also wanted to ask if it were safe, but although only the laymen and the driver didn't know about her identity, she didn't want her ignorance to shine.

Arsenio and Vanni pulled the metal slab upright, nudged it closer to the edge and pushed it so it fell across the chasm.

"Who wants the honour?" Vanni asked, making a sweeping gesture from his companions to the bridge.

"I'll go first," Teo said. She didn't particularly want to, but she'd come across like a rookie several times already. Besides, it was perfectly safe. They wouldn't let her go otherwise. Not only were they her friends, but they would also have to tell her father that they'd brought his only daughter outside the city and watched her plummet to her death. And possibly apart from Vanni, she was the lightest of them all. So she stepped onto the slab and walked across the ravine, holding her arms out for balance and making sure to glance straight ahead.

Once on the other side, she studied the others as they crossed. Arsenio was first, striding across the gulf like he did everything else, purposefully and confidently. Next came the laymen. They balanced carefully under the load they were carrying. One of them stumbled slightly, and Teo felt her breath catch in her throat. But they made it. Vanni brought up the rear. He had never been good with heights, but Teo doubted the others noticed his hesitation.

The party continued across the rocky ground. Now that they were traversing it on foot, the whole place appeared to be even larger than it had from the truck. Perhaps because there was so little to put it into perspective. The landscape was void of vegetation except for clumps of trees and bushes scattered on the ground at intervals.

4:
Teo

If Teo had ever thought the spaces between the domes of Florence were dry, it was nothing compared to the dusty, rocky plains. The party had good boots, even if Teo's were a size too big, and they had caps and scarves to shade their eyes and keep out the dust. She, Arsenio and Vanni also had goggles and canteens with water, and they had a truck waiting for them not too far away. Still, Teo felt exposed and naked and so incredibly tiny in this vast, merciless landscape. The sun glared down at them, and their feet stirred up dust that made her cough more than once. And yet, there were nomadic tribes who wandered for days or weeks at a time as they migrated according to the seasons or where there was food to be had. It had always seemed strange to her, but now a sense of awe was creeping into her view of them as well.

After a little while, the group reached their goal. It was a big hangar like Arsenio had suggested, brownish red with rust in places. One end of it was practically gone, and dust and debris had blown into the hangar's maw. It was dark inside.

"We go in teams of two," Arsenio instructed while he

and Vanni retrieved the necessary equipment from the laymen's bags. "Move carefully. There may be rats or other pests in there. Call out if you find something that could be of value. Fuel tanks are the most important things. Tech of any kind that looks salvageable. Each team brings a torch."

Vanni handed out electrical torches to the others and demonstrated how the switch worked in case the laymen were not familiar with the contraptions.

"Teo, you're with Vanni. You two go together. And I'm with you," Arsenio decided, pointing at the last layman. He hadn't even bothered to learn their names. Not that it was strictly necessary. They were just day laborers. Still, Teo felt slightly embarrassed that she hadn't thought of it before now. She flicked on her torch and shone it at the gaping cavity as Arsenio began to move.

"Wait!" Teo said and reached out to keep him from entering.

"What?" he asked.

Teo pointed the light beam at the ground. "Footprints," she said. "Someone else must have been here recently, or the dust would have covered them."

"Hmph," Arsenio said and squatted, studying the prints. He looked back the way they had come.

"Should we just head back, then?" asked Vanni.

"No!" snapped Arsenio.

"Why?" Teo said, frowning. "Do you think... they're still in there?" she added in a whisper.

"No," Vanni said. "We would probably have seen his vehicle if he were still here... Besides, these prints point the other way. He left again."

"He?" echoed Teo. Yes, judging from the size of the oddly detailed prints, it was likely to be a man. Still, there was something in her friends' voices that suggested they were referring to a specific person.

"Let's go in and see if anything is left," Arsenio said and stood up again. He gestured for the laymen to go with him. "Come on. We aren't paying you to stand around out here," he added.

Vanni shrugged and smiled at Teo as if to apologize for Arsenio's behavior.

The torch only lit up the immediate surroundings in the dim interior. There was something dreamlike about wandering into that space, catching glimpses of shapes along the walls and dividing the huge room into smaller sections according to the torches' reach. Whoever had been here before them had left a set of footprints on the dusty floor, and Teo and Vanni appeared to be following, literally, in their footsteps. The two other torches sometimes showed where the other parties were, like enormous glowbeetles performing an erratic dance in the air.

Most of the geometrical shapes in the hangar turned out to be racks along the walls. The majority of the shelves were empty and, judging from the layer of undisturbed dust, had been for a long time. At intervals, something sat on one of the shelves, and Vanni and Teo stopped to examine the items.

"I don't know what this is," Vanni muttered as he turned a rusty contraption over in his hands.

"I think some of the parts are missing," Teo replied, wishing she could be more precise, more professional, but no one had ever brought an object like it to her worktable before. There were little levers sticking out that seemed like they ought to have been connected to something else.

"Probably. It's like this most of the time," Vanni replied. His voice was calmer now that they were alone and far away from the city. "I hope you aren't too disappointed."

Teo shook her head. "Of course not. As interesting as it would be to find something valuable, that's not the reason I wanted to go with you."

"No... I know," Vanni said, slowly.

"But?"

"No buts." He flashed her a smile as she ran the light beam over him. As a result, his expression looked eerie rather than friendly. "I'm... glad you asked to come," he added.

Teo let the beam linger. It wasn't only her company he was fond of. There had to be something else behind that statement. "It feels wrong never to venture outside the domes and the wall," she said, hoping it was the right answer.

"What would happen if councilman Terzi found out?" Vanni asked as they began to move on, studying the useless leftovers on the shelves and, occasionally, on the floor.

"I'm an adult. I should be free to go where I please. But," Teo added, "despite that, I imagine he would set an arbiter on me to make sure I stay safe. Perhaps find a way to cut the funding of R&R so they can't afford non-essential personnel such as me. And have you and Arsenio sacked for bringing me with you, of course."

Vanni cringed. "Let's make sure that doesn't happen. We're very good at keeping secrets."

"I'm glad. So am I," Teo replied. She stopped and shone the torch on an empty space on the shelf. "What's that?"

"Nothing?" Vanni suggested.

"No, it's the absence of something," Teo told him and kneeled to better see. Yes, the dust was gone.

"Huh," Vanni said. "Well spotted. I'm beginning to think you're as good as Arsenio. So what was here?"

Teo shook her head. "That I don't know..."

Vanni bent closer and studied the empty shelf. There was a dustless area, round and with a diameter of about thirty centimeters. The object appeared to have been dragged forwards and picked up, and there were clear footprints on the floor. A lot of them, as if someone had stepped back and forth here. And then, in the dust next to the empty place, someone had drawn two dots with a curved line under it. The line had a small U-shape attached to it.

"Is that... a smiling face sticking its tongue out?" Teo asked, feeling daft even as she did so.

Vanni groaned. "Yes... Yes it is." He ran his hand over his face as if to wipe off the annoyed expression, but it didn't quite work.

"Are you or Arsenio going to tell me about it at any point? You know who took that thing and drew the face, don't you?"

"Yes, we do," Vanni admitted. "There's a kid out there... He's looking for old tech just like us. And he knows we're searching. To him, it's like a competition. That is his way of taunting us."

"Well, is it a competition?" Teo asked. "Who is he? I thought only spotters and sentries went out of the city."

"He's not from Florence."

"But nomads don't use tech, do they?"

"He's not a nomad, either." Vanni said. "And he does use tech. But..."

Another light beam fell on them as Arsenio and his layman came round a row of racks. "Any luck?" Arsenio called out.

"No!" Vanni replied. The way he turned and stood in front of the empty shelf suggested he didn't want Arsenio to see what they had, or rather had not, found.

Teo stood up. "And you?" she asked.

"Nothing. I bet he stripped this place of value a few hours before we got here." Arsenio raised an eyebrow. "What are you hiding?"

Teo almost grinned. The whole thing felt silly.

Vanni cleared his throat. "He took something from a shelf here, but we have no idea what it was," he admitted.

The muscles in Arsenio's jaw tightened. "All right. Let's get out of here. Find your friends and tell them to meet us at the entrance," he said to the layman and handed him his torch.

"Someday," Arsenio said under his breath, "I want to catch that pest in the act and wring his neck."

"Why not bring him back to Florence instead?" Teo suggested. "If he is looking for tech, he could be a valuable asset."

"No," said Vanni and Arsenio together. Vanni added, "He is not likely to want to work with us."

She wanted to ask why not, but Arsenio was fuming and Vanni seemed so put out by the failure that she thought it was probably better to wait for a more opportune moment.

So they left the hangar practically empty-handed. One of the laymen had found a rolled up cable that Teo examined to see if it could be of any use. One end of it was rusty and could never aspire to anything but smelting, but the other could be cleaned and put to use with a little luck. It was odd and exciting to be doing her job in the field for once instead of back in R&R, and she couldn't help thinking that it would be a lot more efficient to bring out technies with the spotters than having the spotters bring back salvaged tech. She had been told that it was too dangerous and had not questioned it before. But now it seemed pampering and a little bit stupid.

The trek back to the truck was as dry and hot as on the way out. But the vast, blue sky above them and the unknown terrain waiting to be rediscovered made it more than worth the effort. Even the sensation of grains of sand between Teo's teeth and in her nostrils could not quell her mood. When she glanced down, she could spot their footprints from earlier, but in places they had already been obscured by the elements.

Vanni and Arsenio decided to let the driver take a different route back to Florence to see if they could spot anything else of interest, and Arsenio sat with his binoculars, scouting most of the way, exchanging a few words with Vanni who had brought the map out again as the sun began to sink towards the horizon and the light grew soft and orange.

Teo sat looking at the sunset and tried to take in as much as possible before the daylight disappeared. Who knew when she would get out here again? Who knew, a small voice in the back of her head remarked, if she ever would?

As the truck rolled down the hill towards Florence, it was dusk, and the lights of the inner city were glowing below, some clear and others dulled by the domes. The slummers had lamps, too, but they were lanterns dangling from poles and ceilings and smelled of oil. There was something even poorer, even shabbier about the houses and the beggars.

"All right," Arsenio said and reached into the pouch attached to his belt to pull out a handful of coins. "This is where we part. And here's the payment we agreed on."

Agreed on meant, Teo mused, that Arsenio had told the laymen what the financial compensation would be and they had accepted, desperate for work.

The truck came to a halt, and Vanni unlatched the rear gate so the laymen could get off.

"Thank you for your help today," Teo called after them.

One of the laymen turned to give her a quick smile before he pushed through the crowd forming around the vehicle.

"All right, we have nothing else for you," Arsenio shouted.

Teo leaned forward to see who he was talking to. The crowd was surging around the truck like ants around a piece of cake.

"What do they want?" Teo asked under her breath.

"Work, money," Vanni replied and stood up to join Arsenio at the rear.

"Hey!" Arsenio yelled and clapped his hands twice. "Move it! Don't stand in front of the truck!" He jumped to the ground and moved around the truck behind Teo.

She pushed her back against the railing and tilted her head to catch a glimpse of the proceedings. Arsenio had barely disappeared out of sight, shouting at the crowd, before Teo felt a sliding sensation on top of her head. Damn. She reached up to pull the cap on properly again, but suddenly it was gone, and a hard tug on her hair made her yelp and bang her head against the railing.

"Teo!" Vanni exclaimed. "Let go of h—"

Teo gritted her teeth and grasped behind her head for a hold of her own hair. She touched another set of hands, the ones pulling her painfully back, forcing her to stare up into the sky and arch her back. She dug her nails into the other hands, wishing for once that she had the vicious claws that several of her female friends sported.

"Let go or I'll shoot!" Vanni warned. Teo could see him out of the corner of her eye. He had drawn his gun and was aiming it at someone behind her.

Someone, the driver judging from the direction yelled out, "Sabbadin!"

The next shout was more of a ferocious growl than actual words. It was Arsenio's response.

There was a rush of noises then, a cry of pain, and the tug on Teo's hair was released. She twisted around to catch a glimpse of a figure on the ground, a handful of people running away, and one frantically trying to pull the fallen person to his feet. Arsenio had his gun raised, but he was holding it more like a club than a firearm. He bent down, snatched something from the ground and strode around the truck. It bounced as he jumped up. "Go!" he roared to the driver, and Vanni was still closing the gate as they began to move towards the wall.

"Are you all right?" Vanni asked Teo.

"Yes," she said. The back of her head smarted, and she was sure she'd lost a fistful of hair. Her heart was pounding. Worst of all, she felt humiliated and stupid.

"What the hell were you standing there for?" Arsenio yelled at Vanni. He didn't wait for a reply. Instead he turned to Teo and thrust a muddy, disfigured cap at her. "And what the hell were you thinking? Get that hat on your head unless you plan on getting us caught too!"

"I'm sorry!" Teo shouted to be heard. She tried to make her hands stop shaking as she put the cap on her head and unceremoniously stuffed her hair back into it.

"You better be," Arsenio growled.

"I am." She knew she had been careless. She also knew that Arsenio was only shouting because he was concerned, but that didn't make the situation much better.

"It's all right now," Vanni said, ever the diplomat and negotiator between his two friends. "You both need to get your tempers under control. We're coming up to the checkpoint."

Arsenio sent Teo another seething glare, then sat down on the bench opposite her. He folded his body into a comfortable, relaxed pose and made his expression neutral.

Teo attempted to copy his body language. She could not let the sentries at the gate suspect anything.

The truck slowed down, its brakes complaining as it stopped at the checkpoint. Teo could hear someone talk to the driver, and then the sentry in question came around the truck.

"Hello, sirs," he said, nodding at them all in turn, but clearly addressing Arsenio. "Any luck out there today?"

"We found a newly uncovered building," Arsenio said in an admirably laid back tone. "But there was almost only junk in it. No tech. One coil of cable for R&R."

"You can't win them all, huh?" the sentry said. "Well, you don't seem to be smuggling anyone in, so carry on."

Vanni and Teo laughed, hopefully convincingly. Arsenio just grinned and bid the sentry a good night. They all knew the man had meant it as a joke and had, in fact, not been alluding to Teo, but to slummers. Still, Teo's heart was trying to get into her mouth while the truck went through the gate.

No one said anything until they reached the surveyors' garage and were back on the ground. The driver knew Teo wasn't a spotter, but Arsenio had led him to believe she was cousin of his who had begged to go on a mission outside the wall with him.

"Time for your costume change," Arsenio said as the three of them walked towards the locker rooms.

"Thank you for taking me with you. I really..." Teo began.

"Not now," Arsenio interrupted.

Vanni cleared his throat. For a moment, Teo thought someone was listening in on their conversation, but there was no one in the vicinity. Instead, her friends were having a silent exchange consisting of little nods and raised eyebrows.

"We should talk about the trip. Tomorrow," Arsenio finally said.

"Of course. I'd like that," Teo replied.

"I'll pick you up from work. You're working tomorrow, right?" Vanni asked.

"Yes. I'm off at five."

"Good. I'll see you then," Vanni said, smiling.

Teo felt a rush of relief and happiness that she'd really managed to go outside without being caught, without being hurt by the dangers out there, welling up in her. "Yes. Thank you. See you tomorrow."

5:
Mender

Mender opened nir eyes.

The timepiece had stopped at 14:57:05 on May 25th 2217.

It was not likely to be May 25th anymore. It was not likely to be 2217, either. That was the exact time when the power ran out. Mender recalled being low on energy, getting things in order and telling nir clients what would happen in a manner that was not too upsetting, but also did not conceal the fact that there was very little energy left to sustain the facility.

Now the power was back. The receptors outside must have been covered rather than broken, then, and now at least some of them were not obscured anymore.

Priority protocols sprang to life inside Mender. The most important thing was the clients' well being. After that, ne would assess the general state of the facility, contact CerEvolv and then tend to nemself.

But first ne would need to stay in the recharging unit for at least a few minutes. Nir own power supply as well as the solar panels embedded discreetly in nir head were of no use yet. So Mender waited and monitored nir power level as it slowly climbed. It was inadvisable to move away from the recharging unit before fifteen percent was reached. Still, given the circumstances, ne rose at ten. "Hello?" ne called.

Ne began to walk cautiously through the home. Emergency lights illuminated the corridor, giving off a dim, yellowish glow that was barely sufficient to let humans find their way. This confirmed Mender's theory. There would only be energy for the emergency lights if the solar panels had been uncovered recently. Perhaps it meant that it was possible to go outside now if this part of the building was no longer covered in debris.

The first rooms Mender passed as ne proceeded through the corridor were empty. That was unsurprising as their occupants passed away shortly after the impact. Mender had laid them to rest in the coffins in the designated room according to orders from CerEvolv. Mender was to look after the clients for as long as possible, help them eat, assist them in their use of the sanitary facilities, make certain they did not fall or lack oxygen. And keep them company in a calming, soothing manner. Mender was good at all this. It was, after all, what ne had been created for.

Ne entered the first room, which had hosted a living person when ne had last been active. A visual examination was more than sufficient to determine the state of the woman. The bed she occupied when Mender tucked her in that last time before awaiting complete power loss was now void of its flowery fabric. Only tattered pieces remained. Upon it was a heap of human remains. Depending on the humidity, temperature and atmospheric conditions, the amount of time that had passed since the timepiece ceased to function was impossible to ascertain. One thing, however, was quite clear: It had been years.

A fine layer of dust covered everything, from the eyeless sockets to the vase on the bedside table where flowers once stood. Now there was not even a trace of the stems.

Mender returned to the corridor and continued to the next room although ne had already drawn the logical conclusion. Usually ne would be present to make their passage easier, to keep them company in their final hours as one by one they ceased to function. Permanently. Mender nemself had ceased to function as well, but only for a limited period.

It was the imminent death of all the clients, which had caused them to be left in this home and in Mender's care. In a world frantically preparing for disaster, for changes so immense that no one could predict what would happen with certainty, there were no resources to spend on those who would be dead within months. Putting the terminally ill or fragile elderly into stasis was not an option, partly because there was already a shortage of cryo pods, and partly because their bodies would not be able to withstand the conditions of the rapid, extreme temperature changes.

They all watched the feed from GNM when the impact happened. Mender attempted to comfort nir clients in accordance with quality-tested methods, but there was no reigning in the vast array of emotions. A few wept silently as they watched the world go to pieces and the cameras failed one after another. One client fainted. Another shouted in anger, yelling for the lunacy to stop, perhaps not, Mender suspected, realizing how appropriate that word had become. A few screamed.

Only one laughed. Laughed so hard that tears came to her eyes and she was coughing and wheezing and had to put on her oxygen mask for a moment, only to resume laughing when she pulled it off again. Mender had not understood the laughter.

One of the clients who cried did understand, though. A few days later, when the laughing woman was laid to rest, he explained it to Mender. The dying always knew that the world would go on after they were gone. But for a dying person to see the world end all around them, when they were on the brink of that abyss, that was ironic and darkly funny in a terrible way. At the time, Mender reassured the man that the world was still out there.

Two weeks later, they lost the connection to CerEvolv.

And after that, it was not long before it was evident that they had been cut off from the rest of the world not only digitally, but also physically. Presumably dust and debris covered the external sensors and with them the solar panels.

The rest of the rooms proved void of living occupants as well, of course. Mender stood for a moment in the stillness of the common room where they had watched the impact. The screen was still there, spread out across the end wall, silent, pictureless, a dark, semi-transparent film waiting to be activated.

Now that the top priority had been taken care of, Mender raised nir wrist to nir mouth. The com had not turned back on when ne had, so ne touched the panel. Still nothing happened. Ne studied nir hands. Not strange that the com was not reacting. Mender's unique thumbprint was not visible on nir left hand. The right one appeared intact, but the skin on the left one had suffered greatly. Mender did not know how it had happened, but the fact that the skin was torn and tattered hinted that more than a few years had passed.

Mender punched in nir security code. The com flicked to life. A red circle shone in the middle of the panel, rotating while it tried to establish a link to CerEvolv. After a full minute, the com informed nem that there was no connection available.

Well, there was a com panel for emergencies by the door in the sanitary facilities, and it lit up promisingly when Mender touched it.

"This is CerEvolv, how may I help you today?" asked a pleasant voice. It was used for several of CerEvolv's appliances. Hearing it now in the quiet home was strange. It was only the two of them now, but only one of them was a sentient. The voice was merely a recording, and the reason that it sounded clear was not necessarily that the connection to CerEvolv worked, but simply that it came from the device within this facility.

"This is Minder 3431-B," Mender replied with nir mouth close to the panel. Unlike the com's voice, Mender's sounded different. As if dust had gotten into the vocal cords. "I wish to contact the department for sentient feedback."

"Please wait a moment." There was a short pause while the signal bounced from the home to the relay station and onto the nearest CerEvolv department. "It is not possible to establish a connection at this time," the voice said. "Is there anything else I can do for you, Minder 3431-B?"

"Please connect me to the department of artificial intelligence," Mender replied.

The result was the same.

"Can you connect me to any available CerEvolv department? It does not need to be the local branch."

"Please wait a moment."

This moment was longer. With every second passing, Mender knew the odds were dwindling down.

"It is not possible to establish a connection at this time," the voice informed nem.

"Please enable manual connection," Mender said, although ne didn't really expect a different result from calling anyone directly. Ne let nir fingers run across the touch pad on the panel, trying one number stored in nir memory after the other. None of them came through. "Thank you," ne finally said and shut down the com again.

Mender was cut off from CerEvolv. Once there were no more clients in a given facility, ne was to report back to CerEvolv for new orders. Ne could not reach CerEvolv by com. So ne would simply have to physically go to the local branch, but ne needed to make preparations first. Ne would not need food or water, but since some of nir skin was gone, ne had to make sure it didn't get worse and to wear protection in order not to get damaged by rain or dust. But first ne would make certain that it was possible to get out at all.

Ne walked down the corridor, away from the living quarters towards the storage rooms. There was a staircase around the corner...

Mender stopped. Light was pouring into the corridor from above, and in that shaft of light was a heap of debris. No, not just debris. There was a person... Mender approached the body. It was not another sentient. And all the clients had been accounted for.

Mender bent down. It was a young man of perhaps twenty. His attire did not resemble the fashion Mender remembered. It was also worn and dirty, and not only from the fall. Around him were bits of shattered concrete, a crumbled bag of leather and a long staff of smooth wood. The boy was not dead, but unconscious. His breathing was shallow, and there was a drying pool of blood originating from his head.

Getting to CerEvolv automatically moved to a lower priority. Mender picked up the lifeless body. The boy was built sturdily, and he had well-developed muscles, but he was quite lean. He had wild, tangled hair, some of it stiff with dried blood.

Mender carried the young man to the examination room. Like everything else, it looked like it had before the shutdown, even in the dim emergency light. There was not a lot of dust, but there had been no humans around, and most dust inside homes came from dead skin and particles brought in from the outside.

Very carefully, Mender placed the boy on one of the two beds. Ne was not a doctor, but as a caretaker and nurse of dying people, Mender was qualified to make a diagnosis. Ne deftly stripped nir new client, briefly noted that his undergarments were of a surprisingly primitive sort and didn't appear to be mass manufactured. His ethnic heritage was unclear, but under the dust, his skin was several shades darker than Mender's.

The ceiling lights flickered on. They ought to have been activated right away by Mender's movements, but the power supply was only gradually replenishing. Ne reached up for the scanning equipment hanging from the ceiling. It took a little while to activate it, but like everything else in the facility, it still worked. And it showed that the left ulna was fractured. Not a serious injury. There was a gash on the back of the young man's head, but when Mender directed the scanner to it, the cranium proved to be intact.

The client would need to be monitored, have the various injuries treated and the cuts and wounds cleaned and, Mender added to nir list as ne worked, it would be advisable to administer antibiotics since the client was quite dirty. Mender had to use nir code instead of nir fingerprint for the vacuum cabinet where all medication was kept. At the time of the facility's construction, Mender thought it was not necessary to have such a cabinet here because all the clients would be deceased before the expiration date on any of the bottles. Now, however, it turned out to be a good thing.

Mender put a cardiometer onto the chest of the boy and found a vein in his uninjured arm to begin medication as efficiently and quickly as possible. Ne had almost completed the most pressing tasks and was about to decide, based on the client's condition and physique, how much analgesic to use when the boy stirred.

Mender took one step back to give the young man a little room since it may confuse him to see a stranger standing over him. His eyes flickered open and became aware, attempted to focus. When finally the young man's gaze fixed on Mender's face, his eyes widened. The cardiometer indicated that his heart rate was climbing rapidly.

"Please don't be alarmed," Mender said.

But the boy did not appear to register the words. A sound escaped him, not quite a scream and not quite a growl. His fingers gripped the sides of the bed to pull himself up, but when he attempted to use his injured arm, he hissed in pain. Before Mender could stop him, he had thrashed so violently that the IV needle was torn from his arm.

"I am not going to hurt you," Mender said, taking hold of the young man. Ne was not built for fighting, but ne was stronger than most humans because ne needed to be able to carry them and care for them. "Please calm down."

The young man snarled something that Mender could not decipher, but it sounded like a threat although he was in no position to make threats.

Mender held the taut, struggling body as still as possible and reached out to take the syringe ne had been preparing. Ne plunged the needle into one of the veins standing out on the young man's forearm although ne had meant to administer it through the IV in smaller doses.

It only took a few seconds before the client's muscles relaxed and his face grew expressionless. He slumped back into the bed.

Mender let go of him and straightened up. The cardiometer's soft beeps grew slower and resumed a steady pace. What an extreme reaction. Mender could understand the boy's confusion, but he ought to feel at ease to see a nurse caring for him.

Mender carefully slid the needle back into the boy's arm and fastened it, more securely this time. The analgesic would keep him sedated for a few hours, but perhaps it would be better to keep him calm for a while longer so he could recover without endangering his own safety.

6:
Renn

The first thing Renn became aware of was a dull pain in the back of his head. Then came a grinding ache in his back and his left arm.

He took a slow, deliberate breath and willed his heavy eyelids apart. His surroundings were fuzzy and strange and somehow out of place. Or perhaps he was out of place. He must be injured. Must have been unconscious. But... There was a ceiling above him. It looked nothing like the inside of a cave or a tent or one of the buildings in the dead cities.

He breathed again, calmly. Too calmly. He ought to feel more alarmed. He ought to get up, find out where he was and whether he was in danger. But instead he lay there, staring at the ceiling, slightly alarmed that he was not alarmed. He blinked. And finally he moved his head a little. There was a... thing on the wall. How could he name it when he did not know its nature and purpose? It was a black rectangular shape with a pulsing light and a line moving up and down. Could it be a working masheen? He had seen them broken and inactive, littering the ground and the floors of abandoned houses.

A long, thin tube emerged from the masheen. Renn followed it with his gaze and found to his horror that the end of it was stuck into his right arm. It had been fastened with bands around his arm. As he studied it, willing himself to keep still, he could see the blinking light grow faster out of the corner of his eye.

Renn slowly lifted his left arm to see if he could remove the tube, but not only was it uncooperative; it was also covered in a light pink substance. A kind of bandage? But it was hard, almost like stone.

"You are awake."

Renn jerked his head around. A figure was standing a few paces from him. It resembled a human being to the extent that it had a head and a body and extremities where they ought to be. But its face was grotesque.

"I am not going to hurt you. Please do not be alarmed," the figure said.

It was speaking in an accent Renn couldn't recognize. He knew he ought to get up. And yet... He lay injured in the lair of this creature who even resembled the masheens. Would he stand a chance in a fight?

Renn looked around for his staff. He realized he was naked to the waist and most likely below as well, but a thin and shiny blanket was covering him.

"I am attempting to help you," the creature said. It moved closer, and Renn curled his hands into fists. But the creature only brushed its hand over the masheen on the wall.

A warm calm washed through Renn. His mind felt woolen, and the pain turned into merely an irrelevant ache.

"Good," said the creature. "That feels better, doesn't it?"

Renn peered up at it. He really ought to feel more alarmed, but now curiosity was the dominating sensation. What was he looking at? It was a face. The mouth moved when the creature spoke, but it had no lips. It had no skin. No eyelids. No eyebrows. But Renn saw no bones, tendons or muscles. Just a silvery-grey surface with odd lines crisscrossing its surface.

"It appears that you fell down here by accident and were injured. I am doing my best to help you, and I believe you will recover fully. But you still need rest." The creature paused, studying him with eyes that looked more like a depiction of human eyes than actual eyes. "Can you speak? Do you have a name?"

Renn was not certain he wanted to speak. But he was already at the mercy of this stranger. What could possibly change by talking?

"I am Minder 3431-B, but I am usually called Mender," said the creature.

Renn opened his mouth to reply, but no sound came out.

"You must be thirsty," the creature, Mender, said. "In anticipation, I have looked over the reserves and prepared some water for you."

Mender moved away from Renn. It walked like a human, but there was something unnatural about its mannerisms. Was it nervous around him? Or was this simply its way?

"I boiled the water, so you need not worry about infection," Mender continued as it returned with a transparent cylinder.

Renn wanted to take the water and found that he couldn't. He also could not get into a sitting position. It was not only because of his injuries. Mender was doing something with those masheens that made his mind and body dull. But there was nothing he could do. So he allowed the creature to lift up his head and assist him as he drank. It tasted exactly like boiled water, the sharpness and any taste of it gone in the process, although it was perfectly cool now.

"I have kept you hydrated, but intravenous solution will not keep your mouth and throat from getting dry," Mender said in a matter-of-fact tone. Or so it sounded. Renn still had trouble understanding the accent. "Will you tell me your name?"

"Renn," Renn croaked. "Who... are you?" Or what.

"I was assigned to this facility as a nurse before the impact." Pause. Then carefully, deliberately, "Please understand that the original purpose of this building bears no relation to your situation. You will recover well. But this was a hospice, and its original inhabitants have passed on many years ago."

A nurse was someone assigned to taking care of children, often in the event of their parents' death or their mother's inability to feed them as babies. Renn did not know what a hospice was. "I don't... I don't understand," he ventured. "What happened to me?"

"I found you in a collapsed corridor," Mender explained. "The fall, I assume, knocked you unconscious. Your appearance coincides with my reactivation, so I believe you to be the cause of it. Quite lucky for both of us." The creature studied him as he attempted to make sense of what it said. A human being would have frowned or shrugged, but Mender stood perfectly still, regarding him with those inhuman, lidless eyes.

Renn frowned. They were speaking the same language, or something very close to being the same language, and yet Renn could not understand half what Mender said. He wanted to ask questions, but where to start? "How long..?" he began.

"I estimate that I found you shortly after you fell down here," Mender said. "I have kept you sedated for almost 48 hours."

Renn's mouth opened. Two days? Then his Covey would be far away. How was he going to find them now?

"I am sorry. It was the best way for you to heal. I can assure you that I have done my best to keep you safe and comfortable."

Renn closed his eyes. The fog in his mind kept hiding thoughts and conclusions from him. Perhaps if he slept, all this would turn out to have been a dream.

He knew that would not be the case even as he felt himself slipping into sleep.

Some time later, Renn was sitting. He had been offered a short, brown stick, and for a while the words 'you must be hungry' did not appear to have anything to do with it. Then Mender explained that the stick was food. Words like 'compressed' and 'nutrients' and 'proteins' were involved in the explanation.

"Are you not going to eat?" Renn asked. His mind felt clearer now. It would have been hard to accept that a stranger had found him injured and taken care of him, was offering him rest and nourishment without asking or expecting anything in return under normal circumstances. That a stagnant would live all alone and was in possession of working masheens made it even harder. And that the stagnant in question almost made mockery of human anatomy added to the already staggering tower of doubt. Renn could not help wondering what it was that this stranger expected in return for its help.

"I don't need it. Is it a surprise to you that I don't eat?" asked Mender.

Renn paused with the stick halfway to his mouth. He was hungry, and Mender had explained that the removal of the tube in his arm meant he would have to eat on his own. It was with that removal that his mind became clearer. His head and arm had started hurting a great deal more, but even the pain was subsiding after he had swallowed two small pebbles that Mender called pills.

"Everyone eats," he replied. "All living creatures eat."

"That is not entirely true," Mender said. "Some creatures take in nourishment in different ways. In any case, I only need solar power to operate. I am alive, but I am not biological like you. You are aware of this?"

"I don't understand," Renn said. But it was in that moment he finally did understand. "You are an Other," he breathed. "How…"

"I am a sentient," said Mender.

They stared at each other, Renn desperately trying to remember everything he knew of Others, trying to merge the image of this creature with the Moon servants of long ago.

"Your calendar is probably different from the one I was taught," Mender commented. "Mine is based on the birth year of a religious leader. What is yours?"

"After Moon's flight," Renn replied. He only knew because his father had come from a scholarly stagnant family and left to join Renn's mother's Bevy. He taught Renn to read the old script and passed on some of his knowledge before he died.

"Renn," Mender spoke, "will you help me understand the period of time in which I have been inactive?"

Was this the payment for Mender's help? If so, it was no great price. Renn cleared his throat. "I can try," he said. "I only know what has been passed down to me from our elders, and… I think a lot of time must have gone by. I mean, the ruin of the old cities… Things have changed. I don't know where to begin." He had never been a storyteller.

"Can you tell me what the area outside looks like? You mentioned ruins?" Mender asked. "I know the surroundings have changed since the impact. I think that is probably what you call Moon's flight. Perhaps you can begin by telling me how you fell down here."

7:
Renn

Renn described the ruins above, how he had tried to outrun the dust storm and failed, how the floor had given in. Then Mender asked him to go back and talk about his journey, and he did, working his way backwards through the wasteland to the abandoned city, only stopping when he reached the Other he had found in pieces. How would Mender react to learning the fate of the Others who had not been preserved underground for all these years? Renn would be distraught to wake up one day and learn that humanity was gone.

But before he could decide whether to omit that part, Mender asked, "You called me an Other. Is that your name for sentients?"

"I have not heard that word before," Renn said. "Can you... explain to me what you are?"

And so the proverbial talking stone was back in Mender's hands. Through what was undoubtedly a simplified explanation, Renn understood that a sentient was not a human being, but a being created by humans in their image to look like them and act like them, or rather on behalf of them. Mender took care of elderly and very ill people. A great catastrophe had been foretold, and Mender was going about this task when it occurred.

"Perhaps you should rest now," Mender interrupted the tale. "We can talk more later. You need to sleep and relax in order to heal and regain your strength."

"I'm grateful for your help, Mender, but I have to move on soon," Renn said although he did feel annoyingly weak.

"Oh, that is true," Mender said, "you haven't told me where you are going. But you should not be going anywhere right now, regardless."

Renn wanted to get up and put on his clothes and leave, but he knew Mender was right. The only thing more dangerous than wandering alone was wandering about with injuries that weakened him and made him easy prey for scarvhes or packs of starving rats.

The next time he woke up, Renn felt considerably better. He also had his clothes back, cleaner and smelling a little strange. At this point Renn also noticed that he himself was a lot cleaner than he had been for weeks. Probably since his Covey left the coast to migrate north. The fabric felt soft against his skin, but the left sleeve of his tunic had to be bundled up to make room for the light pink bandage on his forearm. Mender explained that it would have to stay there for a few more days at least to make sure the bone set right. It was working some strange magic on his arm, allowing it to heal faster than any bones ought to mend. It felt awkward, but it was better than a splint of wood.

"I have studied the hole you fell through," Mender commented when Renn was dressed and experimentally walking about in the room, "and it seems that you upset the ground quite a lot."

Renn stopped. What an odd thing to say. Was Mender

blaming him for breaking the roof of this underground building?

"It would explain how the solar panels were uncovered," Mender continued. "I believe I owe you a thank you for fixing the problem. After all, this facility and I have been without power practically since the impact."

"You are welcome," Renn replied although essentially he was being thanked for falling through the ceiling. He turned to study the shelves on the wall next to him. There was a row of identical boxes, and words in the old script were on them. He could make out the letters and read what they said, but only a few of them made sense. Still, the labels made more sense than the story about the catastrophe that Mender claimed was the same as Moon's flight.

Working masheens and a sane Other was stretching Renn's perception of reality, but he could accept them because he could see them. The catastrophe, however... That idea was going directly against the stories he had grown up with, against the belief he was living with, violently trying to shake the foundation of his very world... And to what end?

Renn looked away from the boxes and back at Mender who had gone quiet and stood studying him.

"It upsets you to hear me speak of the past," Mender said in a tone that sounded worried.

"No," Renn replied. "No, I only... I can't understand parts of it. It doesn't matter."

"I am meant to assist and soothe the mind as well as the body," Mender persisted, "So it matters to me if I am upsetting you..."

"You asked me where I was headed when I fell down here," Renn changed the subject. "I was on my way northeast. I was separated from my Covey some days ago..."

"Will you be able to find them again?" There was kind curiosity in Mender's voice now.

"I hope so," Renn replied. "We were migrating because of the weather by the coast this time of the year. Coveys and Bevies move north at regular intervals, and we follow roughly the same routes. They left me a sign to point me in the right direction, so..." He faltered because the chances that any more signs left for him were still there now were slim. He cleared his throat. "Well, I need to find a Covey to join, and I know stagnants who trade with wanderers, so I intend to head in their direction. If they have not seen my Covey, perhaps they have encountered another." Renn searched Mender's face for a hint of emotion or an opinion. It had to be there, but reading a face with no skin, no eyebrows, no lips and strange eyes was difficult. "What will you do?" he asked.

Mender tilted the head back and stared at the ceiling. A quick glance told Renn that there was nothing there, but Mender stayed in the posture for a while. "I must go to CerEvolv," it then came.

"I don't know that place," Renn said, admitting for at least the fifth time that he had no idea what Mender was talking about.

Mender shifted the gaze back to him. "CerEvolv is the name of my maker. The closest branch is located in Florence. Do you know where that is?"

"No," Renn said. "I have not heard of it."

"The world," Mender said with almost a sigh, "really must have changed a great deal while I was deactivated. We knew it would, but I don't think anyone could predict to what extent."

Renn didn't reply.

"Well, I will leave this facility when you do. Taking care of humans is my primary function. When you are gone, there is nothing else here to override the priority of contacting CerEvolv," Mender continued.

Mender had probably saved Renn's life. And the strange

being was still asking nothing in return. Instead, Mender would be facing a changed world all alone. "Where is this Florence you speak of?" Renn asked.

"North of here. North-north-east to be exact. I don't expect to find working means of transportation, so I will walk. I imagine it will take me a few days." And even if it was hard to see emotion on Mender's face, the tone of voice sounded more than a little uncertain.

"I am heading north as you know," Renn said. "Would you like us to form a Covey for as long as we are going in the same direction?"

And without lips and without human eyes, Mender's face still seemed to smile. "I would be very happy to, Renn."

Renn smiled, too. He had no idea what to expect from Mender as the other half of a two-person Covey. After all, Mender had not been outside for a very long time. Would Renn be the one who made all decisions, fended off attackers if they were assaulted and read the wind? Well, regardless, it would be safer to travel together for both of them. "Good. It is settled, then," he said and offered Mender his hand.

Mender glanced at the hand for a moment, then shook it. "Yes. Thank you. I am glad to see handshakes are still in use," came as an afterthought. "Then perhaps I am not entirely as socially inhibited as I feared."

Renn suppressed a shudder. A handshake meant an arrangement to be honored, it brought you physically close to another and there was a bond of trust between the parties since a handshake could easily be turned into an act of violence. But Renn had not prepared himself for that dead, cold sensation of Mender's hand. No, not dead. It did not feel like touching a dead person or animal. It was like touching something that nor was and neither had ever been alive in the manner a person or an animal was.

But breaking a handshake was an insult at best and a

sign of untimely termination of the arrangement at worst. So he forced himself to clasp the hard, unyielding hand in his and meet Mender's gaze before letting go. "When will you be ready to leave?" he asked.

Mender glanced around them as if the answer were written on the walls of the room. "Tomorrow. Will that be adequate?"

Renn would have preferred to leave right away, of course, but he still agreed that it would.

"I need to make a few preparations," Mender said. "And you will be better off then, too. In fact... It would be better for you to wait a little longer..."

"No," Renn said quickly. "We leave when you are ready."

"As you wish," Mender said with a small nod. "Tomorrow, then."

8:
Luca

In retrospect, Luca knew he should have paid attention to the heat steaming off the metal. But he was so focused on his work that he hardly noticed. What he did notice was a sudden flash in front of his eyes and a curious sensation like IV fluid rushing through his veins, through both of his arms, and colliding somewhere in his chest before he could even blink.

And then he was on his back coughing as if someone had tried to strangle him, struggling to get control and sensation back in his limbs. His heart was doing something odd and irregular, and as Luca wasn't a stranger to a textbook electrical shock, he knew exactly why. Just because he didn't always adhere to the damn security protocols didn't mean he was oblivious to how things worked. He scrambled to his feet, still fighting for breath. The circuit board in front of him was in flames. How much time had he lost? Hopefully only a few seconds or the whole thing would be fried.

He stumbled to his workbench, pulled out the fire extinguisher under it and aimed it at the drone that lay there innocently with its belly open and exposed entrails. A fine, white mist spouted out of the nozzle and drowned the flames to a sizzling mess and then a smoking ruin.

"Shit," Luca finally managed as he dropped the fire extinguisher. That was days of work literally up in flames. "Shitfuck..." His knees buckled, and he let them. Maybe if he could black out for a while, the mess would have fixed itself when he came to.

"Master Luca!"

No rest for the wicked. The reproach in her voice cut through his attempt at ignoring what had just happened. Luca opened his eyes and blinked up at her worried face. "I'm fine, Nanny" he said. The air smelled of smoke and burnt wires and circuits and... skin. He held up his hands. "Oh."

"You were not wearing gloves," she said as she helped him to a sitting position. "Again."

"Gloves make it worse," he mumbled. "I need to feel what I'm doing."

Nanny held his wrists, efficiently inspecting his burnt fingers and feeling for his pulse at the same time. "You need medical care."

"I need to assess the damage," he said.

"There is going to be no change in the condition of that machine from waiting. There may be a change in yours."

Always so damn sensible. He bit back a reply before he could say, "I should just reprogram you," because he knew it was never an option. Not with her. Semis and demis, sure. The sentients he dragged home for repair, sure. But he could never tinker and mess around with her and Alfredo. They were the only ones left, along with Luca. "We're all relics of a lost civilization," he muttered. An echo of the electric current punched him in the chest for good measure, and he winced as he got to his feet once more.

"Can you feel your hands? Is it something else?" Nanny asked.

There was the merest ghost of pain in his hands as well as in his chest. Judging from the blistered, burnt skin on five of his fingertips, this was one of the times he should be grateful for whatever nerve endings had been severed or frozen away. Though, without that little kink, he would have noticed the heat in time. "I said I'm fine," he sulked, but he followed Nanny inside the house.

Before they moved in, just after Luca turned sixteen, his parents had referred to it as the base. They spent a couple of years perfecting it before then, turning it from an old vineyard into a state-of-the-art fortress with everything one could possibly need during a siege. He sometimes wondered if they knew what they were preparing for, if his mother's position in the security service had warned her before the general population was told.

By the time they did move, everybody knew. GNM looped the same footage of the meteor over and over, and every possible social media was going crazy. As Luca and Leo were picked up from their respective schools, panic was spreading like wildfire. No one in the Capello household panicked, of course. Their parents because they had anticipated it, or something like it, the two boys because they trusted that everything was under control, and the rest because their programming didn't include panic.

Worry was a different matter. Nanny kept a close eye on Luca as she brought him to the ground floor infirmary. The only infirmary at this point, bearing as little resemblance to the technological wonder that once stood downstairs with its salvaged parts and battered equipment as Luca's workshop did to the facilities in the Institute of Robotics and Artificial Intelligence.

"What happened this time?" Alfredo asked in his curious, polite tone. He was approaching them from the direction of the stairs. Like Nanny, Alfredo was wearing plain, clean clothes and had been given dark hair and a kind face, not too handsome and not too ugly. The sentients were perfect contrasts to Luca in his dirty jeans and faded black t-shirt, with his bleached hair and perfect smile.

"You're making it sound like I screw up all the time," Luca sighed. "Can you just... take care of this and let me get back to work?" He held up his hands as Nanny carefully pushed him onto the metal table.

None of the sentients was a doctor. There had been one, but... Luca focused on his hands. A lot of good that had done anybody. Suddenly he wanted to punch something. Hard. But he allowed the servants to fuss. Measure his vital signs, clean his hands with something that almost stung, bandage his fingers with sterile rolls of a thin, rubbery material that would speed up the healing process but also make it impossible to work on his projects for the next few days. "What?" he asked when both sentients paused and were looking at him questioningly.

"Do you need something for the pain?" Alfredo asked.

Luca considered this. He could feel his hands now. And his whole body felt a little weary, but he was hardly in agony. He made use of the perfect smile. "What have we got?"

"I think rest is the best remedy," Nanny said.

"I think fixing the mess I made is the best remedy," Luca mumbled.

"I'm afraid there will be none of that," she retorted.

"I think I do need something for the pain, after all," he said.

They had plenty of advice for him on what to take and how much of it, but they also knew he was every bit as knowledgeable as they were in this field. They both had basic first aid training, but he had had almost two years to experiment now and they all knew the two of them had no real authority over him.

As far as medical supplies went, the base was fairly well-stocked. Luca had enough antibiotics and vaccines and bandages and painkillers to last him a lifetime or two. So he chose a nice blue pill that was part of a batch he had picked up somewhere on one of his treasure hunts. They were unlabeled, so he assumed they were probably recreational. Alfredo and Nanny frowned upon the use of drugs, but he was too smart and had survived enough shit not to get addicted or kill himself. He swallowed the pill, reassured the two of them that he was fine once more, and left the house.

Luca kicked the front door open and scowled at the offending piece of machinery on his way to the storage unit. Hopefully the shell of the drone and a bit of the hardware inside it would be all right. He hadn't salvaged it from that warehouse just to burn it to cinders a few days later. Sure, he had spare parts that could be fitted in there, but not for every component of the drone. Even disregarding all the hardware related complications of 3D printing these days, he lacked schematics and would have to build everything from scratch since the internet had basically ended with the rest of the world. And Luca was trained in making awesome things by putting together building blocks, not in making the stupid blocks to build with.

He shouldered the door of the storage unit open and stepped down the flight of stairs to the underground lair. A smell of oil and metal and chemicals wafted towards him as he reached the last step and pushed open the door to the facility itself.

This was Luca's treasure chamber. In a way, it had been his family's treasure chamber before the impact because this was where their cars and backup generators were stored. Below it was an even deeper cellar with food in the shape of protein bars and nutrients with no expiration date, as well as vacuum chambers containing water, in case the manual pump upstairs dried up. Luca hadn't needed them yet. Half of Tuscany may practically be a desert now, but the base's architects had drilled deep enough for water supply not to be an issue even now.

There was also a wine cellar which, the first time Luca ventured down there alone, punched all trepidation out of him and made him laugh until tears rolled down his cheeks and he had to sit down on the floor at the absurdity of a backup wine cellar just in case wine was a sparse commodity after the goddamn apocalypse.

Luca began to stride along the row of salvaged artificials like a general inspecting his army. Yes, he thought, exactly like a general. He didn't know which war he was preparing for, or if it would ever come, but he knew he wanted to be prepared.

The cars were still there. Two flimsy vehicles that wouldn't last a minute in the terrain outside and the Rover next to them, pockmarked with small dents and scratches. Luca kept it as clean as possible and made sure it didn't rust, but it certainly wasn't as pretty as the first day he'd taken it out for a spin. Next to it was his motorcycle. Unlike the other vehicles, it was not part of his parents' collection. He found it on one of his treasure hunts almost a year ago and fell for it immediately. It was a sturdy vintage model, locked up in another garage along with a year's supply of fuel near a residence where the inhabitants hadn't been as lucky as he had. He shrugged off that thought, ran one of his bandaged hands over the weather-beaten, but well-groomed, surface and then continued his inspection.

Two years ago, it was only him, Nanny and Alfredo. Now the household included two semis whom he kept mostly deactivated in a spare bedroom next to what was supposed to be Leo's room. They were for personal use. And then there was the collection out here. All salvaged by Luca. So far, the army consisted of an assortment of semis, demis and plain robots, twenty-one in all. Not exactly a big army, but considering what some of them were capable of if equipped with enough firepower, they could kick some serious ass.

Luca couldn't help grinning as he stopped in front of his pride of the bunch. The figure hulked all of two meters and was so broad and heavy that Luca hadn't been able to load nem onto the Rover and had been forced to drag nem on a makeshift sled. Nanny and Alfredo had been as furious as their programming allowed them to. The soldier's solar panels were completely useless, so ne wasn't really a danger. But the nanny and the butler had tended to Luca's injuries the first time he'd encountered a rogue sentient and not known what he was dealing with, so they were pretty upset that he would bring home such a dangerous specimen.

Fixing the power was easy, but restoring the soldier's programming had not worked. Luca was forced to remove a good chunk of nir personality and independence, so now the soldier was nothing but a demi in a sentient's body.

Next to the soldier stood a couple of ex-rogue sentients. One of them had been a police officer who had outlived nir own programming when there was no one left to serve and protect, or so Luca assumed. That was one way ne could turn completely mad. Luca had to take it down with force. He glanced down at his left arm. He still had a scar from the valuable lesson it taught him.

He scowled, then smirked as he passed the next sentient. That one had been ridiculous. One thing was going up against a former police officer, but to be attacked by a defunct kindergarten teacher who insisted that he should give the other, non-existent, kids his toys... Yeah, not that sentient's finest hour. Not Luca's either.

He reached the end of the line and stood for a moment, just staring at these marvelous creatures. He'd get more. Probably right now wasn't the best time to go looking for that kind of trouble, though. He decided to have a shower and play with the semis in the house instead.

9:
Luca

Luca peeled off the bandages on his hands in the shower. It didn't hurt much, but he would need fresh bandages and they would still make it impossible to do delicate work today. Had he really deserved this just because he was a little cocky when it came to electricity? At least he didn't need to shave today, he thought when he stepped out of the shower stall and studied his own face in the bathroom mirror.

"Hey, handsome," said a voice behind him.

Luca shifted his focus to look into a pair of eyes even more green than his own. He knew he was kind of cute, but behind him stood one gorgeous piece of machinery, one of the two well-preserved semis he had excavated from the ruins of a once high-class establishment in Arezzo.

"Want to take a shower?" asked the impossibly beautiful semi. He was naked, and so much thought and care had gone into the realism of every single part of him. His skin felt more real than that of most other artificials, too.

"I just had one," Luca replied. Why was the semi turned on? Luca rolled his eyes at his own, unintended, double entendre. Oh yes. He'd forgotten to deactivate him last night.

"Why is Luca so boring today?" called a sing-song voice from the bedroom.

Luca sighed and adjusted the towel around his waist. "Okay," he said and padded past the semi.

"Okay?" both of them echoed. Their voices were perfectly tuned to each other. It probably wasn't a coincidence that he'd found them together. They used to sell those in pairs. Nice deal, if you were stinking rich and wanted some variation.

Luca took in the sight of the other naked semi languishing in the bed, one of her perfect legs resting on top of the sheets. "Okay," he repeated. "Thank you both for last night, it was fun. Please get dressed and go back to your room. Self-deactivate timer on Sia in five minutes. Self-deactivate timer on Simon in five minutes."

They did what he asked without further complaints. Of course. They were semis, not sentients, and as such their programming was easily accessible with a simple user interface and no complaints unless that's what tickled the owner's fancy.

Luca dressed, asked Nanny to put fresh bandages on his hands, and then sat down to have his breakfast. It was never very exciting. He was slowly working through the supplies that had been stored for as long as he had been asleep. He swallowed a protein bar with a big mug of coffee. Luckily, they had enough instant coffee to last him for years.

"The weather seems good for laundry," Nanny said in a conversational tone.

Luca shot a glance out the window. All the panes had been boarded up to begin with, but he had uncovered a few to feel a bit more human. "Yeah," he agreed. It was a quiet day which meant that if the laundry was hung up outside, he wouldn't end up with a million little sand grains in his underwear. "I'm going out," he added.

"Where to?" Nanny asked, refilling his cup with water.

"Just taking the bike out for a ride," Luca replied.

Soon after, Luca brought the motorcycle up the ramp on the far side of the garage and was clumsily strapping on his helmet. He'd fitted a respirator onto it to spare his lungs the dust. The whole thing made him look more like an astronaut than a biker, but no one was around to see it, anyway. At least no one who counted.

The engine revved happily to life, and he steered towards the closest highway. Well, it wasn't really a highway anymore, but because of its former career as one, it was a flat expanse easier to traverse than other surfaces.

The last time he'd gone from the city to the base before the end, everyone else had gone about their daily commutes like normal, marching towards the man made disaster they all expected to lurk in the future. The thought made Luca laugh. Everyone went on about the environment and global warming and nuclear waste, and in the end, it was a goddamn rogue asteroid that dark horsed its way to the front of the catastrophe queue and beat the human race to it.

But he was still here. Luca swerved around a gaping hole in the ground. He was going east today. Since he didn't plan on treasure hunting, he thought he'd check up on his old home. It only took him a couple of hours to get there on a day like this, after all.

As he got closer to his destination, he slowed down and took his time to make sure no one else was about. He could not be bothered to meet a team of scouts from the city.

He left the road and found a suitable place to park the bike, so it was hidden from view from any busybodies out there. He lowered the respirator and took a swig of the canteen he had brought with him, then got his binoculars from the compartment under the seat and started towards a good vantage point on foot.

And there it was, nestled in a valley below him. He lay down on his stomach, propped up on his elbows and aimed his digitally enhanced sight at the city. He liked to go here, just once in a while, to make sure they hadn't completely fucked up Florence yet.

The sunlight bounced off the transparent domes above the roofs, an idea they had come up with to shelter the inhabitants and the ancient buildings from harsh weather and meteor showers following the destruction of the Moon. He didn't remember the formula they had used, but they had fortified some kind of acrylic substance with millions of thin wires, creating the most durable kind of plass possible. In addition to the domes, a wall had been built around the inner city, almost as an afterthought, saying, "Oh, by the way, we also want to keep other people out."

Luca scanned the skyline. There was the dome of the cathedral, looking much the same as it had in Luca's time and probably more than a thousand years before. He spotted all the landmarks, one by one, ticking them off like beads on a rosary. Palazzo Vecchio, Skyline Hotel, the Uffizi, Ponte Vecchio, the CerEvolv tower... Whatever that was used for these days. He let his gaze follow the Arno, then veered off and found his old home. It was hard to see the details from up here, but the house was still standing. His house. His property. His parents had not sold it when they moved to the base, so technically it still belonged to him. This was almost as good as pulling up a street view map online.

Movement at the edge of his vision made Luca turn his focus to an area north of the central gate to the inner city. Some kind of commotion was going on. Since this was outside any dome, it was possible to see more details without the glare of the sun getting in the way. He increased the zoom to its maximum capacity.

A gathering of people were pushing and shoving at each

other, shouting angrily from the look of it. They were fighting over an object he couldn't make out since everyone was trying to claim it and kept getting into the line of sight. It was probably food or water or something bestowed on them by the elite on the other side of the wall.

Luca scoffed. Okay, so Florence wasn't a paradise when he lived there. It had the kind of problems every big city had. Pollution, crime, overpopulation, people complaining about not being able to afford sentients or even semis, other people complaining about too many sentients and semis taking their jobs... But things had gone downhill from there. They'd made the place so shitty that he preferred to live in the base instead of moving back.

Three people broke away from the clutter and ran, one of them carrying a bundle and the two others fending off the crowd. Luca lazily followed their progress through dusty roads, away from the most populated areas and past once respectable housings that had now fallen into a derelict mess.

He had visited Florence once in the past two years. When he found himself the only human survivor at the base, he'd had to deal with a lot of shit before he even considered going back to the city. But one day he decided it was time to suck it up and start actually living. That's when he took the Rover to Florence.

He was shocked to see it like this. But they were even more shocked to see him. All the slum dwellers outside the wall stared at the car and the guards at the gate were clueless. In the end, they contacted their superiors and asked what to do with him, and Luca was escorted to the city hall, still located in Palazzo Vecchio, to be interviewed by some big cheese. By the time he entered that building, he was beginning to realize how much everything had changed in his absence. Not just the wall and the domes. Not just that people spoke differently. Not just that fashion in clothing had changed. But they had abandoned artificials, social media and practically every bit of technology invented after the First World War. Probably. Luca wasn't really into ancient history. All he knew was that everything was so damn old-fashioned and that they considered themselves the last civilized community in the whole world.

Going on his own without bringing Nanny or Alfredo was something he felt he had to do. Probably as some kind of lame rite of passage that he'd needed at the time, but it turned out to be a good move. Not only had Florence abandoned artificials. All kind of robotics above the level of a waterpump had actually been outlawed although he never learned the reasoning behind it.

The trio that Luca was studying disappeared from view, and he shifted his gaze to the perimeter of the slums. The wasteland was creeping down the hillsides, ever so slowly taking little bites of civilization and giving them a good chew before spitting them out again.

He supposed it was a small miracle that they had let him leave again. They told him he could stay, that he was a valuable resource. He was someone from their past who may possess knowledge that could be useful to them. Not about sentients, of course, but they had lost a lot of skills through the centuries. No shit. Luca didn't need them to tell him that. They praised him for being a contemporary Lazarus. It didn't sound too bad at first, but being allergic to bullshit, it didn't take Luca long to start metaphorically sneezing.

It wasn't just that he couldn't bring Nanny and Alfredo with him. They also told him that his robots, the offensive term not helping at all, would have to be destroyed and he wouldn't need them anyway since he would be living in a protected environment. He tried to explain that his staff were sentients and that killing them was not an option. He also guessed that the protected environment in question meant not so much his protection, but making sure that he didn't pollute the minds of the common man with outrageous ideas.

Luca lowered the binoculars. It was a brittle society they had reduced themselves to after generations of inbreeding or whatever went on down there. He knew he could do wonders for Florence. Da Vinci, Macchiavelli, Basella, Capello. Not alone, of course, but with help from either the right combination of sentients and semis or people who weren't so narrow-minded, he could revolutionize the place. He'd get rid of the wall and educate people. There was no reason why they should live in a strategically ridiculous medieval fortress and not a flourishing, expanding city. Basically, the descendants of his contemporaries had completely forgotten that Florence was the cradle of rebirth, a scientifically and culturally innovative place.

He stuffed the binoculars back into their case. Florence ought to be his. And someday... someday.

10:
Teo

The Centre of Rediscovery and Restoration felt different. Teo knew it hadn't really changed. It was the same heavy building squatting in one of the outermost domes where most industries and manufacturers were located, aptly called the Industrial Dome. Once most of them had been placed outside Florence, but when the domes were constructed and the ancestors of the current inhabitants were forced to cut their losses, they moved in there. The Centre, colloquially nicknamed R&R, had existed for a shorter amount of time. The plaque above the entrance said 378 AF. That was when someone had decided that it was a good idea to begin organizing the finds from the past.

If anything had changed since the previous day, it was Teo. Every object she inspected and prepared for storage or sent on to restoration carried a meaning she had never sensed as strongly before. She knew where these items came from now. She had more firsthand knowledge than most other employees in the R&R now.

It was a strangely hard secret to keep. Not that she was in any danger of blurting out, "Oh, by the way, I disguised myself as a spotter and went outside the city yesterday," during the lunch break. But R&R felt restrictive, and the excursion meant more to her than she had realized it would.

The ending of the trip had been awful, but even without that incident, she had not enjoyed going through the slums. As much as she would like to be able to go outside whenever she wanted, she had to admit that she felt safe and snug in the inner city. But it was a privilege. She had always known this, but being confronted with the slummers brought one of her old questions to the surface. Why was it that some people were inside and others outside? Who had decided who went where when the wall was built?

It was impossible to find a reliable, historical source. And it was not for lack of trying. But whenever Teo consulted a book on the subject, it either completely left out anything beyond stating that the wall, like the domes, was built to protect the inner city from the elements, or went needlessly biblical in its treatment of the matter.

"Do you have anything for me today?" asked a voice next to her.

Teo almost jumped. She was so deep in thought that she hadn't heard the woman with the trolley coming up to her.

"Yes. Sorry, I'll just wrap it up for you," Teo said, smiling. She did have a few objects for filing. One was a piece of scrap metal with a number on it, but Teo was certain the number was a serial number and not significant in any way. As much as Teo hated trying to destroy the past, there was no reason not to smelt it into something usable, so she tied a yellow ribbon around it and put it into the trolley.

The other item she had inspected today was more interesting. Teo was fairly certain it was an intact mechanism for securing the shovel on one of the digging machines used in the Green Dome. Even if that was not the case, such a part could be used for other purposes as well. So that got a green ribbon.

"Thanks for waiting," Teo said.

"Have a good day," replied the trolley girl and moved on.

Teo looked up at the clock on the wall. Her shift would be over in a few minutes. She could hardly wait. Perhaps it was her friends' no-nonsense manner. Vanni and Arsenio were both down to earth and some of the least aloof people around her, especially of anyone in authoritative or high positions. But having been outside with them made them even more... She searched for the right word and settled for sincere. She felt she could even bring up the subject of the wall with them. As someone who traversed it on a regular basis, they may know a little more about its origins than she did. She was going to be cautious, though. Not because it was a crime to ask questions, but it was frowned upon. Teo asked her father about it once, so she knew exactly how these conversations would go if one talked to Florence's elite.

Her father had leaned back in his chair with his hands on his stomach. It was a clear sign that he was about to make an important statement. As if he needed to lean back in order to take in air enough to shout out his words. He didn't shout, though. He just spoke with the authority of a man who thought he knew he had the one and only truth.

"When the end came," he began, referring to the catastrophe, "Florence, once more, became the city of rebirth." He paused for effect. "It became an ark. Like Noah and his kin, we were spared destruction."

Teo nodded. "But does that mean... Did God tell the first council whom to bring?"

Her father sent her an admonishing glare. "It is not as simple as that. Perhaps He did. Perhaps He used the elements to show His will." He tapped the table between them with his forefinger, emphasizing every single word as he went on, "Humanity was in decay. You see evidence of it in your work every day, Teodora. Our ancestors worshiped themselves, and they worshiped the tech. They elevated themselves to godhood by creating robots in their own image."

There was no way of proving him wrong, but being used to dissecting her father's words, it was clear to Teo that he was not answering her question. Someone built the domes and the wall. Someone decided who went inside and who didn't, and she had a hard time imagining that any god would personally attend to that task.

"The people of Florence were meant to survive God's wrath," her father hammered home his postulate.

"But there are other survivors," Teo said, meeting her father's gaze. "They're right outside the wall. And that's only some of them. There are nomads out there..."

"Teodora," he cut her off, "They, the people out there, are in Purgatory. We were spared. Why can't you just be happy and grateful for that?"

Because someone made the call, and it wasn't God. She didn't say this. Instead she said, "But Noah went on to re-populate the Earth."

"When the flood was gone," her father said, nodding sagely. "The flood that removed all the sinners."

Teo began to see where he was going. "So we are waiting for everybody else to die?" she exclaimed. "But that's... Who says they even are dying? Who says we're the last city? I find it hard to believe that only Florence survived the fall."

"You take it too literally," her father said, chuckling a little as if she were an ignorant child.

She bit back a remark that in her opinion, he was the one taking everything too literally. There was a lot of that when your father was a councilman. Biting back answers and behaving politely and orderly. Well, at least in the open.

Teo's shift was officially over, so she put her pen in its holder, stacked her papers neatly and left her table. R&R may be a big place, but most of it was used for storage. They were only a handful of people assessing and labeling items, a few more like the girl with the trolley who made all the figurative cogs turn by moving objects around and then the board who did the literal cog-turning. Teo automatically glanced at the door that led to their department as she passed it on her way to the entrance hall.

The ruling body of R&R consisted of historians and technies. Every employee in Teo's department adhered to their rules, going through a virtual checklist of features to look for in the artifacts they were presented with. And the items that did not appear to be useless junk ended up with the experts.

The corner of Teo's mouth twitched into an involuntary smile. Experts. Oh yes, they undoubtedly knew what they were talking about, but they weren't alone. Teo liked to muck about with the objects she was given before passing them on. But she wasn't expected to attempt to impress anyone. After all, she ought to get married and retire from her job and, her father had told her more than once, sooner rather than later. He hadn't been fond of her working at R&R in the first place, but she had convinced him that it would look good for his daughter to show an interest in contributing to the city's well-being. Politics always won him over. Unless it was the wrong kind of politics.

"Goodbye, Miss Terzi," said the woman at the reception desk.

"Goodbye," Teo returned with a smile as she passed through.

It wasn't that Teo wanted to be famous. It wasn't even that she hoped to make a discovery that became famous. She only wanted to work with tech and to be good at it. She wanted to make things work that would never otherwise work. She wanted to salvage scraps from her ancestors and turn them into engines or pumps or other useful machines. To replace old and worn out cooling systems instead of just patching them up. But she was officially stuck cataloging artifacts until the day she bit the bullet and married.

She shook her head in an attempt to clear it. Now she was meeting Vanni, and they'd be talking about their adventure, and she'd better leave her moping behind.

11:
Teo

Vanni Alesi was leaning against the wall of the building opposite R&R. The street between the houses was empty. Not everyone was allowed into this section of the Industrial Dome. The council didn't want people to be able to wander in from the street and take a look around R&R because although most of the dangerous items were immediately destroyed, such as old, defunct robots, they did have a lot of things considered unsuitable for the general public. Vanni, of course, had the necessary clearance to get in anywhere he pleased.

Teo paused before she crossed the road. Vanni hadn't noticed her yet. He was standing in the shade of the building, playing with something in his hands. A small ball?

A cloud passed overhead, and Vanni glanced upwards. The roof of the dome must have been so clear once that it would be possible to see every little detail in the sky, but now the surface had been scratched and dented. At times it was hard to see anything, but the wind had blown sand and dust away today.

Teo crossed the road, and Vanni looked away from the

sky, noticing her. He pocketed the ball.

"I hope you didn't wait," Teo called out.

Vanni disengaged himself from the wall and shook his head. "No, it's fine. How was work?"

Teo gave him a quick hug. "Nothing out of the ordinary," she said. "Dusting off old stuff that someone like you brought in from the outside."

Vanni smiled. "You should be doing more than that," he muttered.

"Thanks," she replied. Vanni had listened to her going on about ancient tech and examining the parts that were brought in often enough to know she was a pretty good technie. "So where are we going?"

"Arsenio is meeting us in the Green Dome."

"All right." They began to make their way down the street. It was a good place to meet if they meant to talk undisturbed. It was easier to catch someone eavesdropping in a park than in a crowded café.

As they got closer to the edge of the dome, more people began to appear. It was late afternoon and work shifts were over. Now everyone needed to get home. And although motorized vehicles were restricted inside the domes, a lot of people on bicycles and on foot were gathering and moving in a slow mob towards the exits, creating a bit of a traffic jam.

Vanni smiled and gestured for a group of people to go on when they stopped, obediently, because of his uniform. Teo couldn't decide if it would be nice and useful to instantly have people respect her, or if she would rather stay in anonymity. Not that she was that anonymous, really. Whenever she went somewhere with her parents, strangers treated her differently. Even on her own, she was sometimes asked if she was councilman Terzi's daughter. Vanni was noticed not because of who he was, but because of what he did. She was noticed not because of who she was or what she did, but because of what her father did.

They opted for the most direct route to the Green Dome and went through the corridor between the domes, but with the amount of people there, it would have been just as fast to choose an exit with an unsheltered path. There was nothing out there as the exposed streets and houses had been abandoned long ago. But on clear days, Teo rather enjoyed being outside, breathing the unfiltered air and feeling the dry wind on her skin. As used as she was to life inside the domes, there was something tantalizing about being outside, even in a mere passage between transparent walls.

The passageway split in two, and Vanni and Teo steered down the left-hand path. A moment later, they entered the Green Dome. Teo took a deep breath. Once everything around Florence looked like this. Teo knew because she had seen depictions, photos, of it. They were made by a machine called a camera that captured detailed images exactly as reality looked without any of the artistic freedom of artists and painters. Teo had seen cameras, but never a functioning one.

"You always do that," Vanni interrupted her thoughts.

"Do what?" Teo asked.

"You go quiet and sniff the air like that," he explained, "whenever we go in here. You did it when we were kids too."

Teo grinned. "I did?" She had always loved the Green Dome. When she was a small child, she imagined the Garden of Eden just like the Green Dome. She dreamt of becoming a farmer when she grew up, and although she ended up pursuing tech instead, she still enjoyed the atmosphere of this place more than any other. "So where are we going?"

"Arsenio is meeting us in the clearing," Vanni said.

The clearing was a place for picnics and day trips situated in the forest that made up the middle of the dome with tall trees that obscured the roof when you walked among them. It was a place to sit on a bench and pretend the greenery around you was endless. It almost was. The Green Dome was the biggest of all the domes of Florence. Of course there were small parks and plots with vegetables in the others to keep the ecosystems healthy, but the Green Dome was more than a park. It was the agricultural center of the city and the only place to find livestock.

Teo and Vanni found a footpath and walked through the forest to the clearing. There were several tables with benches scattered around the grassy ground, with enough distance between them to give the illusion of privacy. Only a few of them were occupied. Teo spotted Arsenio immediately. He was lying on his back with his arms behind his head on one of the tables, looking up at the canopies above him.

"Hey! Slacking on the job, Sabbadin?" Vanni called out.

Arsenio turned his head towards them. "Hey," he called back, ignoring Vanni's joke.

"Hi," Teo said. It had occurred to her that he may still be upset with her for what happened on their way back to the gate the previous day and it was a relief to see him smile as he got up from the table and greeted them.

"All clear?" Vanni asked.

Arsenio nodded. He had chosen a table conveniently near the edge of the clearing. "We can talk. Have a seat."

They all sat down, Arsenio and Vanni on one side of the table and Teo on the other. It felt a little like an interview. As if they were making a distinction between themselves and her. Weird. When she spent time with them, they were just her friends. It usually wasn't important that they were men or that they were arbiters and spotters and she wasn't.

"Did you enjoy the trip yesterday?" Arsenio asked.

"Yes," Teo replied. "It was incredibly interesting. Thank you again."

Arsenio made a dismissive gesture. "You don't need to thank us. That's not what we're here for."

"All right…" Teo raised an eyebrow and looked from Arsenio's unreadable expression to Vanni's slightly worried one. He was biting his lower lip. "So what are we here for? You said you wanted to talk about the trip."

"We do," Vanni agreed. "Certain aspects of it…" He cleared his throat. "When we came through the slums…"

Teo held up her hands. "Look, if it's about the mistake I made, I get it, and I did apologize. I understand if you're upset, but…"

"It's not about that," Arsenio interrupted. "We want to hear your thoughts on the town outside the wall."

"You know what I think," Teo said. "They're people. Like us. Only less fortunate."

"Do you still think so? One of them attacked you."

Teo met Arsenio's gaze. "Do you still think so, Arsenio? You beat that man down."

He didn't flinch and there was no hesitation in his eyes. "I did what I had to. It does not change my general view of the conditions out there. I'm trying to find out if it changed yours."

"Well, it didn't. Was I frightened? Yes, I was. Did I feel sorry for the man you beat? In a way, yes I did. Because he was a product of that place. There is a physical wall separating them from us, and the idea of it runs deep in all of our minds, but we are all human." She crossed her arms over her chest. "Why are we talking about this? I thought we were going to talk about the trip, but you two clearly have an ulterior motive."

Arsenio scratched the short, black bristles at the back of his head. She was better with words than he was, and he knew that.

Vanni snickered, then coughed to hide it.

Arsenio noticed and glared at him. "Well?" he said.

Vanni wiped the smile from his face and leaned across the table. His voice was so soft that Teo had to strain to hear him speak. "Well, you are not the only person who thinks like that. In fact... there is a group of people within the wall who would very much like to see some changes."

"A group?" Teo echoed. And things began to slip into the right places in her mind. It felt like a row of light bulbs on the same circuit being lit up one by one in rapid succession. Her father tearing a poster from the door of the council building and crumpling it a month ago. An overheard conversation about someone never getting political power. Vanni's cryptic comment that it would be interesting to bring her outside instead of telling her that it would be interesting for her. Arsenio and Vanni exchanging glances before asking her to meet them today. "You are... talking about a..." she began.

Arsenio and Vanni looked at each other. Again. It was a quick exchange, but there was no way she wouldn't notice.

"No," Teo corrected herself as more pieces eased themselves into the bigger picture. "No, you are trying to recruit me for a movement that you are both members of. Some sort of rebellion against the council... That's it, isn't it?"

"The reason we decided to take you with us on that mission yesterday," began Arsenio.

Teo nodded and finished for him, "It was that you wanted to see my reaction to the people who live out there. It had nothing to do with the actual mission. And here I thought you were doing it because we're friends," she added, not completely certain if that would have been better or worse.

"I'm sorry," Vanni said.

"What kind of arbiters would we be if we took everyone out there with us just because they asked?" Arsenio mumbled.

"Excuse me?" Teo turned on him. Her voice was squeaky and she cleared her throat to get it under control. "Everyone? I'm not everyone."

Vanni sighed. "No, you're our friend, but—"

"That's not what I meant," Teo bit him off a little more harshly than she intended. "I'm in R&R! I may not have a high position, but you know what I can do!"

"Of course," Vanni said, holding up his hands as if to deflect an attack. "Of course. And that's part of the reason you could be..."

Arsenio smacked the palm of his hand flat on the table. "All right," he said, leaving no room for interruption, "we brought you because you share our views on certain political issues, and we would not have done it if we weren't close to you personally. We know we can trust you."

Teo didn't reply. She knew he was waiting for her to confirm it, but she was going to let him stew a bit, even if it was childish. Vanni looked tortured, and Arsenio's eyes bored into her skull. "Yes," she finally said. "Of course you can trust me. Go on."

"You would be a valuable asset," Arsenio said.

"To... the rebel group you're part of?" Teo asked.

"Yes," Arsenio said, not missing a beat.

"Because of your job as well as your connections," Vanni added.

Teo nodded, slowly. Her father, that's what they meant. They wanted her to spy on her father. They wanted her to betray him.

"It's not only about the conditions out there," Arsenio added. "There's a lot of issues we disagree with."

"The shunning of technological advancement and use of earlier inventions," Vanni said.

"You know I'm with you there," Teo replied.

"And the council keeps insisting that it's not safe to attempt to expand the city or even establish settlements in other locations," added Arsenio.

They were pushing all the right buttons, as the saying went. It was one that Teo appreciated. "But why is all this so secret?" she asked. "Why don't any of you run for council?"

"Do you think we haven't tried?" Arsenio almost

growled.

"Not the two of us, personally," Vanni clarified. "But we have associates who have. But it's not as easy as that. Even if you have the age and status required to be eligible, the current administration needs to give you their approval as a candidate before you can run. That makes it pretty hard to get any opposition to the people already in power."

"All right. So who is involved in all this? What are you planning to do?" Teo asked.

"Well, we're..." began Vanni.

Arsenio held up a hand to silence him. "We've told you as much as we can right now. Are you in?"

"Wait," Teo exclaimed. "Hold on! How can I make that decision when I don't even know what you're planning? Do I want to see some changes? Yes. Do I want to help planning the assassination of my own father? No!"

"No one is going to assassinate anyone," Vanni said. "We want to solve Florence's problems without bloodshed. We want to influence the council politically and help the people in the slums."

"I need to think about it," Teo said.

"Of course," Vanni replied.

"Friday," Arsenio simply said. "Meet us at the Mezzo Pieno at eight if you're in. If you don't show up, we'll assume you aren't interested, and we'll forget this conversation ever happened."

12:
Mender

Although ne was programmed to be sympathetic, Mender was not capable of the wide range of reactions that some humans were susceptible to. Being level-headed and well-balanced was important when taking care of the terminally ill and dying. So when finally Mender and Renn had found a safe passage to the surface and stood in the rays of the morning sun, Mender did not panic. Ne did not break down because of the shock and ne did not refuse to go anywhere but back down where it was relatively safe.

Instead ne took a moment to absorb the devastation. What had once been a town with neat rows of houses and small, well cared for gardens and a quiet stream of motorized vehicles and pedestrians alike now lay in ruins. Buildings crumbled by years of neglect, streets deserted, covered with sand and dust, plants that would once be considered weeds struggling to survive.

It really had been centuries. For the first time, it occurred to Mender that the connection to CerEvolv may not be down. If the whole of Tuscany looked like this, perhaps even civilization on the whole continent or all over the planet had fallen, then CerEvolv itself may be long gone.

Mender had no choice but to find out. Ne knew that. And ne knew that leaving these ruins behind was the first step. Yet, for a while, ne did not take any steps. Ne was processing everything, reconfiguring protocols to adapt.

"Mender." Renn's voice was level.

Mender turned and saw him waiting at a respectful distance with his wooden staff in one hand and the other sticking out from beneath the cast. This was his world. Everything about him made instantly more sense now that Mender saw him in the right context. This was the environment he was negotiating. These were the surroundings that had shaped him.

"Yes. We should leave," Mender replied.

"Yes," Renn agreed, but his tone was quiet, unintrusive. It suggested that although he did want to move on, he would accept it if Mender needed more time.

"Please," Mender said, describing an arc around them with nir hand. Ne had a physical map and a homing device inside nir head, but ne was well aware that the routes on the map may not be available anymore and that nir companion was the expert on navigating here.

Renn inclined his head, then looked up for a moment, using the sun's position to navigate, Mender assumed. Then he began to walk, and Mender followed.

In addition to Renn's own belongings, Mender had given him protein bars and water. Mender had prepared for the trip as well as ne could. This not only meant dressing in a sensible way with gloves to keep the damaged hand safe, a coat with a hood and a scarf. Hopefully it would keep sand and dust away from the exposed parts in nir face. Ne also carried a bag stuffed to the brim with items that may come in handy. Preserved foodstuffs and drinkables, antibiotics and painkillers and plasters, materials for constructing a shelter, torches and any tools ne could find.

Mender did not have any physical money. Ne had decided not to attempt to explain to Renn how transactions took place in the past with payments transferred from one device to another, an invisible currency that worked because everyone believed in it. Renn had explained that there were settlements where wanderers sometimes traded, rested and brought news from other parts. Trinkets from the past were valuable to the stagnants, as Renn called them.

"It is very different from what you remember," remarked Renn after they had left the ruined town and found themselves wandering a vast and dry expanse.

Mender nodded. "Yes. Very much so," ne replied. "I did not realize the changes would be this great."

"How did it look?" Renn asked. His voice betrayed measured curiosity. He was not blurting out questions; in fact, Mender was surprised at how little he asked. Perhaps he was still timid of Mender or not certain if he could trust nem yet. Or perhaps he was trying to be polite.

"There were a lot of people," Mender said because ne had to begin somewhere. "Humans like you and sentients like me." Ne shot Renn a look to see if he understood. "And semis and demis too."

Renn's brow furrowed.

"Other kinds of artificials. Like me, but not as independent," Mender explained and decided to move on to something more relatable. "The houses in the town were functioning buildings with window panes and furniture and water for bathing and flushing the toilets. Lights came on when you moved or touched a panel in the houses and the electricity came from photovoltaic power stations or solar farms," Mender continued, then realized ne should stop before the descriptions became too detailed to understand without any prior

84

knowledge. "If I am not mistaken," ne continued, "this path we are walking now was a large road with room for many people going back and forth between the cities and to the smaller towns and villages. There were lamps along it so they could see at night."

Renn nodded. "Were there many trees?" he asked.

"Yes," Mender replied, glad that he was finally asking more questions that made it easier to anticipate where his interests lay and how much he knew. It would make future conversations easier as well as help Mender understand the new world. "This place was greener. And people in towns had gardens. And there were vineyards where wine was produced." Mender glanced at Renn for confirmation that he knew what wine was.

"It sounds fertile," he mused. "And easy."

"Food and drink were easy to come by for those who had wealth," Mender explained. "But some people were poor."

"Do you think it is always like that? That some people will go hungry while others have plenty?" Renn asked.

Mender walked for a moment in silence. That was a very insightful question, one that pointed to knowledge of complex societies. "I think it is a danger of any society, yes," ne said. "Back then, many humans strove for financial equality, but some people lived in large houses and had servants to work for them while others could hardly afford to pay for modest lodgings. Do you have experience with this problem?"

Renn made a half-shrug. "Wanderers don't consider worldly possessions important," he said. "We carry with us what we need in order to live and objects that may be of value to others in order to trade. Stagnants are different. Many of them like to... own things." The last bit sounded hesitant. As if he hardly knew what it meant.

"We have something in common, then. Sentients like me did not own anything. We were granted the means to provide for our needs, but we were satisfied carrying out our occupation. But that is far in the past now," Mender added. "Now I am here and I'm glad that you are sharing your knowledge with me."

"You are very knowledgeable in some areas," Renn said, eyes darting to the cast on his arm as he spoke, "but the world must look very different to you now. I don't know what you need to be told, so I welcome your questions."

"Thank you," Mender said. It was a relief because he appeared guarded most of the time. "And I yours, of course."

"Do you... miss the people you knew?"

Mender thought for a moment. Given nir occupation, it would have been illogical to program nem with that sort of sentiments. But in order to interact with grieving family members and understand bereavement, ne did have a sense of empathy that made nem able to acknowledge loss. "My purpose was to take care of very ill and very old people, and so I am used to losing those around me... But," ne added, "I have never been bereft of centuries before."

Renn regarded nem in a way suggesting that he thought Mender may be the only one to have experienced this. Mender wondered if ne was. "I imagine that you miss your Covey."

Mender had come to understand that it was the name of the group of wanderers that Renn had traveled with. Ne wasn't sure if they were his family or a bigger unit that migrated together.

As if he understood what Mender was thinking, Renn replied, "I miss the security and company of them, but we are not close. Our Covey is one of convenience, not of family."

"I see," Mender said. "But you want to find them for practical reasons."

"Yes," Renn said, but he hesitated a little. Undoubtedly there was more to these customs than Mender could immediately comprehend.

They walked for a while in silence. Mender was not constructed to feel fatigue, and Renn clearly was used to hiking across the unwelcoming terrain for hours every day. Despite his injuries, he kept a good, steady pace. He studied the horizon and their surroundings, navigated by the sun and read the wind for sudden changes in the weather, like the dust storm that brought him to Mender. It was the first time Mender saw anybody rely so fully on themselves and their own senses instead of electronic equipment.

"I have much to learn about your world," Mender broke the silence, "but you could probably not tell me everything even if you talked for a week."

Renn smiled at that. It was reassuring. Mender was meant to help and soothe nir clients, and often a smile was a good indication that ne was fulfilling nir purpose.

"I could say the same," Renn said, briefly meeting Mender's gaze, another small gesture to establish a more comfortable relationship between them.

"I probably should ask you what dangers we could run into on our journey," Mender continued.

Renn dipped his chin in agreement. "Dust storms are our most common foe," he said. "If one approaches, we will have to take cover. Rockfalls can be dangerous, but they are not frequent."

Mender could guess what a rockfall was. Although most of the tiny fragments left in the wake of the meteor that hit the Moon were expected to burn up in the atmosphere and only be detectable as shooting stars, more meteorites would make it to Earth in the centuries after the impact than ever before in the history of mankind.

"Some animals like wolves attack if they are hungry and sense weakness. And rats in packs," Renn continued, "and scarvhes of course."

"Scarves?" Although neither wolves, nor rats were a

threat in nir days, ne knew of them. Scarves, however, could not possibly be their wearable namesakes gone feral.

"You don't know of scarvhes?" Renn asked.

"No," Mender said. But now ne could discern a guttural sound in the word that likely signified a different spelling and meaning of the word. "Are they predators? What kind of animal are they?"

Renn thought for a moment. "They are like snakes, but with a hard shell like some insects. Hard like bone," he then explained. "They lie in wait in the sand and have wings. They are very fast."

A flying snake with an exoskeleton? That sounded fantastical to Mender, but Renn appeared to be serious. "How big are they?"

Renn brought up his staff. "The biggest are almost as long as this."

"Are we likely to encounter scarvhes?" Mender asked.

Renn shrugged. "I don't know. I have killed a few before. You need to strike at the top of their head. They have a soft spot."

"I will remember that," Mender said, "though I hope I won't need it. Is there anything else that may attack us?" Mender was half expecting Renn to mention tribes of violent people or robbers, but Renn was quiet for a while.

"Others," he finally said, discomfort evident from his tone of voice as well as his furtive glance at Mender.

Others. That was Renn's name for sentients, but he had been reluctant to talk about them. Something made them a sensitive subject. Mender assumed it had to do with the fact that they were thought to be defunct or dangerous and that Mender clearly was neither. "Have you been attacked by Others before?" Mender probed.

"No."

"But you think they are dangerous?"

Renn shook his head, but it didn't seem to be in response to the question. "The legends say they are. Everyone is told to run if they see one." His eyes searched Mender's face for a moment. "They are not supposed to be like you," he added.

"I see. But," Mender added, cautiously, "I think perhaps they are." Who knew what happened to a sentient after being active for centuries without maintenance and, especially, a duty to fulfill? It had never been tested because they were such a recent step up in the robotics industry that there simply was not enough data. Mender was only a few years old at the time of the impact and in a manner of speaking, ne had not experienced the time ne was without power. Ne had not been without a purpose in nir entire existence. Even now, ne was following nir instructions.

Mender rummaged nir mind to find a way to explain this. "Others are like tools," ne began. "They have a purpose, and they will fall apart if not taken care of. The Others in your legends, I think, have been neglected for a long time, and as such they have fallen into disrepair and may have become unreliable."

"How are you different?" Renn asked, obviously understanding the comparison, possibly a little too well.

"I was not active until you activated me. I was in a safe place. I will last for many years yet before anything of the sort happens to me." This Mender could not know for certain, but in any case, ne would part with Renn and reach CerEvolv before any crisis was likely to arise.

"Good," Renn said. Then, after a few minutes, he added, "We should look for a place to camp for the night."

13:
Renn

Renn woke with a start and the feeling that he had slept for far too long.

"Good morning," said a calm voice, so reassuringly that it was difficult not to accept that it was indeed a good morning.

Renn found himself staring at the now familiar shape of Mender sitting on the opposite side of the embers of last night's fire. The Other ... No, the sentient, he reminded himself, was studying him with that unreadable, almost metallic face. "Good morning," Renn replied.

"Did you sleep well?"

Renn almost laughed. He could not remember the last time anyone asked him if he had slept well. He also could not remember the last time he had a full night's sleep during migration.

They had found a suitable campsite the previous evening, managing to put up a bivouac using curiously light metal rods and strange fabric Mender had brought along. The material appeared thin and fragile, but it was waterproof and kept the wind out well.

They gathered twigs and roots, and Renn built a fire while Mender watched. Then Mender produced a strange tinderbox, demonstrated how it could quickly be ignited with no skill or technique at all, and Renn allowed the peculiar being to set fire to the pile.

After that, it was time to eat. Mender had brought a number of those curious meals and several bottles of water. Renn still marveled at the fact that sentients didn't need other nourishment than sunlight. As if that wasn't unsettling enough, Mender also announced that sentients did not need sleep either and therefore offered to keep watch through the night.

"I slept heavily," Renn replied for despite his resolve to keep an eye on Mender, he had slept all night.

"Good. Then you are rested for today's trek," Mender replied.

Renn only nodded. Lack of sleep never caused him to halt a migration. But from what he gathered, Mender had never done this before.

As Renn collapsed the bivouac and packed up their belongings, he could feel Mender studying him. Again. In the beginning, Renn assumed it was caution, the same feeling that made him shoot glances at Mender at intervals. But it was something else. It was... curiosity? Or perhaps his companion was merely trying to learn from him. That could be it.

The landscape gradually changed in the course of the day, taking them across a hilly terrain with what almost amounted to a forest surviving in the lee of higher ground. There were traces of a stream there, but it had dried out, and only a brittle surface of lined and cracked mud was left. There were no signs of his Covey.

Throughout the day, Mender studied a curious map full of roads and towns that only existed as letters on the smooth, colorful paper.

It was early evening and they were back on the flat

expanse of windswept plains, when clouds began to race across the sky, casting dark shadows with their pregnant bellies.

"Rain is coming," Renn said because although it was obvious to him, he could not be sure if Mender noticed it.

"Do you think we need to find shelter?" Mender asked.

For the second time that day, Renn almost laughed. "Yes," he said. Of course a downpour was not as immediately devastating as a dust storm, but every sudden change of the weather was not to be taken lightly.

"Well," Mender commented, "it is awfully dry. It will do the plants good with a little rain."

"Perhaps," Renn said, stopping to look up at the sky for a moment. The wind wasn't strong, but it was coming from the west and the clouds were blowing in from the mountains to the east. It was going to be a thunderstorm. "But it is rarely a little rain."

Renn mentally went through their options as he walked, faster, in the direction they had been going all day. They could stop where they were and use the strange fabric to cover themselves and hope it would keep them dry, but water would seep into the ground under them. And they were still going to protrude on this flat expanse. That meant danger of lightning strikes. The nearest hills were an option, but they were now closer to the stagnant dwelling that Renn was headed for.

"You can move faster for a while without getting exhausted, yes?" he asked. Mender had not seemed troubled or sore from hiking so far.

"Yes," Mender replied. "I am constructed to carry more too. If we need to pick up speed, I can carry your bag."

It would be unwise to give a stranger his bag... But Mender was hardly a stranger any more. "We will try to make it to the nearest settlement," he said, carefully slipping out of the straps on his backpack. He handed it to Mender and hesitated a little. There was no polite way to approach this. "Will you cover your face as much as possible? They have not seen a sentient before."

If Mender was offended, it did not show. "Of course," was the only answer Renn got as Mender adjusted the bag. Then, almost as an afterthought, "I was not meant to look this way. I know it is strange to humans."

Renn made a noncommittal sound. He couldn't very well pretend that he hadn't screamed in horror at the sight only a few days ago.

They set off at the fastest pace Renn could muster without exhausting himself too quickly. Mender appeared untroubled by the speed and the extra burden. As they hiked, the clouds overhead grew darker, and guttural growls began to emerge from the sky, rolling back and forth in the distance.

The ruins of what Mender's map showed as an inkblot with a printed name above it crept into view and Renn turned away from the ancient road they had been following all day. It may culminate in that city eventually, but there was a more direct path to the part of it, which the stagnants called their home.

The air felt alive around them as the wind picked up and the clouds raced towards it, and the clashing of wind and clouds brought the roaring of the heavens closer and louder and ever more frequent. Blinding lights began to flicker, still too far away to strike, and Renn counted his heart beats against the space between lightning and thunder, but his heart was beating out its own thunderous rhythm in his chest now.

"Have you been to that settlement before?" Mender asked without a hint of exhaustion. They may as well have been casually strolling.

"Yes," Renn replied, "they will give us shelter."

The first drop fell on Renn's hand. A tentative reminder of the storm chasing them. Renn had hoped to make it to the settlement dry, but it was a foolish hope.

The next drop came, and then another, faster and faster, raindrops the size of pebbles pelting from the vast bellies of the clouds above to make a pattern of dark dots on the ground until there were no more dry patches.

Renn had pulled up his scarf and his hood to provide a little protection, and beside him, Mender had covered as much of the strange face as possible, pulling the hood of the coat down and arranging the scarf so only the eyes were visible.

A whiplash of white tore across the sky, leaving an impression so vivid that Renn could still see it when he shut his eyes against a gust of wind that carried grit and water with it. Only a few seconds later, the roar of a thunderclap reverberated through every bone in his body.

Mender made a noise that sounded like, "Oh." It was muffled by the scarf and the sound of the rain pounding the wanderers and the ground now. Renn assumed it meant that Mender finally understood some of the dangers of the rain.

Renn pulled out his flask and uncorked it, holding it out to the elements with his injured arm. Despite the heaviness of the rain, it would soon be absorbed by the earth and leave this place as dry as ever. It was wise to collect some for later use.

He squinted, droplets falling from his hood and splashing around his feet. In the murk of the downpour, ancient buildings suddenly loomed in front of them. They were grey giants like every other derelict city, but stagnants had made it theirs and changed it into a patchwork of new and old.

"Stay behind me," Renn shouted over the rain as they approached the settlement. Mender would both be safer behind him and less likely to cause any trouble.

The noise of the storm was amplified by the buildings in front of them. Water was pattering on the rooftops, and the wind was rattling every loose brick and board.

The settlement was protected by a wall of scraps and rubble balanced in piles and filled out with dirt where there would otherwise be gaps. Renn aimed for the nearest break in that wall. He put the lid back on his flask and shoved it into his belt as he went through. The ground was slippery, muddy and soggy here in the way it only became when several people had trampled a path and stirred up the dirt as it turned wet. And the smells were almost overwhelming. They too told a story of many people living close together. Waste of all sorts, smoke, food and dirt, and behind it an underlying scent of animals.

But the streets were empty. The downpour had driven the stagnants inside. Renn swatted water away from his eyes and tried to get his bearings. He knew the settlement spread across only a corner of the old city. Last time he was here, his Covey stayed for a while in some suitable ruins near the stagnants, but not within the invisible borders of their town. They had traded, talked, exchanged information, but they had stayed separate. Now it was too wet for that. They needed to get dry. And the best place for outsiders to go would always be a tavern or an inn.

He glanced over his shoulder to make certain Mender was still following him, then ducked his head against the rain and splashed towards the most public-looking building in sight.

14:
Renn

There was a sign nailed to the door of the building, welcoming 'thirsty citizens and weary wanderers alike'. The door creaked open when Renn pushed, and he stopped just inside while Mender carefully shut the door behind them. Renn was breathing heavier than he had realized, and his panting was the only sound in the tavern. It was dimly lit by lamps hanging from the ceiling, giving off a smell of burning fuel that mixed with those of sweat and draught. All faces in the room turned towards the newcomers, some open-mouthed, others narrow-eyed.

"Good day," Renn broke the silence. This settlement did not have sentinels guarding the perimeter, but it did not mean newcomers were not assessed. He was talking to everyone and the keeper of the bar in particular, asking their acceptance of his presence. His presence and that of his silent companion who undoubtedly looked very out of place here.

"Good day, wanderers," came the reply after a drawn-out pause.

The tension began to seep out of the room, through

every crack in the dusty floor and rough stone walls. And although Renn was better at reading the wind than reading people, he knew they had both been officially accepted. He nodded, more to himself than anyone else, pushed down the hood of his cloak and stepped forward. The room was still quiet and his boots sloshed with every step, but a faint murmur came from the dark corners of the establishment now.

"We seek shelter from the rain," he said and stopped close to the bar itself. The top of it was shiny with wear and from being polished. It seemed to be the only really clean surface in the room.

The woman in charge, not only of the bar, but of the stagnants' opinions of strangers, did not try to disguise her gaze as it traveled from the top of Renn's head to the soles of his boots, searching for weapons and wealth. Renn studied her in return, though slightly less overtly. She had the look of a stagnant. Paler, less weatherbeaten, less muscular. Her gaze was calculating, but not unkind. She cocked her head and peered around Renn. "Only the two of you, then? That's the smallest Bevy I ever saw."

"Yes, only the two of us," Renn confirmed, not bothering to correct the mistake.

"Your friend doesn't talk much," she commented.

Renn made a discreet gesture, hoping that Mender would understand the encouragement to speak up, but not too much.

"Hello," Mender said, and it sounded like Mender was smiling. "We're happy we reached your town. It's a horrible weather outside."

The woman's face split into a sympathetic smile and Renn realized that for whatever reason, Mender's approach was exactly the way stagnants spoke, emphasizing universal facts instead of moving the conversation along. How could a sentient who had been asleep for hundreds of years know? Probably because in a way Mender had been a stagnant. Mender had never had to worry about food or water or being killed by predators or the elements. The only thing Mender really needed was sunlight.

"You two look half drowned," the woman replied. "If it's just you, we can put you up so you can get dry and get something to eat. If," she added, "you can pay."

Taverns like this one often had spare rooms, but Renn had never understood why. His various Coveys never visited them, partly because they would not pay for a place to sleep when they carried their own homes with them, and partly because there was never space enough for more than a couple of people in the taverns. And the town people all had homes near the tavern, didn't they? Perhaps the stagnants weren't so stagnant after all and sometimes went to other settlements. "We have wares to trade," he replied and turned to Mender again. The sentient had insisted on carrying a number of items along for the purpose.

"Show me," the woman said, crossing her arms over her bosom in a way that suggested she may not find the things they brought particularly valuable.

Mender put the big bag on the floor. It looked soaked, but the items inside it were dry.

Renn glanced over his shoulder. They were still attracting some attention. He had intended to talk to Mender about the value of the items they brought along before they had to trade. But when the weather changed, there was no choice but to get to safety as quickly as possible, and now he had to trust that Mender was capable of this. And preferably quickly because the heat he had built up hurrying towards the settlement was leaving Renn now, and he was starting to shiver.

"I think you may be interested in this," Mender said and placed a small box on the bar. If Mender was out of place, it was nothing compared to that. It was shiny and smooth with only a red cross bulging up from its surface.

Renn studied the woman. She was trying to hide surprise behind a skeptically raised eyebrow. "Where did you get that?" she asked.

"In an intact basement under the ruins of another town," Mender replied, which was perfectly true and not true at all.

The woman reached out, ran her fingers across the lid of the box. "Does it open?" she asked.

Mender hesitated, then said, "Yes. The items inside are what we are looking to trade."

Renn kept his gaze on the woman, but he could see Mender's fingers, although gloved, easily pry open the box and take out a small package. "There is something inside each of these packs that can be put on scratches and small wounds. They are called plasters. They stick to the skin and treat the area for infection. I am not going to open one because then it is no longer entirely clean."

Disbelief crept over the barkeeper's features now. "How do you know it works?"

Mender turned to Renn. "Could you..?"

Renn held out his injured arm. The pink cast dripped water, but it was not soaked.

"This is a bandage made from a similar material. It is much larger and tougher than a plaster, but it works much in the same way."

Renn allowed the woman to touch the odd cast on his arm and hoped he didn't appear to doubt how it worked or what it was.

"How many plasters are in the box?" she inquired.

"Ten. We also..."

Renn cut off Mender, "Will it do as payment for a room for the night and a meal?"

A calculating expression flickered across her face.

"We can share one meal," Renn added.

She nodded. "We have a deal, wanderers."

Renn shook her hand in agreement, and Mender handed over the box. Renn would have been sorry to see such a thing go if not for the fact that he knew Mender had more in the bag as well as other medical wonders that had not yet been explained to him. "May we go to the room? I will return for the meal," Renn said.

The woman directed them towards a staircase in the back, and they went past curious glances as they made their way to it.

The room was small and furnished with only a narrow bed and a three-legged wooden table. They both put down their bags.

"I expected to pay more," Mender said, unwrapping the scarf and pulling off the gloves.

Renn didn't know what to reply to that. Even if Mender had several of those boxes, it was a valuable and useful item to part with. He began to undress, peeling off soaked clothes and deciding to drape them wherever they could be draped. He wanted most of all to strip entirely and wrap himself in one of the blankets on the bed in order to get some heat back in his body. But he needed to go downstairs for his meal first.

A sound he couldn't identify made him turn to Mender again. It sounded a bit like a gasp. Mender was studying one hand.

"Is something wrong?" Renn asked.

"There is meant to be a protective layer of artificial skin covering my whole body," Mender replied. "I... think I detected a leak..."

"Of..." Renn trailed off. He suspected that Mender did not actually have blood inside.

"An undesired electric charge," Mender explained, and Renn felt no wiser. "It is not dangerous to you. But perhaps I ought to undress and let my clothes dry so no damage occurs."

"Oh. Of course," Renn said. "I... will go downstairs for the food."

On the way, he wondered if Mender needed the privacy. The Coveys he had been in were not usually stringent with who was allowed to see whom undressed, but he knew some stagnants were very keen on men and women not being around each other unless properly dressed or on intimate terms. And he did still not know the gender of his companion.

His stomach growled as he descended the stairs and the smell of cooking wafted towards him. He decided to ask a few questions now that he was there. If anyone heard gossip in a stagnant settlement, it was the barkeeper.

"Your meal needs to boil for a bit longer," said the woman behind the bar. She was surrounded by a handful of people who were examining the box Mender had given her.

"Thank you," Renn replied. "May I ask you a few questions while I wait?"

"You may," she agreed.

"Do you have more of these?" interrupted a man, pointing at the box just as the barkeeper snatched it up and put it into a pocket in her apron.

"No," Renn said although he was a reluctant and rather bad liar.

"But you have other things like it?" guessed the man.

"It belonged to my companion who was very lucky to find it. I own nothing of the sort," Renn replied, a bit more truthfully. "Please, if I may?"

The woman gestured for him to continue.

"We are looking for a Covey who may have come through this place. Do you know if any wanderers besides us have been here recently? It would be a few days ago. Less than a week."

"What did you say your friend had packed in that big bag

of hers?" asked the man.

The barkeeper scowled at him. "An answer to a question doesn't cost anything in this place," she said. "And yes. A group of wanderers came by some days ago."

Renn smiled. As certain as he had been that he was following in their path, it was nice to have it confirmed. "How many? Do you know?"

"Seven," said the woman. "A small child was with them."

So it was probably the old man who had died.

The woman served one of the men at the bar a cup of draught. "They were headed towards the domes," she offered.

"The domes?" Renn echoed.

"The city," the woman said, pausing before she realized he still did not know what she meant. "The city in the valley with the domes. I don't think they were going there, and right they would be not to, but they were headed that way. North-east."

"Thank you," Renn replied. "Is there a reason they should avoid that city?"

"Haven't you heard of it?" asked the man with the draught.

"The hermit told us," the man who had been so eager to get his hands on Mender's wares chimed in.

All Renn had wanted to know was whether his Covey had come through the settlement, and now everyone seemed to be telling him things he could not relate to anything.

"It's like this," the barkeeper cut through the chatter. "There's a hermit who lives by himself out there. He comes to us every few months in a wagon that makes a lot of noise and drives without being pulled. He comes to trade with us. He talks of the domes and the city under them and warns us against them because the people who live there would steal everything we own and turn us out."

Renn nodded.

"The hermit speaks in a strange way. Not like you," said the man with the draught and sipped it carefully. "More like your friend, really."

"I see," Renn said although he did not. He had more questions now than when he arrived, but the most pressing one had been answered.

A man in an apron came through a door behind the bar with a steaming bowl.

"Your food," the barkeeper said, pushing it along the bar towards Renn. She took another glass and poured draught into it. "And something to drink."

"Thank you," Renn said, picking up the items and trying to will his stomach not to growl again.

He balanced the hot bowl, a wooden spoon and the cup as well as he could with his broken arm on the way up the stairs. They were talking about him as he went, in hushed whispers that they probably assumed he couldn't hear.

Renn pushed his back against the door to push it open, and it was only when he turned around that he saw Mender. He almost dropped the bowl.

Mender had undressed. The parts of the body that had been covered by clothes had skin. It was paler than Renn's by far, but not so much compared to many stagnants. It was smooth and unscarred and there was not a single hair on it. Despite his efforts not to stare, it was impossible for Renn to not take in the whole of Mender. And Renn found that his question about gender was not answered. Or perhaps it was. Only not in the way he might have expected.

"Oh, I am sorry if this is awkward for you," Mender spoke up and quickly pulled a blanket from the bed to drape it like a sleeveless robe.

"No, I..." Renn began with no idea where the sentence was going.

"I understand. Many humans find being unclothed only

appropriate for intimate situations. I meant no offense," continued Mender, "but I do apologize. I assumed it would not be an issue since I am a Minder model."

"I did not mean to cause you to feel..." Renn began again. "To feel uncomfortable." Sentients were Others. According to the legends, Others were created by mankind, not bred. Renn understood it now, and it seemed strange that he had assumed his traveling companion must be male or female.

After Renn had slurped up the last of the meal and drunk the draught, he felt relaxed and tired. Going to sleep not only with Mender keeping vigil, but also inside a building where no predators or storms could surprise them was a luxury he was not used to.

15:
Mender

Before the impact, Mender would sometimes put nemself on standby. Ne did not need the downtime, but once in a while there would simply be nothing to do in the home, and if an emergency arose, alarms would immediately reactivate all nir senses.

There were no alarms to tell Mender if something happened to Renn. And Renn was Mender's client, at least until Renn decided to cut the ties or Mender reached CerEvolv. It was hard to tell if Renn understood this or not. He seemed to trust Mender, but did he realize that Mender's primary purpose was to care for him now?

The previous night was Mender's first time watching over someone outside. It was also nir first night after emerging from the relative safety of the home and venturing out into the broken world. Despite the amount of unknown data and the dangers Renn had warned against, it struck Mender as a peaceful night.

Ne familiarized nemself with all the new auditory inputs and took care of the primitive fire. At intervals, ne studied the sky. There was no Moon, of course. Ne had known this all along, but visually confirming it under the vast sky was a new experience. If ne had been programmed to feel nostalgia and loss, it would probably have provoked such emotions.

The second night was proving different. The tavern was not quiet. Laughter and drunken shouts found their way to the small room, and Mender sat on the floor, listening in the darkness. Ne hoped to catch bits of conversation that would reveal more about the society in which ne now found nemself, but the voices were warped and only the loudest exclamations could be made out clearly. They only informed Mender that alcohol was flowing and that humanity still liked to play games and gamble. Whatever the game, it was undoubtedly a far cry from the betting systems that some of Mender's clients had enjoyed.

Later, the tavern became quiet, and Mender could easily hear Renn's regular, quiet breathing on a backdrop of rain and thunder. The storm rolled across the heavens, appeared to circle overhead for a while, and then, well past midnight, it began to fade.

Mender was running a self-diagnostic, now that ne was completely dry again, to make sure none of nir circuits had suffered any damage when a sound at the door caught nir attention.

Hushed voices were discussing something, urgently. Nervously? Mender sat quite still. Fragments of the conversation reached nem. They included words like 'treasure' and 'kill' and 'if necessary'. The combination of these words and the near proximity of the persons speaking made Mender's sense of danger spring into action. Ne reached out to touch Renn's arm and warn him, but before ne managed, the door opened.

Despite the stealthiness of everything that was happening, Renn woke. It was more like a sentient being activated than a human waking up from deep sleep. One moment he was most certainly sleeping, and the next, he had rolled over, nearly knocking Mender aside, and was reaching out for the staff he always kept close.

"Don't even think about it!" hissed a voice from the doorway.

Mender turned to see three figures silhouetted against the dim lamplight in the corridor outside. One was holding what looked like a club. Another was wielding a contraption that, judging from the way she was aiming it at Renn, was probably a sort of firearm with an arrow instead of bullets.

"What do you want?" Renn asked, not a trace of sleep in his voice.

"Stay quiet and still if you want to keep your lives," the unarmed of the trio told him. Mender was reminded of the kind of interactive media entertainment that those of nir clients who could move enough to engage virtual foes would partake in. But this was not the least entertaining.

"Where do you keep your artifacts?" asked the unarmed man and began to creep into the room.

So that was what they wanted. Mender did recognize the man with the club as one of the patrons in the bar earlier. Mender attempted to calculate the possible outcomes of this encounter. Perhaps it would be advisable to let the thugs have what they wanted as not to endanger Renn further. But in the long run, if they took everything Mender had carefully chosen to bring, Renn could also be endangered by the lack of supplies...

"I told you I don't..." Renn began. His voice had dropped to a lower tone that Mender identified as threatening rather than frightened.

"Yeah, and scarvhes are soft," snorted the woman with the primitive firearm. There was a scraping noise as she drew back the string further, readying it to shoot

"All right," Mender spoke up. Ne glanced at Renn and made a small nod, hoping that Renn would understand what ne was doing. It was against protocol to make decisions for clients who had their faculties intact, but it was in accordance with said protocol to protect a client at all costs. "It's all in that bag." Mender pointed at Renn's backpack, which was resting on the floor very close to the bed.

The unarmed thief approached, made it past Mender who did nir best to stay in the shadows so that he would not notice nir face, and bent down to examine the bag.

Mender rose and tossed the blanket away, into the woman's line of sight so Renn was obscured for one short moment. Three fast and precise steps, and Mender was so close to the two in the doorway that they were within an arm's reach. Their reaction was exactly what ne hoped for; Shock at the skinless face. The man actually stumbled backwards with a cry and hit the doorframe. The woman swung the weapon around, but Mender intercepted it, wrenched it out of her hands and threw it aside. Ne pushed her back against the wall to keep her pinned there as a potential hostage if Renn needed it.

Renn did not need it. Mender's attack took few seconds, but when ne turned, ne caught a glimpse of Renn, swinging his staff with one hand at such a speed that his weapon was a blur. A loud crack told Mender when it hit its target, and the thief practically flew backwards. He landed sprawled and unmoving on the floor near the table. Renn's staff was clearly not only meant for hiking. It was a weapon, and its wielder was an expert at using it.

"What are you?" the woman gasped.

Mender studied her for a moment. The people of this settlement were as unused to sentients as Renn was, and ne was not certain which reply would be the least risky.

"Mender!" Renn shouted. A second later, something solid connected with the side of Mender's head so hard that ne stumbled forward, almost colliding with the woman. The surroundings seemed to blink out of existence. The synoptic connections failed because of the impact. Nir auditory connections did not fail, however. As ne was regaining nir balance, ne heard rapid footsteps, a whooshing noise, and then almost simultaneously a thud and a cry. Someone shouted, and something rushed past Mender as ne was trying to make sense of the situation. Then nir sight returned.

The man with the club was now a man without a club, and he lay motionless on the floor. Renn was holding the tip of his staff at the woman's throat, supporting the weight of the weapon with his bandaged left arm and aiming it with his right.

"Stop! You win! I'm not stupid," the woman breathed. She was still holding the weapon, but the string was slack and the arrow on the floor.

"Are you all right?" Renn asked, ignoring the thief for the moment.

"Yes," Mender replied. Despite the momentary lack of visual connectivity, there appeared to be no serious damage in nir circuits. It was advisable to see an engineer about it, but ne would do that when ne reached CerEvolv. "Thank you."

"Drop the weapon," Renn told the woman, and she obeyed without argument. "Sit down." The nomad lowered his staff and turned to Mender again when she slid to the floor without protest. "We need to go. Dress quickly."

"Should we not contact law enforcement?" Mender asked.

Nir companion frowned. He stood with the staff in his hand, stripped to his undergarments and with hair tousled from sleep and wind and rain, and he had never looked less like Mender's previous clients. If Mender was an expert caretaker of the dying, Renn was an expert at surviving. "I don't think there are any laws here that would favor wanderers," he spoke. "Please. We need to leave."

Mender argued no further. Instead, ne pulled on nir still damp clothes.

The wind howled outside the building, but the patter of rain on the roof had all but ceased.

The man who had attacked Mender with a club, remained unconscious on the floor while the other stirred and moaned. The priority protocols battled inside Mender. Ne was programmed to help humans, and the two men clearly were injured and in need of medical assistance. But treating them may very well endanger both Renn and Mender further.

Renn picked up the woman's weapon and handed it to Mender as they were about to leave. He pointed his staff at her. "Don't follow us."

She barked out a mirthless laughter. "Not for your skills with that staff, wanderer," she replied. "But for that abomination. Moon only knows how you came by an Other."

Renn seemed to consider a reply, but he bit it back and gestured for Mender to follow him out of the room.

16:
Luca

Luca sent out his recently restored drone, a plump little fellow of thiry centimeters across with happily blinking lights, a brand new camera and every bit of sensory equipment that Luca could fit into it. His parents paid a fortune to get him schooled in one of the leading institutes of robotics and artificial intelligence, a direct ticket to a top position in CerEvolv someday if combined with brains, nimble fingers and hard work. But they probably had not imagined that this was the way he would end up using the skills acquired at IRAI.

The drone hovered through the courtyard and hurled itself into the sky, and Luca soared with it into the thunderstorm. He was sitting comfortably in the chair in his workshop, wearing a visor, a headset and holding what was once a controller for *EverMist Isles XII* that was rendered obsolete when MMOs were no longer a thing.

The downpour created a constant noise in his headphones, every so often to be drowned out by thunder that left Luca with a temporary case of tinnitus. At one point, lightning struck a tree right next to the drone, and Luca circled, watching through the drone's camera as it burst into flame. The fire only lasted for a few seconds before the rain quelled it.

Luca decided to stay closer to the ground after that. He had not recovered the drone, burnt his hands fixing it and spent countless hours programming it to lose it in the storm. The ground could not absorb the water fast enough, and whole rivers of rainwater filled every crevice in the usually hard and dry earth. In one place, the drone witnessed a landslide as a hill succumbed to the elements.

He circled back towards the base. Since the disaster that brought him into this world, the base had not suffered significant damage from quakes or storms, but he wanted to make sure everything was in order. The rain was draining from the estate as it should and the lightning conductors were intact, so Luca returned the drone to his workshop and took care of it so it didn't catch a mechanical cold.

Then he waited for the rain to stop. He busied himself for a while recording a vlog although he didn't really feel like it. To begin with, it had just been an extension of what he'd done before the impact, although the thrill of watching the number of views and likes and subscribers to his channel go up was gone. Instead he was recording for posterity, making an archive of footage that showed how he lived and survived. He was a rare commodity nowadays, so it may become a valuable historical source someday. But as time passed, it began to feel pointless, and now he only did one recording every second month.

Still, he changed into a clean t-shirt, teased his hair into the best do he could muster, put on his best smile and turned on the camera. "Hey, strangers. Welcome to *Luca's Lab*," he said to the blinking red dot on the side of the recording device. "Be quiet for a while and listen... That is rain! And that was a thunderclap. We're having an actual goddamn thunderstorm. Sooo, what's new since last time?"

It was still raining when he finished the vlog. Luca had

plenty of other toys to entertain him indoors during the downpour, but he hated feeling holed up. Hated feeling trapped.

The next morning, Luca loaded his gear onto himself and the motorcycle. Mostly, this included water, a spade, a CEW gun and an actual gun. He told himself he was looking for technological things, gadgets that the rain might have uncovered, but as usual, he kept a faint hope in the back of his head, not allowing it to grow because that would only cause disappointment.

The Capello family's base was not the only of its kind. Most people planned on ensconcing themselves inside cities, building walls and domes to preserve a hospitable environment, or hoped to wait out the worst of the repercussions of the impact in well-stocked facilities underground. But some of the wealthiest people decided to hibernate through it all.

In hindsight, Luca was really skeptical. How would anyone know when to set the timer to? And how could anyone make sure the cryo pods were actually safe from environmental changes? Sure, sentients around the premises were pre-programmed to leap into action if anything happened, but even that did not ensure safety. Just look what happened to Luca's whole family. It may have been better to stay in Florence. But then again, he was alive here and now, and so who was he to complain? And besides, he could not possibly be the only one.

After he had done his bit of grieving and moping, after pulling himself out of the rut, Luca had checked the locations he knew of as the next logical step. His parents knew a few people who did what they did, but one place had malfunctioned, and there was a mushy soup of human remains inside the stasis pods. The other place had been abandoned a long time ago, and Luca could only make theories as to when and why and what had happened, but from the look of it, whoever had been in there had left the premises generations ago.

The most remarkable thing about being outside after a

thunderstorm, Luca mused as he sped down an almost clear stretch of road, was that there was almost no dust. Despite his efforts, he had minuscule grains of sand everywhere after a day outside. It was a special kind of peeling. One that left your skin raw rather than smooth if you weren't careful. But today he could drive without a mask and still not get his lungs full of the stuff.

The empty expanse went by on both sides as he made his way in the direction of Empoli. If he recalled correctly, there were some hills or dunes in that area that had not been there in his time, that weren't on any of his maps, and that he'd meant to check out for a while. Maybe the rain had uncovered something. There could be buildings hidden between the hills or even under them.

The sun broke through the veil of clouds drifting across the sky, almost blinding Luca before the visor on his helmet reacted and darkened. He slowed down and turned onto an invisible road that was so slick that the tires could hardly gain traction. Mud splashed from the wheels, staining his boots and trouser legs, and he was reminded of off-road racing before the impact. Back when survival was a sport and a lifestyle and not just life. He'd barely learned to drive before the world ended. But at least there was no one around to notice when he broke ancient speed limits or ignored rusty road signs.

Something caught the sun, reflecting it in short, Morse code-like glints. Something, Luca thought with a triumphant grin, that had not been there the last time he was out here. He revved the engine.

The hills were still there, but a few of them seemed to have experienced a landslide. They were oddly lopsided, and what had caught the sunlight was a metallic structure, sticking out at an angle from the hillside. As he got closer, Luca could see it was indeed the corner of a building, and there was a door inserted into it.

He parked the bike and shouldered his bag of equipment. It took all his willpower to saunter up to the newly exposed building at a laid-back pace.

The door was glorious. He knew the door. Well, he didn't know that exact door, but he knew the type. It was the same kind of door that had sealed the part of the building where his family's cryo pods had been. He told himself not to get his hopes up. Still, his heart made a happy, excited little dance inside his chest as he wiped dirt off the access panel with his sleeve and put his hand on the surface.

Nothing happened. He found the solar panels above the door and took out the spade from his bag to assemble the lightweight tool. Then he removed a rag from one of his pockets and fastened it around the handle of the spade to reach up and wipe the soil from the solar cells.

A few seconds later, the panel in front of him lit up in faint red.

"Hello there," Luca said, not really expecting an answer. Instead he put his hand on the panel again.

Red letters told him to fuck off. Or rather, they told him he was not authorized to access the facility. So it was time to get down and dirty and mess with the wiring behind the panel.

Every kid knew the kind of action movie where someone hotwires a car to steal it or breaks into a secret lab by meddling with the programming of the lock. Not all kids knew how to actually do these things. Luca did. Of course. He worked quickly, despite wearing gloves to shield him from electrical charges, cutting a wire here, connecting another there. A small spark, a flashing warning on the panel, though it was kind of pointless to show that someone was breaking in to the person who was breaking in.

And then the door began to grind open, so painstakingly slowly that Luca was starting to wonder if it would fall off the hinges and crumble to a heap of rust before it was open. It didn't.

The lights did not turn on. Luca's heart sank. But it could just be an electrical malfunction local to the lights. After all, the door worked.

17:
Luca

Luca flicked the switch on his torch. The thin beam showed him a cavernous space with crates stacked against each wall and no less than twelve pods on podiums in the middle of the room.

"Please," Luca whispered. His breath came out in a cloud of vapour. It was cold in here. It was a good sign. But the displays on the pods were dark. There should be something. A tiny blinking light on each of them at least. Perhaps they were on the other side...

He shone the torch around, but there was nothing on the floor except cables running from the cryo pods to the walls. "Please," he whispered again.

The transparent lid of the first pod was frosted over. Luca wiped at it with his gloved hand. But it made little difference. Inside was one big, white mass, a block of ice. That's not how it was supposed to look. He examined the pod and found the panel. When he touched it, it did light up, and for a moment he thought everything was all right after all, but then disappointment hit. The temperature was too low even for long-term cryo sleep. How had that even happened? The light that indicated life was not on. So whoever was inside had frozen to death.

Luca took a deep breath. It could be a local error. He would check each of them to be certain...

A sound behind him made him stop. A click... and then a voice.

"Step away from the pod and put your hands behind your head."

Shit. Luca knew better than not to comply. It sounded too much like a semi guard with a gun not to be a semi guard with a gun.

"Turn around slowly and identify yourself."

Luca put the torch on the ground and turned with his hands behind his head. "My name is Luca Capello," he said.

The guard was indeed a semi. Ne looked a lot like a human, as most semis did, but Luca could not discern nir features. The guard had a light attached to nir forehead that shone right in Luca's face and made him squint. "Luca Capello. You are an intruder," the guard said, which was true. "Intruders must be destroyed."

"What? No!" Luca replied. "Detained! Detained!"

The semi didn't bother to answer. Ne just raised nir firearm and shot.

Except nothing happened. The weapon was defunct. Luca breathed a sigh of relief. He lowered his hands. Either someone had messed with the semi's programming, or else it had malfunctioned sometime during the past few centuries. Either way, Luca knew where this was going.

The semi tossed the useless weapon aside and lunged at him, closing the distance between them so fast that Luca barely had time to draw. The light beam coming from the guard's forehead flickered, and ne came at him in flashes. He brought up his CEW gun, slammed it against the bulk of the semi's chest and pushed the button.

The light went crazy, jerking this way and that. Luca had done a few changes to the components inside the weapon to give it a few extra settings so it would never fail to take out any kid of artificial. It worked this time too. The semi's light went out and when nir body was done twitching and seizing, ne grew limp. And heavy. Luca didn't have time to get out of the way before ne collapsed against him and brought him to the ground.

"Shit," Luca coughed. Everything had gone dark around them. He reached out, but his torch was not where he thought it would be. Okay. He'd have to get out from under the fucktons of robot and grope around for it. He holstered his CEW gun and grimaced. The guard's hip was pushing against his crotch and any movement caused it to grind against him. "Shit," he muttered again. And then, as he pushed the prone shape of the semi to get away, it slid against him again, not at all unpleasantly. "Under different circumstances," he panted, cursing whoever had thought making these things so goddamn heavy was a good idea when more lightweight materials were actually available, "I'd have been up for it, but I'm not here to jerk off against a defunct fucking semi guard."

All of a sudden, he heard another noise. It was an exhausted sound, a rattle and a whine like a door swinging on creaking hinges, somewhere to his right along the row of cryo pods. Luca lay in the darkness, listening, trying to breathe silently.

A vague thumping sound accompanied the rattling and whining. Footfalls. Regular, marching, relentlessly getting closer. Okay. Luca slowly lowered his hand from trying to push off the fallen semi, back to the holster on his thigh, awkwardly twisting underneath the lump of robot and trying not to make a sound.

The footfalls came closer. Luca closed his eyes. He knew robotic sounds. He had listened to so many of them... The rattling was a loose joint or body part. The whine was mechanical and not of the vocal sort. Could be related to the loose part. Underneath the other noises, there was a dragging sort of sound. Yes, the approaching entity was dragging one foot slightly. And being bipedal, it was likely to be a sentient or a semi. He was pretty sure it was a guard like the first one, left here for centuries to fall into disrepair and deterioration.

Luca opened his eyes again and tried to spot the guard, but he couldn't see much without turning his head and risking exposure. And besides, it was so damn dark. Would it have killed them to make sure the lights switched back on when the door to the facility was opened? Probably not, he thought, but something else had. He continued the slow and stealthy process of getting hold of his CEW gun.

Now he could feel the vibrations from the guard's every step in the floor. Maybe it would pass by him and go to the door and sort of just continue into oblivion, marching on until it eventually broke down completely... That's what some artificials appeared to have done anyway.

Luca took a deep breath and held it when the footfalls were almost right beside him. Go on. Go on, go on, go on...

The guard stopped.

A new sound penetrated the darkness around Luca, a moan of metal stretching. And now he saw the guard. A silhouette above him with two tiny dots illuminating the face. And Luca knew the guard saw him too.

The minutes that had been stretched out like an elastic band reached the maximum length and now they crashed back together on a mad collision course with Luca's life. The guard reached down, took hold of the fallen semi and effortlessly pulled it off Luca.

The disabled semi was hurled through the room and crashed to the floor. Not two seconds later, the guard's fist came flying towards Luca. He rolled, avoiding the punch, and sprang to his feet.

The guard turned and Luca was grateful for the noise it made since it helped him discern where it was. Now that he was standing, it was evident that this was not the same model as the other guard. This one was unarmed, but it was so enormous it wouldn't fit through his front door.

"Deactivate yourself!" he shouted, knowing it was a long shot.

Without even pausing, the guard advanced on him and attacked.

Luca made a dash for it, turning and taking hold of the closest cryo pod. Adrenaline was rushing deliciously through him now, making it almost impossible to be really scared. Luca had been raised on a healthy diet of action flicks and viral videos and interactive entertainment, and when stuff like this happened, he found he automatically switched to action mode.

So he jumped onto the pod and balanced there as the huge guard turned its beady glowing eyes on him again. It came at him once more, aiming for his head, but Luca jumped in a moment of abandon and insane inspiration, practically landing in the guard's face.

"I'll reprogram your ass!" he yelled as he finally pulled out the CEW gun and thrust it between the guard's eyes.

One of the guard's hands came up to pry him away. It closed around his shoulder, grinding bones together and threatening to break them, but then the pressure released as the guard convulsed and twisted. Luca hung on, pressing the gun into the face until the lights in the guard's eyes began to flicker and the whole artificial wobbled.

Luca let go and threw himself to the side, landing hard and rolling a few paces.

He lay there, panting and gasping, as the guard fell over and crashed into the cryo pod, actually breaking it in a cacophony of splintering as the lid and the ice inside shattered.

That was close. Way too close. "Holy fuck," Luca

coughed. Then he listened. But apart from the creaking of the broken cryo pod and his own ragged breathing, the room was silent. And despite the pain in his shoulder and general ache all over, he started laughing.

A few moments later, Luca got to his hands and knees and began to search for his torch, a task not made easier by the considerable lack of sensation in his fingers. Eventually, he found it and turned it back on.

Wow. The place was a mess. Luca stood up, swinging the light beam appreciatively over the floor. Two semis down for the very long count and a ruined cryo pod... Luca turned abruptly, not wanting to see what was inside the ice. He did not want to face bits of shattered human.

So he inspected the rest of the pods. He didn't expect anyone to be alive, but even telling himself that, it was a little disappointing when he reached the last coffin and concluded that all twelve of them were entirely void of vital signs.

Okay... He rubbed his sore shoulder. This just put one more place for him to salvage on the map. But not right now. He wanted to get out of here. So he'd go, lock the door behind him and come back with the Rover and proper light and tools for disassembling the guards another time. There was a slim risk that the soldiers from Florence would discover this place in the meantime, but they wouldn't necessarily know how to open the door. And even if they did, they would run away screaming at the sight of the two artificials.

And if he was taking the car anyway, he might as well make it an overnight trip and go to one of the settlements further west to trade. He could use some flour and milk and whatever else they could offer him for the useful stuff he brought them. Who knew, it may even be fun to talk to some living human beings for once.

Luca nodded. Fine. He had a plan. Plans were good.

18:
Teo

At first, only an irregular tapping sound far above Teo indicated anything out of the ordinary. She would have missed it if she hadn't taken a detour on her way home from work. The noise from the larger streets were filtered out by houses cradling the narrow alley, and she heard the rain and stopped to look up.

As she watched, the color of the sky beyond the dome turned from blue to a murky grey. A flash of lightning whiplashed across the sky. A low growl of a thunderclap rolled after it moments later, and then the rain really began.

Teo was not the only one who noticed. Front doors were opening into the alley to let out a host of curious people, mostly children, who wanted to see. And suddenly Teo had the impulse to do what she did as a child whenever it rained.

She dashed through the alley, crossed the closest street and ran down another alley towards the nearest edge of the dome. It was not an exit she was looking for. It was simply a place to put her hand against the clear surface of the dome and watch the rain. She found a space between two buildings large enough for a person to squeeze through. The sloping side of the dome was right overhead. Teo steered towards the very edge where the transparent wall met the ground as the noise of the rain grew so loud it drowned out everything else.

It seemed almost wrong that the ground should be entirely dry when the rain was pouring down an arm's length from her. Teo sat down on one of the rocks that were often arranged near the domes' edges as if to mark them. She reached out and put her hand against the cool, smooth surface that looked like glass but wasn't. It was awe-inspiring that mankind had built this, had worked with materials such as these centuries ago. Where was that knowledge now? And what had it been traded for?

She traced a line of water running down the outside of the dome with her finger. The ground was all puddles and mud already. And she had the strongest urge to be out there. She smiled. As a child she had wanted to go out there. To feel the rain on her skin. She had imagined the rain to be warm like bath water. Now she was fairly certain it wasn't. And she knew there was a good reason that everybody, even arbiters and sentries, were told to stay inside the domes during thunderstorms.

Lightning flashed across the sky and a crash of thunder followed it closely, so loud she could feel the surface under her fingers vibrate. There was nothing to see outside this dome but the vague, distorted outline of the next. She thought she could make out someone standing near the edge over there as well, looking out like she was.

For everyone safe and sound inside the inner city, the rain was a welcome change, a rare occasion when they looked at the outside with interest. There was a system of containers and funnels around the edge of the city that collected rain for use inside the domes. But how did the slummers handle the rain? Did they collect it too? Or was it not possible for them? One thing was certain, Teo thought. The houses out there would not be able to withstand a thunderstorm like a dome did.

She sighed and rested the side of her head against the dome. She may have been reminded her of her childhood, but now the present was grinding against her mind so relentlessly that she could not ignore it.

"Forget the conversation ever happened," she whispered and pressed her head a little harder against the dome. Another thunderclap rang out, reverberating inside Teo's chest. Arsenio knew she couldn't forget. Vanni did too. Was that part of the plan? To leave the question inside her mind to roll back and forth until she did something. Until she made a decision.

Clearly the houses outside the domes could withstand a bit of rain. The slummers had to know how to handle it. They had methods of surviving whatever the weather threw at them without the protection of domes. If anyone didn't know how to handle the rain, it was not the slummers, but the people of the inner city. How would she react to actually being out there in a thunderstorm? Or a dust storm for that matter?

It wasn't only the people in the outer city who dealt with the elements unprotected, though. She had seen the settlements marked on Vanni's map. Those people lived in the ruins of other cities. They made it work without a transparent roof to shield them. But they still did have houses, didn't they? And yet, somewhere out there were nomadic people, tribes roaming the continent. They had... what, tents? Huts? As a child, she had been fascinated by the thought that there were people living outside Florence at all. She asked her teachers so fervently about the subject that they brought it up with her father and he explained to her that there were only savages out there. Some stories had it, her father conceded, that once there were other civilized cities, but they were gone. There was only Florence. And everything outside Florence was dangerous territory according to her father. According to the council and every person of authority... except perhaps Vanni and Arsenio.

Still, was that reason enough to mount some kind of rebellion? If they were only objecting to protection, what was there to rebel against, really?

Teo pulled away from the transparent wall with a sigh. She would have to work this out, and preferably before she drove herself mad thinking about it.

She stood up and adjusted her clothes. It was time to go home and get dressed for dinner at her parents' house. If nothing else, it would be an excellent way to listen to what some of these old men who ruled the city had to say.

The Terzi residence was located in the Posh Dome. This was not its official name. It wasn't even the name that other people called it by, at least not when the daughter of the Terzis was around. But it was what Teo called it. Not only the Posh Dome, but the posh part of the Posh Dome. Her own flat, frowned upon by both of her parents, was located in a nice neighborhood not that far away, but it was still inside a building with different families and singles like herself occupying separate living spaces.

Her parents could see no reason that Teo should not just have stayed in their house. There was plenty of room. But she wanted to be something more than only her father's offspring. She wanted to be able to do what she wanted and see whom she wanted without her mother being nosy and her father advising against the company of certain kinds of people.

But she did have duties to her family. One of them was showing up in a respectable dress with clean fingernails and a pleasant smile to show that her father was the sort of man who had sired an attractive, clever daughter who knew how to wear a respectable dress, scrub her fingernails and smile in a pleasant way. She only felt thoroughly confident about two out of three.

Her boredom at dinner parties was not a reason to

mount a rebellion against the rule of Florence, Teo thought as she ascended the stairs to the front door, but one of those parties would be an excellent opportunity to take a closer look at the elite of the city.

The front door opened before she had time to knock.

"Welcome home, Miss Terzi," said the man who opened it.

"Hello, Filippo," Teo replied, smiling. Filippo was a servant of the house and, not for the first time, Teo wondered what he would have been doing for a living if this had been the old days before the fall. Back then, robots would have carried out his work. "Pardon?" Teo said, realizing that Filippo had asked her a question.

"May I take your jacket?" he repeated.

"Please. Thank you," Teo said and shrugged out of her jacket.

"Teodora!" a voice trilled from the top of the stairs leading from the entrance hall to the upper floor.

"Hello, mom," Teo called back.

"Teodora," her mother repeated, coming down in a flurry of dress and carefully arranged hair. She was the only person Teo knew who could make her already too long name sound like it had at least five syllables. "Look at you! How are you?"

Hugs and air kisses and trivial exchanges of politeness followed. It wasn't that Teo didn't like her mother. She just liked her a lot more when she wasn't in her present shape. The carefully molded Mrs Valentina Terzi shape.

"Your father will be right down. The guests should be arriving any moment too," her mother continued, linking arms with her daughter and leading her towards the dining room.

Sometimes when Teo looked at her mother, she wondered if she were staring at her own future. They had the same dark, wavy hair and the same nose. The exception was

Teo's eyes. She had her father's eyes, people said. This was always remarked with a certain respect, although really, Teo was certain his were a cooler brown. But no matter how hard she tried, Teo could simply not picture her future including marrying a councilman and becoming an accessory to rule.

"If it isn't the prodigal daughter," her father's voice boomed behind them, and the two women abandoned their admiration of the wonderful dining table decorations.

"I have been away for maybe four days, and I practically live across the street," Teo replied.

"Nevertheless," Mr Terzi said and went through the hugs and kisses routine as well. When he stepped back to study her, Teo knew he was looking for imperfections. Work clothes, trousers, unkempt hair, anything that would disturb the image he wanted to project to his guests. "You aren't wearing earrings," he said.

"No," Teo replied. She had forgotten, but she wasn't going to let him know that. "I had a reaction last time I wore a pair." She almost winced. Really, wasn't she old enough to tell him she didn't wear jewelry at work and couldn't be bothered to remember it only because he wanted the perfect daughter package?

Before any of her parents had the time to reply, they heard the front door open and voices of the first few guests arriving.

Teo straightened her back and steeled herself for an evening of tiresome politeness and feigned interest. At least there would be plenty of good food. And wine. Lots of wine.

19:
Teo

Halfway through the dinner party, Teo lost count of how many times she had discussed the weather with someone. It definitely rivaled the number of times she was complimented on something her father had said, done or suggested at a council meeting.

It was still pouring down outside the dome, and the streetlights had been turned on early to compensate for the darkness. Every flash of lightning and thunderclap distracted at least one of the guests from what they were saying, caused someone to shriek or make a comment about water supplies or earth slides or make a toast to the safety of the domes.

"I do wonder what it must be like to be outside at a time like this," Teo ventured at one point during the main course, a lavish selection of meat inside little nests of finely spun pasta.

As she had assumed, the party consisted of councilmen, judges and other people of importance. She was seated between a jovial, fat man whose name she could not for the life of her remember and a young doctor called Gabriele De Felice who served as a health adviser to the council. It was the doctor Teo directed her comment at since her other neighbor was engaged in discussing the red wine with his wife and the couple on the opposite side of the table.

"Wet, I imagine," the doctor replied and concealed any facial expression that went with the statement by pushing his spectacles up the bridge of his nose.

Teo raised one eyebrow. "I do believe you're right," she said. "But do you know how the people in the outside city handle it?" As she quickly scanned the guests around them to see if anyone was taking her bait, Teo noticed her mother smiling encouragingly. It was no accident that she had been placed beside an unmarried man. And a fairly handsome one at that, with intelligent, blue eyes and strong, slender hands that dissected the food on his plate with a surgeon's precision. But Teo felt pretty sure she would not attract any romantic attention from him.

"I'm sure they have their own ways," Gabriele De Felice replied. His eyes met hers and despite his noncommittal reply, he continued, "What makes you think of them?"

"I say it'd be better for all of us if the flood made them leave," commented the wife of one of the councilmen on the opposite side of the table.

"Or drown," added her husband. "Just kidding! Just kidding!"

Next to Teo, the doctor's laugh sounded as forced as her own.

"But on that subject," the offensive councilman continued, leaning forward to address Teo's father at the other end of the table. "Perhaps this dreadful weather will be helpful, don't you think, Emilio?"

"Indeed," replied Mr Terzi.

Teo opened her mouth to ask how, but another woman beat her to it. It was a short woman with a kind, round face and a necklace gleaming at her bosom that matched a considerable gem on one of her fingers. "How do you reckon?" she asked.

"Well, the climate has been fairly stable for a while," Mr Terzi said and then added the one comment out of every conversation that night that would stick to Teo's mind, "Those loafers tend to get too confident when they don't have anything to occupy them. There was another riot a few days ago. The arbiters had to shoot a couple of them. If they see a bit of natural tribulations, it usually makes them grateful for what they've got."

Teo felt color rising in her cheeks. She wanted to talk. She wanted to tell her father how horrid he sounded and ask him if he really meant all that. If he could think of no better way to keep the poor slummers happy than hoping they would have their hands full surviving. But she knew now was not the time. She picked up her glass of wine to keep herself from blurting out something.

Next to her, the doctor mimicked her gesture, and to her horror, Teo saw the whole table following suit, thinking she was raising her glass to her father.

"Hear, hear," someone boomed.

"Good fellow," another concurred.

Teo quickly drained most of her wine and gestured for the waiter to bring her more. She gulped down a big mouthful of the new contents.

"Are you all right?" the doctor asked her when conversation was resuming all around them.

"Yes! I'm fine!" Teo said. "I mean..."

The waiters were beginning to take the plates from the table, and Teo knew there would be a break before dessert was served.

"I think I need some air," Teo continued.

"Would you like some company?" her neighbor offered.

"No, I'm fine. Thank you," she said and left the table trying not to stomp off.

It was not the first time she heard that kind of talk. But she had never reacted so strongly before. That was the worst part. How had she sat through these things for years and never said anything? She relived previous occasions, her father's hateful words, her mother's approving nods and smiles.

Was it her trip outside that opened her eyes to the fact that the slummers were not just a mass of troublesome individuals who had to be kept at bay and occasionally used as laborers when hard or dangerous work had to be done? Or was it the talk with Vanni or Arsenio?

No, she thought as she stood in the garden outside the house with nothing but the rumble of retreating thunder to keep her company. She had known all along. She had chosen not to protest too loudly because there was nothing she could do. And now—Could she do something now?

Teo wrapped her arms around herself. She could go to that meeting on Friday and see what it all was about. She could try to influence the council or put pressure on them for changes. And with that, Teo knew she had made a decision. There wasn't really a choice. Not if she wanted to do the right thing. She drew in a deep breath and released it in a long sigh.

The Mezzo Pieno was located in one of the popular districts in the Central Dome. Teo's father would have called it a questionable quarter. Her mother would have called it rowdy. Luckily, they were not here. The Mezzo Pieno was sparsely lit with lamps in the corners and candles on the tables. It was half full of patrons talking either in hushed voices or laughing and singing. Most of them were in uniforms in various states of unbuttoned disarray, and arbiters' and sentries' hats littered the space on the tables between glasses and bottles. The place was notorious as the favored drinking establishment of lawmen and, as such, considered a safe place although they were all off duty.

Teo scanned the room for any sign of her friends, but they were nowhere to be seen. So she turned to the bar instead. Here a line of patrons sat on stools, but one was standing, leaning against the bar and sipping a glass. He looked at Teo and nodded at her, then seemed to lose interest and left towards the back of the room.

"What can I get you?" the barman asked.

"Beer," Teo said, fishing her wallet out of a pocket.

"Light or dark?"

"As dark as you got," she replied.

The barman nodded, approvingly, and turned to find a glass and pour her a drink.

"Hello, stranger," said a familiar voice behind her.

Teo turned, relieved, to see a familiar tall figure in a spotter's uniform. "Hi," she replied. "I couldn't find you..."

Arsenio leaned in to give her a hug. "The private party is downstairs," he murmured. His breath smelled of alcohol. "Pretend we're flirting."

"You'd like that," she replied and pulled back with her coyest, most playful smile.

Arsenio smirked at her and sized her up. "Nice shirt."

"You've seen it before," she replied. "Nice uniform."

"You've seen it before," he echoed.

"Your beer," interrupted the barman as he put a foaming glass on the bar and winked at them. "You've seen beer before, too, but you'll find the taste better than anywhere else in all of the domes."

"Allow me," Arsenio said and put a few coins on the bar.

"Are you trying to buy me?" Teo asked.

"Of course not!" Arsenio exclaimed, grinning. "You're not that cheap. Come on." He reached out for her hand and tugged at it for her to follow him.

A few catcalls accompanied them.

"It's right this way," Arsenio said in his normal, brisk

tone when they had left the room through a door in the back. Kegs and crates were piled as tall as Teo out here, and there was a sink where a boy no older than fifteen was washing a stack of glasses. He and Arsenio exchanged polite nods, and then Arsenio opened a door to a narrow stairwell. "Watch your step," he said.

Teo let go of his hand and reached out to steady herself against the wall. This place was so secretive that they hadn't bothered with light, apparently.

But when they reached the end of the stairs, she saw light pouring out of an open door down a corridor. When they entered, Teo saw a big wooden table full of bottles and papers. Around it, twenty people turned or raised their eyes almost simultaneously to study her.

Vanni waved at her. "Teo! I'm glad you made it," he said as if this were a card game club or a birthday party.

Teo smiled. There she was with her beer in one hand, facing a group of aspiring rebels... No, actually joining a group of aspiring rebels. She had plunged into this out of anger and frustration, and now that she was here, she felt oddly deflated.

She glanced at each of them in turn and was surprised to find that Arsenio and Vanni were not the only people she had met before. Not only was the man she had encountered at the bar there. The young doctor from her father's dinner party was smiling at her from his seat, and it took her a moment to identify a woman at the end of the table as the kind looking wife of one of the councilmen. She looked different with her hair in a simple bun and with a tunic instead of an evening dress. The only lavish thing about her now was the ring sparkling on her finger.

"Welcome, Miss Terzi," said the woman. "I'm glad you could join us. Please have a seat."

"Thank you, Mrs Basile," Teo said. She found an empty chair between Arsenio and an elderly man with thinning grey hair and a beard to make up for it. "Just Teo is fine," she added.

The woman smiled. "And you can call me Patrizia." There was something behind the smile and her calm, brown eyes that Teo had never noticed before. Something hard and determined. She was the group's leader, Teo realized.

"Thank you for inviting me," Teo added.

Patrizia acknowledged this with a nod. "We think you can be an asset to the group," she said. "I believe Arsenio and Vanni have already told you what we do?"

"Not in detail. I'm not sure..." Teo trailed off. Not sure what? That she knew what she was doing here? That she knew if she could be of any help at all?

"You will be," the leader said. "Now, let's get started."

20:
Teo

There were no introductions or easing her into the group. Teo tried to follow the discussion and catch everyone's names too. They were talking about a new law that would make it easier for sentries to quell riots in the slums outside. The conversation went from there to the problems faced by the slummers due to the recent downpour and to the rising prices of produce from the Green Dome.

Some were of the opinion that overthrowing the council with the help of the arbiters who agreed with them was the only way forward. Others reminded them that someone tried that fifty years ago, and the instigators had mysteriously vanished after it failed. They believed in applying pressure by handing out leaflets. Yet others suggested organizing citywide strikes as a means to showing the elite of Florence that the citizens stood with the slummers. Vanni argued that collecting useful items and taking as many people as possible outside the wall to help with medical care and building better housings was the way to go. The doctor agreed with him, but Arsenio claimed it would only have the effect that no one would be allowed back in. One thing they all agreed on: It was time to take action.

"All right, then we do it discreetly," the doctor said. "They need our help, and it will make them sympathetic to our cause as well if they see we make a difference."

"I agree," said Patrizia. "If you are willing to take the risk."

Gabriele inclined his head. "I am. The downpour caused damage to their houses, but the illness is worse. Simple antibiotics will make a huge difference."

Teo listened to the talk of smuggling medical supplies outside the wall, marveling at the fact that these people were discussing ways to help the slummers as matter-of-factly as her father had joked about the misfortune of the very same people.

"If we are doing this," a young woman said, "we ought to take another look at the list." She hadn't said much up to this point, but Teo had seen her taking notes. She was slender, had short hair and didn't look older than twenty. A silver crucifix dangled on a necklace whenever she bent over her notes. In a way, it surprised Teo because her own father's dismissal of the people outside the domes was so often based on a religious view. But then, it was a pleasant surprise that her father's idea of God's will was not the only one.

"I agree, Clara," Patrizia said and began to shuffle through her own papers.

"The list?" Teo asked.

"We have a list," Clara, explained, "of things Arsenio and Vanni have noticed on their trips through the slums. Broken items and such. Just small spare parts that some of us may have in our own homes or be able to get." She smiled, confidently and, Teo noticed, quite attractively.

"Oh, that's nice," Teo said, more than a little impressed that her two friends had apparently been working on something like that while doing their jobs.

Patrizia pulled out a sheet of paper and placed it on the

table, sliding it towards Teo. "The items marked with red are crucial," she explained.

Teo scanned the paper. A few of the items underlined with red ink were not common items, but parts of ancient tech that were still in use. At the bottom of the list was a connector for a certain kind of pump that the domes employed for their hydration systems. "We get these in for repair and for cleaning up now and then in R&R," she said.

"Would you be willing to take one?" Patrizia asked.

"Yes," Teo said. She couldn't very well say anything else now that she'd brought it up. Besides, that was what she was here for, wasn't it? If she wanted to be part of this, she had to make a contribution. "It's small enough to put in a pocket. I can do that." She noticed Vanni staring at her with a concerned expression. She tried to look confident.

The plan began to take shape. Gabriele would steal some medical supplies from a pharmacy and take the rest from his own office over several days so no one took notice. He would then meet Arsenio and Vanni late at night, and they would help him slip out of the domes wearing a uniform.

When the meeting was adjourned, Teo's head was spinning with new information and ideas. The group dispersed slowly. It would be unwise for them all to leave at the same time, so some planned on staying in the bar upstairs for a while, others left straight away to go home, and others yet hung back downstairs.

As Teo was about to leave with Arsenio and Vanni, Patrizia called out to her, "Teo, would you mind staying a little longer?"

Teo caught a glimpse of a grimace on Vanni's face. "She volunteered to get the connector. Do we really need..." he began.

"Yes," the leader cut him off. "We do."

Vanni did not make any further arguments. Arsenio

didn't even try. "I'll be upstairs," Arsenio said to Teo and made a gesture mimicking a bottle being tipped.

Teo sat back down again.

Patrizia moved to a chair right across the table from Teo. The door closed. "I'm happy you decided to join us," she said.

"Thank you," Teo said. "Me too."

"I know it's not an easy decision to turn on the city and the people you loved."

Teo shook her head. She had caught the past tense in that last verb. And it must be like that for Patrizia. Her husband was a council member. Was it easier to betray a husband than a father? And how she wished she could think of a less harsh word than betray...

"We only have your word that you are with us, Teo," the other woman carried on.

"I am not going to..."

Patrizia held up a hand. "I'm sure you aren't. However, you will understand that we need to make certain." She slid out another paper from the stack of documents on the table and turned it around so Teo could see it properly.

Teo's mouth opened. It was a picture. A photo. The fact that the rebel group apparently had a machine that could produce those was not what shocked her, however. The photo showed a truck going uphill outside the wall. There was a backdrop of derelict houses and a few slummers in the foreground. In the truck, a short spotter in an ill-fitting uniform sat between the other officers with the cap pulled down over the eyes. "That's..." Teo began, then trailed off and stared up at the leader.

"Yes," confirmed Patrizia. "That is you. With Arsenio and Vanni and three laymen outside the wall."

"But how..?"

"How is not important," Patrizia said and tapped the photo with her index finger. "What is important is why I'm showing you this."

Teo narrowed her eyes. "You're blackmailing me," she concluded.

"No," Patrizia said, firm lines forming around her mouth. "If you did not wish to join the movement, this picture would not have been shown to anyone. Not to you, and not to anyone you know. But now that you are here of your own free will, I need to make certain that others don't sway you back to their cause."

Teo glanced down at the picture again, and then at the leader. As mild and kind and harmless as she had appeared next to her husband at the dinner party, Patrizia was stern and serious and left no room for argument now. "So... if I betray you, you will show this to my father?"

"Yes."

"But it's not just me!" Teo exclaimed. "Vanni and Arsenio are in that picture too. They would get in trouble..."

"Yes, they would," Patrizia said, calmly, as she took the photo from the table and put it back into the stack of papers. "And since they are your best friends, that would probably hit you as hard as the ramifications against yourself. But," she added, the deceivingly mild smile making its way back onto her face, "as long as you don't tell anyone about us, there is nothing to worry about. Those are the rules. You can even back out of this if you don't think you have what it takes and still nothing will happen. But should you break the rules..." She placed her hand flat on the papers and patted them. "Well, I believe that was it."

Teo nodded. "Yes," she said. "But that wasn't necessary."

"Everybody says that," Patrizia replied, getting up from her chair. "And yet, there is a reason we do it like this."

21:
Renn

Beyond the stagnant settlement lay a few animal enclosures, and then a vast labyrinth of ruins spread out to all sides. Renn had never before ventured into that maze, but after the nightly attack, he led Mender out of the tavern and into the complete darkness of the ruins. Thankfully, the rain was a mere drizzle now, and the angry wind had run away to torment someone else. But the ground was slippery, and the further away from the settlement they got, the more littered it became with debris and robust vegetation.

Mender said there was a fireless torch in the bag, but Renn preferred not to risk it. He could take on a few thugs easily, but if the stagnants went after them in larger numbers, they would be in trouble. So they groped their way through the ruins until they were so far away that Renn doubted anyone else would dare to go out there in the darkness.

They spent the remainder of the night in the ruins, shielded from the stagnants' view by abandoned buildings. Ironically, the only dry wood they could find was the crossbow. It would not make a lasting fire, but Renn needed to boil water to drink. The wood gave off an unpleasant smell and even Mender's tinderbox took a while to ignite it.

When the sun rose, Renn saw they could hardly have gone much further and still found shelter. Beyond this point, the buildings appeared to have been flattened until they rose again in the distance. The ground curved slightly down, and following an almost invisible edge with his gaze, Renn could tell that there was a considerable indentation in the ground. It resembled a giant bowl, in the bottom of which was now a lake of rainwater.

Their only company that morning consisted of rats and cockroaches and one unlucky snake that Renn killed with a quick, hard thrust of his staff.

Mender had a deposit of the edible sticks, but Renn found it wisest to eat what he found to make the rations last longer. And, he quietly admitted to himself, to show his traveling companion that he was capable of taking care of himself. But although Mender had treated him almost like a child to begin with, the altercation with the thieves last night had changed the way the sentient looked at him.

Well, if Mender learned something about him from the fight, he learned something about Mender too. The sentient was fast and had insight and ingenuity enough to use whatever means were available. But every action in that fight was taken to prevent injuries and, Renn was not oblivious to this curious fact, more to him than Mender. Renn asked a few times if his companion had suffered any injuries, but although the club had connected hard with Mender's head, the other insisted there was nothing to worry about.

They packed their things, some of which were still damp, and weaved their way through the rubble and into the shallow bowl.

"This looks like a crater," said Mender.

"Rockfall," Renn said by way of explanation. In the past,

it rained stones more often and more unforgiving than now. By the look of the destruction here, quite a large rock had fallen from the sky, decimating half of the city and probably taking the life of every living being in it. Nowadays, rockfalls were not uncommon, but Renn had only seen the streaks across the sky that heralded chaos a couple of times, and the rocks fell so far away that they could neither be heard nor felt. More often, the fire in the sky only reminded people that once Moon had traveled across the heavens with her lantern, and the sparks were all that was left now.

Renn bent by the pool of accumulated rainwater and filled up his flasks. The dark clouds were nothing but a thin line near the horizon, and overhead only white dotted the blue sky. Renn aimed for the domes of which the stagnants had spoken. There was no point in searching for signs left by his Covey. Perhaps they had gone to the domes, perhaps they had not, but it was his best lead now.

The companions walked in silence for a while, emerging into the last remnants of the city when they left the bowl. Renn was expanding his mental map of the world he knew to include this part of the city while keeping an eye out for anything worth examining. Meanwhile, he was listening for any sudden noises and glancing back now and then for a glimpse of potential pursuers. But they never came.

Mender, too, seemed to be occupied with studying their surroundings. Renn noticed the sentient sometimes jerking the head from side to side in a way he had not seen before. Had Mender sustained an injury, after all?

"The place you are going," Renn said, but he spoke in a low voice to make certain it did not carry too far. "Cere..."

"CerEvolv," Mender replied, pronouncing the word so strangely that Renn suspected it was in a different language. Dialects varied, of course, but he had come across a few wanderers from the North who spoke an entirely different language. Communicating with them was almost impossible and could only be done by using gestures and mimicking actions.

"Yes," Renn continued, "is it a place with domes?"

Mender regarded him for a long moment, only interrupted by that strange, new jerking of the head. Renn would have to address it if it got worse. "Domes... Oh." Mender nodded. "I understand. I remember from the newscast that domes were built to protect Florence from the consequences of the impact. Yes, that is where I am headed."

"It is still there, then," Renn volunteered. "I talked to some of the stagnants last night and they thought my Covey was going in that direction. They called it a city of domes."

"I am glad to hear that. Thank you," Mender said. Then, as an afterthought, "and I am glad to stay in your company until we reach Florence."

"And I'm in yours," Renn replied. A small Covey they may be, but he had already benefited from Mender's company more than once.

"You must be relieved at the prospect at seeing your friends again," Mender said.

Renn made a half-shrug. It was hard to describe the bonds of necessity that sometimes held Coveys together for years. His Covey were not his friends. They were safety. It did not mean he didn't value their company or enjoyed talking to them, but it was long since he was part of a group that he thought of as close friends or family. He had learned that sometimes it was simpler and easier that way. "The stagnants said something else," he added. He relayed the information about the wagon that moved on its own and the rumors of a person with an abundance of treasures from the past. While the puzzling hermit was not relevant to him personally, it occurred to him that perhaps Mender would be interested. "Do you think it could be someone like you?" Renn asked.

Mender's expressionless face took on a puzzled quality.

Maybe understanding the sentient was a matter of reading the silences rather than being confused by the lack of expression. "I am not sure what kind of sentient would live alone and trade with people of the settlements. I can't think of any programming that would require that sort of behavior. But..."

Renn waited for the rest of the sentence as he took one last sweeping glance behind them before they reached the edge of the city. Or rather, the last buildings that had not been swallowed by the elements. The road they were traveling was now flanked mostly by low hills that might once have been houses.

"Perhaps it is someone like you."

"Like me?" Renn echoed, taken aback by the conclusion.

"A human who has stumbled upon functioning technology," Mender clarified. "Someone who has taken residence in a shelter from the past."

"But why..." Renn trailed off. He was about to ask why anyone would choose to live alone when there was always safety in numbers. Then again, just because only one person had come to trade with the stagnants, it did not mean that the person in question lived alone. And who was he to make assumptions? Perhaps it was someone who had chosen solitude. Perhaps whoever it was did not want to share the wealth of such a shelter of the past with anyone else.

"We will probably never know," Mender concluded for him.

"No," Renn agreed. It was not important. It was not relevant. What was important and relevant was the stretch of land ahead. The distance they would have to put behind them before they reached the domes.

22:
Luca

It was another brilliant day with dry air that left you aching for lip balm and lazily floating dust and grit that made you instantly regret it if you put it on.

Luca was packing the Rover with a generous amount of water, some food and an assortment of exotic wares from the past that would make anyone in this second stone age wet their pants with excitement. Okay. That was an overstatement. It wasn't like the stone age. It was a drab throwback to a time between the nineteenth and the twentieth century probably, back when things were slow and boring.

He shut the boot of the car and patted it. He'd almost taken a few t-shirts with statements that the settlers in Pontedera would probably not be able to read, just for the laugh, but then he decided against it. He wanted useful stuff. They probably did too. So he packed things like lighters and toothpaste and a few edible items that he had and they most certainly didn't. And some rope for securing the guard artificials that he would go get on the way back. He was pretty sure he would need to do some disassembling to get one onto the roof of the Rover, so he brought tools for that too. The other would have to be dragged. He also took the drone with him because it may come in handy if he did some treasure hunting on the way.

"Do you have a shopping list for me?" he asked Nanny who had come out to see him off.

She shook her head. "I trust your judgment. You are the only one who is going to eat it," she added.

"True." Luca said. "Well, I'm off then. I'll be back tomorrow, probably."

"Be careful, Luca," Nanny replied in her customary half-stern half-concerned tone.

"Of course," Luca said and waved at her as he climbed into the Rover. He could easily make the trip in a single day, but he preferred being able to stay at the settlement for a while if he felt like it and taking a detour if he got the craving for adventure.

One thing he did miss about road trips from the olden days, Luca thought as he swung onto the remnants of a westbound road, was listening to music. He still occasionally did, but he only had so much music downloaded. Somehow he had not expected that the future may not hold streaming services.

The landscape sailed past him outside the car. Even for a routine trip, this was uneventful. Once he caught a glimpse of a formation of those creepy flying snakes the world had produced while he was asleep. They never attacked the Rover or even his motorcycle, but he once had to shoot one that went for him while he was hiking. Exoskeleton or not, it still couldn't survive a round of well-aimed bullets. But how had nature cooked them up? They looked like overgrown horseshoe crabs crossed with a pterodactyl. And a snake. Perhaps they weren't really a product of natural evolution. With the Moon gone, the magnetic poles of the planet went haywire and that fucked up birds, which had lots of bad effects on the environment. Luca couldn't help wondering if the armored flying snakes were somehow genetically engineered animals supposed to do the birds' job. But what did he know? His field was artificials, not biology.

In any case, the people of the settlements were scared to death of them, but they didn't have firearms. And while Luca usually brought a real gun as well as a CEW gun with him, he wasn't going to hand out weapons. Guns didn't kill people, but people with guns just had a tendency of killing people more than people without guns. Gun crimes hadn't been a thing for hundreds of years and Luca wasn't about to revive that tradition.

He turned off the road and took a bumpy shortcut to the next road that would lead him directly to the Pontedera settlement. The bumps and lack thereof were practically the only way to tell whether you were on a road or not.

It was only midday when Luca decided to stretch his legs and have something to eat. Sitting on the hood of the Rover and staring at the acres of nothing all around him was probably the one time when he felt most alone. Partly because he was, and partly because the lack of other people was so complete out here. He couldn't imagine them being next door, couldn't make up for them with his sentients and semis, couldn't drown out the silence with the roar of an engine...

"Fuck off," Luca told himself and jumped off the hood. Time to move on. Time to actually see some people.

Once in a while he asked himself why he didn't go to the settlements more often or maybe even move closer to them- well, that was a thought quickly cured by going there. They welcomed him with a bit of suspicion, a lot of curiosity and even more greed. But they lived in a completely different world. They didn't get his jokes, they didn't understand his references to the past, they treated him as if he were some kind of weirdo, when really he was pretty normal and they were the weirdos.

But it was okay to go there to trade with them, and although Alfredo and Nanny acted more like real people than the settlers did, they were humans of flesh and blood.

Luca parked the Rover around five or ten minutes' walk away from the settlement. He didn't want anyone panicking at the sight of his magicalhorseless carriage. He put on his backpack, hoisted up a duffel bag in one hand and made his way towards the settlement.

Once, during his first year at IRAI, the class had a retro-science week. The point, officially, was to examine the visions of earlier times of how robotics and computers would develop. Unofficially, Luca was pretty sure, the point was to laugh at the poor sods of the 20th century who had imagined the future as a place of flying cars and time machines, but with every document and newspaper existing only in print and with the exact same gender roles and religious ideas as the men who wrote the stuff were used to. Anyway, the students had watched a documentary called *Bleak Visions of Tomorrow*, and some of the footage from old science fiction flicks that had them in stitches at the time made Luca feel like he was the butt of the joke now.

The city looming in front of him as he lugged his marvelous junk towards it looked exactly like it had been lifted from one of those film sets. Most of it lay in ruins, one part decimated by a meteor that could easily have wiped out Luca's base if it had hit another spot. Other sections of what was once Pontedera had been swallowed by centuries of dust storms or were overgrown with the kind of weeds that gave zero fucks about environmental disasters and changing climates. Only one part was kind of suitable for human habitation. Some houses had been repaired with whatever was available and stood as awkward amalgamations of the post apocalyptic variety. Others had clearly been erected from scratch by people whose imagination didn't lack as much as their architectural knowledge. From this side, Luca could not see the enclosures where the present-day Pontedera inhabitants kept their cattle, but it was there, providing meat and milk and leather to the small community and cropping the vegetation on long-overgrown streets.

As Luca reached the hole in the protective wall, a haphazard parody of the one surrounding the inner city of Florence, he began to hear and smell the inhabitants of the settlement.

When the weather permitted it, there was a market in one of the big streets. Luca had tried to identify it with a map, but it was hard to figure out which part was which without any of the helpful landmarks on the map, and nowadays, it was probably of no consequence. There were only a few hundred people living here, so finding one's way wasn't a big problem.

Luca straightened his back and put on his mysterious-but-benevolent-stranger-smile as he encountered a group of kids playing. They stopped when they saw him and began to whisper, daring each other to speak to him.

"Hello, hermit!" a girl said, coming towards him.

"Hello, kid," Luca replied.

"What's in your sacks today?" she asked boldly as the other children began to form a curious half circle around him. Her accent was different from anything anyone had spoken in Luca's time, but he could understand her.

"That depends. Have you been naughty or nice?" Luca asked.

The girl's face fell for a moment, then she grinned. "Naughty?" she tried.

Luca grinned too. The kids were always easier to get along with than the adults. "All righty, then," he said and put the duffel on the ground. The children stared as he unzipped it, fished out a small, multicolored plastic bag and tossed it at the girl.

"What is it?" she asked.

"It's for eating," Luca explained, then added, "not the bag. What's inside it. You have to open it. The round things inside it are like food."

"Thank you!" the girl said, beaming.

Luca hoped the kids would be smart enough to eat the sweets before an adult saw them and confiscated the suspicious items.

He moved on in the direction of the market. A man with a roll of fabric bumped into Luca and gaped at him with a mouth full of... Well, not full. Judging from his sallow complexion, his rotting teeth weren't the only problem. To begin with, Luca shied away from people who looked ill and practically bathed in alcogel after touching anyone, but his regular health boosting, virus-killing shots administered by Nanny seemed to be keeping him from contracting anything from the people here as long as he didn't kiss them or anything. Which he really, really wasn't going to, he thought with an involuntary shudder.

Giving the fabric bearing creature a wide berth, Luca moved to the closest stall that caught his attention to see if someone would part with some flour for a bottle of shampoo or a lighter.

A little later, he walked away again with everything on his shopping list ticked off and still a few things left in his backpack, so he decided to hit the bar. He would eat and drink there and when he was tired and drunk, he would go back to the Rover and get some sleep.

23:
Luca

The bar was, hands down, Luca's favorite place in present-day Pontedera. Florence had been taken over by technology shunning zealots, Italy was practically a desert, Luca was the only person of his age... But the bar was a bar, and there was something universal about it.

Luca placed himself on a stool at the bar, nodded at the people around him and flagged down the bartender.

"Hello, hermit," she said.

Luca decided not to explain that he lived with two sentients and some semis, so he wasn't exactly the only person around. "Hello," he replied instead.

"What can I get you?" she asked, glancing at the bag propped up against the stool. She knew whatever he carried would be plenty of payment.

"Draught to begin with?" Luca suggested. Civilization could go to hell, but rats, cockroaches and alcohol would survive. And Luca.

She acknowledged the request and turned to get him a drink.

Luca scanned the faces of the people around him. They were curious, but not hostile.

"Have you been at the market today?" asked the man next to him.

"Yeah," Luca replied. "I needed some supplies."

"Do you... need anything else?" the man asked, leaning closer to him, clearly hoping to strike a deal that would earn him some of Luca's possessions. "I can find you a nice lady."

Luca cringed. "No thanks."

"Or a nice man," the man suggested.

"I appreciate the thought," Luca said, "but I don't need that either." He kind of did... Sure, he had Sia and Simon, and he could do a lot more with them by selecting from a variety of scenarios or even tweaking their programming than you could expect from most humans, but that was just it. They weren't human... But hell if he would get a prostitute in this filthy place.

The man shrugged. He seemed a bit disappointed. Luca was about to ask him if being a pimp was a tough job in a place like this when the bartender put the mug of draught down in front of him.

Luca caught a glimpse of something as she pushed the drink towards him and honed in on her hand. "What the... Where did you get that?" he gasped, all his laid-back coolness momentarily evaporated.

The bartender glanced at her hand and held it up for him to see. A knowing smile spread across her face. "Not from you," she replied.

"I know that!" Luca snapped. "Did you find it? Did someone give it to you? Who gave it to you?" That was a plaster on her hand. Not a primitive bandage. A genuine plaster with an antiseptic agent that kept the wound clean. Luca had a bunch of those. But he had not traded them here. He was sure of that.

"A couple of troublemakers," a man who had listened in from the other end of the bar said. He was making his way towards them now. "Friends of yours?"

"No," Luca said.

"Are you afraid of competition?" asked the bartender. "They seemed to have a lot of interesting items."

"No!" Luca repeated. "Look, just... please tell me. Are they here in this city?"

The bartender sized him up and then appeared to come to a decision. "Two strangers showed up during the rain. They gave me a box of those in exchange for food and shelter. They left in a hurry. Not sure it was worth it," she went on.

The rain? That was only the day before yesterday. "Do you know where they went?"

She shook her head.

It didn't matter. He would find them. He got up, took his bag... and then one of the men grabbed his arm.

"Are you leaving without paying for your drink?" the bartender asked.

"Fine!" Luca hissed and shook off the helpful patron. He plunged his hand into the bag, took out a few items and slammed them on the bar. Didn't matter what they were. There was no time for haggling or considering how much toothpaste a mug of draught was worth.

Apparently it was enough because no one tried to stop him again. He ran out of the bar, past the playing children who called after him, out of the settlement and all the way back to the Rover.

He took out the drone and placed it on the roof of the car. Then he sat down in the driver's seat, quickly put on the visor and leaned back with the controller gripped tightly in his hand.

The drone took off and Luca had a clear view of the Rover from a bird's eye perspective before he turned the drone's camera to the surroundings. Okay. So the people he was looking for left Pontedera in a hurry, during or right after the storm. Unless they had a motorized vehicle, they should not be out of the drone's reach yet.

Luca began to circle the settlement, spiraling outwards to cover as much ground as quickly as possible. If they were anywhere within reach of the drone's camera, he would find them. A couple of moving people would stand out in this empty landscape.

He should have brought his draught, he thought after the first few minutes of excitement had passed and he was still going in wider and wider circles. Instead he reached out and groped on the passenger seat for a bottle of water, found it and pulled off the lid with his teeth to take a few mouthfuls.

Since the moment he had spotted the plaster, Luca had not paused to ask himself why he was doing this. But it was obvious, he snapped at the part of his mind that decided to get difficult and ask questions. Someone who had access to a goddamn box of plasters from half a millennium ago was bound to be someone Luca wanted to meet. He'd been hoping to find someone like himself for the past two years. Someone to talk to about viral videos and MMOs and programming with. Someone, that annoying voice in the back of his head chimed in, who had been through the same shit that he had.

Anyway, he might be in for a disappointment. They could be a couple of nomads who had stumbled upon a vacuum-sealed cache of equipment somewhere. Even so, they had figured out what the plasters were for. And the people in the bar had indicated that there was something weird about them. Besides, nomads didn't travel in pairs.

Suddenly something caught his attention. Luca stalled the drone in midair and descended to get a better view. There was a small lake surrounded by hills and a few trees and between the trees… "Fuck off," Luca growled and shot back up to a higher altitude. A pack of mangy wolves.

So he continued while the minutes accumulated into an

hour and then almost two. The sun would begin to set soon. But then they would have to make a fire, right? Luca didn't particularly want to drive at night, though. There were no streetlights and way too many potholes for that to be comfortable.

Just as he was clinging onto the last shreds of enthusiasm and hope, Luca saw them. "Yes!" Luca cried out in triumph. He edged closer. One of them was a regular nomad. The other...

Luca crept closer. The one who was definitely a nomad had long hair and walked with a stick in his right hand. His clothes were made from leather and rough textiles. But the other one was wearing a hooded coat that looked suspiciously synthetic. And there was something familiar about their gait.

In that moment, the nomad turned sharply, staring directly at Luca. The other figure turned as well. Luca let out an involuntary yelp of surprise and instinctively drew back, moving the drone up and away from them at a dizzying speed.

"Holy shit," he panted. He quickly set the drone to automatically return to his coordinates and then pulled off the visor to rest his eyes for a moment before examining the footage in the drone. He let go of the controller and flexed his fingers.

He had found them. They were moving east, and now that the drone had their coordinates, it would not take long for him to get to them by car. But he needed to review the footage.

He put the visor back on and replaced the feed with the recording of the moment when the two travelers turned. Zooming in as close as possible without ending up in pixel hell, Luca played the sequence in slow motion.

The nomad turned, deliberately. It was a man, perhaps a few years older than Luca. Well, older than what Luca looked. He had ridiculous hair and dark, intense eyes that stared straight at the drone and sent shivers down Luca's spine. How did a simple nomad know it was there? How did he spot it that precisely?

But then the second person turned. "No way," Luca breathed. "No fucking way."

Most of the face was obscured by a scarf and the hood, but there was a glint of something metallic, and the eyes... Luca went back a few frames and paused the video. That was a pair of sentient eyes. The skin seemed to be gone, but he would have known regardless. As much personality as they had, sentients lacked that little something that made human eyes... well, human.

What the hell was a sentient doing with a nomad? He could turn that question around too. What the hell was a nomad doing on his own with a sentient for company?

Luca had never come across an active sentient in their right mind on his treasure hunts, but this one didn't seem to be a murderous lunatic. He took off the visor. A good old-fashioned paper map was folded up in the glove compartment, and he pulled it out to have a look. The mysterious duo were going east using a flat expanse which had once been a highway that ran almost parallel with the one he had taken from the base to Pontedera. Perhaps they were going to Florence. "Oh..." he muttered to himself as he revved the engine. Yes, they probably were going to Florence.

He needed to catch up to them before they reached their goal. In fact, he would prefer to catch up before nightfall. The drone would come along on the way there.

Luca swung the Rover around and squashed the accelerator pedal. Good thing traffic police wasn't a relevant concern anymore.

24:
Teo

The beautifully crafted metal connector on Teo's dining table proved that everything really had changed. That she had plunged into the unsafe waters of a budding rebellion against the society she had been brought up to believe in.

Teo picked up her cup of tea, blew at the steaming surface and then sipped it, all the while staring at the treasure. She had seen items like it often enough. Had rinsed dirt off them, carefully dried them and put a neat, green ribbon around them before sending them on to the technies. But it was the first time she had one in her own home.

After she took it from her worktable, it burned hot in her pocket for the remainder of the workday, on her way out of R&R and all the way through the Industrial Dome. It pulsed and bounced and shouted out to random strangers on the way through the Posh Dome until she closed the door to her flat behind her. Still, nobody had noticed anything.

Teodora Terzi was not used to being a thief, and she wasn't sure she liked it. Not because someone would miss the connector. It wasn't filed anywhere yet, and the spotter who picked it up in the first place probably didn't know what it was beyond looking remotely useful. What she didn't like was the risk of being discovered. What would they do if they found out? Fire her, of course. Cause her father to go on a rampage, accusing her of undermining his authority without even knowing exactly how true that was. Ask her a lot of difficult questions that she needed to make up plausible answers for. And then what? Could she go to prison for it? Undoubtedly her father would use his influence to get her out if that happened.

Still, what she did like about being a thief was finally being able to make a difference. This little thing would help constructing a drill to dig for water in the slums. And the people who were facilitating this were due to show up in ten minutes.

They would come to take the burden of her theft away, but before they did that, she needed to confront them with a matter that had been gnawing at her since the meeting in the Mezzo Pieno a few days ago.

She took another sip of her hot tea, then put down the cup and picked up the artifact on the table instead. It was odd to have it here, but if anything, her home was a fitting place for it. She had built up quite a collection of items relating to her job and the broad interest in anything technological and ancient that had made her want the job in the first place. She only owned a few books, but R&R had a lot more, and she had copied illustrations and certain inspiring passages from them. Most of her notes were kept in a thick folder, but she found some of the illustrations so pleasing that they decorated her wall.

The sound of boots on the stairs made Teo get up from her chair. She opened the door so quickly that Arsenio still had his hand raised to knock.

"Hello," she said, a little too sweetly.

"Hello," Arsenio replied.

"Hi," said Vanni, holding up a cabbage.

"Come on in," Teo said and stepped aside. "Why do you..."

Arsenio snatched the cabbage from Vanni on his way through the door and threw it at Teo. "Catch."

She did. "What's the cabbage for?" she asked and closed the door behind them.

"Cover," Vanni explained. "In case anybody asks any of us why we were here today, we all know why. To give you that cabbage you asked us to pick up for you in the Green Dome."

"I see," Teo said. She supposed she could make a stew with it. "Thanks. Would you like some tea?"

"No, we're leaving right away," Arsenio answered. "Is that the thing?" he added, gesturing in the general direction of the table in her living room.

Teo strode past him, tossed the cabbage onto the sofa and picked up the connector. "Yes," she said, "it's the thing." She glared at them in turn.

"Thank you for getting it. We know you took a big risk," Vanni said in his sincerest voice, probably thinking she was angling for gratitude.

"I volunteered to help," she replied, working herself up to ask them the question.

"All right," Arsenio said, "what's the problem, then?"

"When you took me out there with you," she began, "was it only so you would have something to blackmail me with?"

Arsenio groaned. "Is this really necessary?"

"Don't roll your eyes at me, Arsenio, or I will stuff this connector into the most suitable orifice on your body that I can find."

Vanni cleared his throat. "We understand. No need to stuff anything anywhere. Look, Teo, it's not as simple as that. We took you with us because you asked us to. But the reason you asked us to is that you were curious, right? Wanted more, right?"

She nodded.

"So naturally we thought you could make a great asset if you were interested in joining us. Patrizia has something on all of us. It's just for extra security. We trust you. Honestly." He smiled and added, "We would never have taken you out with us in the first place if we didn't."

Teo felt herself deflate a little bit. Arsenio could be blunt and insensitive, a real brusque arbiter, but his heart was in the right place. Vanni was the one who could talk and who radiated honesty. He could have had a political career if he'd wanted it. But he was too nice for that. "What does she have on you?" Teo asked and held out the connector towards Vanni.

"Can we save this for another time?" Arsenio said.

Vanni shot him a glance, then shrugged at Teo. "I'm sorry, but he's right. We need to go. We..." He faltered, then smiled brilliantly. "It's a relief to be able to tell you now. The operation is tonight. It wasn't supposed to be until later this week, but a couple of sentries are ill today, so they need help. I volunteered for a shift. Arsenio is taking your little gift with him and he's joining Gabriele."

"And he is taking medical supplies outside?" Teo guessed.

"Yes," Vanni replied. "So... Wish us luck."

"Good luck," Teo said, putting an arm around each of them in a big hug. "Be safe."

Arsenio squeezed her tightly and mumbled something she couldn't make out. Vanni kissed her cheek. And then they were gone.

And to her own surprise, Teo immediately felt fidgety and nervous. If only she could go with them... Logically speaking, it would not make it better to put herself in danger as well. They were trained arbiters. They knew what they were doing. They must have been keeping their work with the movement secret from her for quite some time. Nothing had changed. Except that now she knew. She would have to get used to it. Everything would turn out to be all right. It wasn't the end of the world.

The next day, Teo went to work as usual. And her theft had, as she knew it would, gone unnoticed. So she was in quite good spirits until her lunch break when it turned out that the world had ended, after all.

When she entered the cafeteria, she had to edge her way around a group of technies discussing in loud, urgent whispers.

"I heard there's least one high ranking official involved," said one.

"I'm glad they were caught. They must be crazy to sneak out," another replied.

Ice began to shoot up through Teo's feet and into her stomach and chest. "Excuse me," she heard herself say, "but what's going on?"

One of the technies turned to her with a frown on his face. "Someone was arrested for plotting a conspiracy with the slummers."

"Oh," Teo replied. She found that she couldn't say anything else.

She left work and headed towards the closest exit from the Industrial Dome in a haze before her mind began to catch up. Where was she going? She needed to know what had happened... But who would she ask? Her father would probably already have heard the news and in a lot more detail than any rumors she could catch. But she couldn't just burst in and demand to know if her best friends had been arrested. That would incriminate them further, and herself too. She needed a distraction... The cabbage. Yes, that would be her excuse.

"Hello, mom. I have this cabbage, and I thought perhaps you had an idea how to make something nice of it." In Teo's head, it had sounded feasible, but the moment she actually spoke the words, she understood the look on her mother's face perfectly. It was one of deep mistrust and doubt and a bit of amusement. "I mean," Teo added, gesturing at the cabbage in question with her free hand. What she really meant was, 'please let me see my dad! I need to know if my friends are all right!' And she couldn't think straight until she knew.

"Oh, Teodora," her mother said, shaking her head. "That's not the reason you're here. It's all right. Why don't we put that cabbage away? You don't need an excuse to visit."

Teo smiled, sheepishly. "No, I just..."

"I know you want to be independent and do your own things," Valentina Terzi carried on, the last bit in a bad imitation of Teo. "But even a grown, independent daughter wants to come home and eat sometimes. Especially if all she has in her kitchen is a cabbage."

Teo heaved a sigh of relief. Even with the suggestion that she wasn't doing well on her own, her mother was better at coming up with an excuse than she was. "Thanks, mom," she replied. "It's been a long day. Is dad home yet?"

Mrs Terzi glanced up at the timepiece on the wall. "He should be on his way. The council was having an emergency meeting. Let us sit. Tea?"

"Yes, please. Emergency meeting?" Teo repeated as her mother took her to the parlor.

"He didn't tell me much," her mother said while she bustled around with a teapot. "It had something to do with those dreadful people outside. But don't worry. Your father said it is under control. No one has broken in or anything of the sort."

"Oh, good," Teo replied, not really meaning it. "Didn't he tell you anything else?"

In that moment, the front door opened, and they heard Mr Terzi exchange a few words with Filippo in the entrance hall. He appeared in the doorway to the parlor a few seconds later.

"Hello, darling," he said to his wife. "And Teodora! What a surprise."

"I missed you a little bit," Teo replied. She sounded embarrassed, but that was fine.

She wanted to ask the questions on her mind right away, but Teo forced herself to wait. To exchange pleasantries, answer a few questions about her own work and such. Finally, when they had sat down at the dinner table and she had complimented the food, she broached the subject. "Mom says you were having an extraordinary meeting today?"

Her father nodded, finished chewing and drank a mouthful of his wine. "Yes," he said, sighing. "It's a terrible business."

"Oh dear. Are the people outside being difficult again?" said Mrs Terzi.

"Well," Mr Terzi said. "If only that was the case. There was a break-in last night in a pharmacy's stockroom."

"No!" Teo's mother gasped.

"Whole shelves of antibiotics were emptied. Medication the citizens of Florence need," he continued with the same air, Teo imagined, he used when speaking to the council.

"Do you know who did it?" Teo asked. Her voice sounded alarmed, but she hoped it didn't betray the cause of her alarm.

"Yes," her father said. He paused, unbearably, and drank again as if he needed something to strengthen him.

Teo tried not to grip her cutlery as if her life depended on it. She did her best to look curious and appalled rather than horrified and scared.

"You remember Gabriele De Felice, the doctor," he continued.

"Yes?" her mother said and then, "Oh no!"

"Yes," Mr Terzi confirmed, anger flushing his cheeks.

"We are all very disappointed. The council trusted him. We trusted him. He was always a little strange, but to think he was sitting in our very home a week ago. The snake!"

"But why would a doctor steal medicine?" Mrs Terzi asked, crestfallen.

"He was taking it out of the city," Mr Terzi replied, his voice shaking a little as he continued, "Sneaking out of the southernmost gate to give it to the wretched outsiders."

"No!" exclaimed Mrs Terzi, one of her hands flying to her mouth.

"How?" Teo asked.

"He had help," her father said. "He must have had help from someone... It stands to reason that it would be a sentry, but we don't know who. And God only knows why any of them would do it. It is very, very disappointing that someone would betray the trust of our community like that."

Under normal circumstances, this was the point when Teo would remark that it was probably to help the less fortunate people outside. When she would ask how the slummers would get medical supplies otherwise... But today she could not risk even lifting an eyebrow. "So it was just doctor De Felice?" she dared.

"The sentries who caught him saw two others, but they attempted to flee. The sentries were forced to shoot one of them."

Teo bit the inside of her mouth so hard she could taste blood.

"That is horrible," Mrs Terzi said.

"It was one of the outsiders. We don't know if he was inside the wall with De Felice or met him outside to distribute the supplies. The other man escaped."

Teo fought hard to keep her expression from changing into something like relief. "Was he a slummer too?" she asked.

"The sentries were not certain, but they think he was

from the city as well."

Mrs Terzi shook her head and dabbed at her mouth with a napkin. "I don't understand it," she said. "I simply don't understand it. Why would anyone do something like this? We live so peacefully here."

"Some people just can't leave well enough alone," Mr Terzi replied.

"What happens to the doctor now?" Teo asked.

"He is in prison now," her father replied. "We are trying to find out with whom he was working, but so far he has proved to be very uncooperative."

"That despicable man," Mrs Terzi said. It was hardly more than a week since she had placed the despicable man next to her own daughter at the table, hoping they would get along.

"We will keep working," Mr Terzi said. "Keep questioning him until he cooperates."

Something in his voice made Teo shudder. The ease with which a trusted member of society, a good acquaintance if not a friend, could fall into such disgrace that councilman Terzi spoke of interrogation as if it were just another task at the job. It made Teo wonder if he would personally be attending this questioning. It made her wonder what her father would say if his own daughter was caught.

Mr Terzi shook his head and went on to say something about the need to find a new man to take the Gabriele's position and about more security being needed at the gates and on the streets as well. But Teo was not listening to him anymore. Her mind was overcome with relief for her friends, fear for the doctor and the urge to get up from the table, rush out of the door and find someone, anyone, from the group to tell them the news.

25:
Mender

They had been convinced no one was following them. After leaving the people Renn called stagnants, a term that seemed derogatory although Renn did not in other ways assert his superiority, both human and sentient glanced back once in a while to make sure.

As afternoon turned into evening, the two companions were beginning to look for a suitable place to camp. Their destination for the day was perhaps half an hour ahead if they kept their pace, a formation of rocks that would provide them with some safety through the night. All of a sudden, Mender noticed a tenseness in Renn. Merely a tighter grip on his staff and a slightly sharper intake of air.

Mender's awareness surged from Renn to their surroundings, but ne did not see what was the matter before Renn spun around, ready to strike. Following his gaze, Mender finally did spot it. A round shape perhaps thirty centimeters across and five or ten centimeters tall hung in midair just above head height and a few paces behind them.

The thing made no noise, and Renn stood so still, staring

at it so fixedly that Mender wondered if he were even breathing. Then their pursuer took flight, zipping almost vertically upwards until it was a small dot. They watched it zoom back in a straight line in the direction they had come.

Renn turned again, making a sweeping motion with his staff. For a moment, Mender was confused, but then ne realized he was looking for more pursuers. There was none.

"It was a drone," Mender offered.

Renn let down his guard. "A drone?" he repeated.

"A remote controlled..." Mender trailed off and began again in an attempt to explain it so it would make sense to Renn. "In the past, humans made not only advanced sentients like me. Drones are a simpler kind of robot. A simple kind of Other. They can move and fly and see and hear, but they have no mind or will of their own. A person controls them to be their eyes and ears."

"Then who is controlling it?" Renn cut right to the most relevant topic. "Who is using it to follow us?"

Mender shook nir head. Who indeed? The drone left too quickly for Mender to make out a logo or any trademark features. It could be a military drone. Or it could be one of CerEvolv's observation drones patrolling the area to register any trouble. Perhaps it had scanned Mender and gone directly back... But CerEvolv's closest department was in Florence, in the direction they were headed... "I don't know," Mender replied. "What makes you think it was following us?"

Renn made a half-shrug. "It came from behind. It was there, hovering above us for a little while."

"How do you know?" Mender asked, hoping that Renn understood it as the question it was meant to be and not disbelief that Renn did know.

"I felt it. You said it has eyes. I felt it looking," Renn replied as if this were the most natural thing in the world. Perhaps it was to him. Mender was not in possession of that kind of sense, but ne had heard humans speak of it. Perhaps the ability to feel when one was observed had been honed over the centuries. "It left when I turned to look at it. Why?"

"I don't know," Mender said again. "Drones are not weapons. We have nothing to fear from it."

Renn cast one last glance around and then thrust his staff into the ground and resumed walking. "But what about the one controlling it?" he asked.

"It could be someone who had the drone handed down through the generations," Mender suggested. "Or someone from a society that still uses that kind of technology."

"But we don't know for certain it's not the stagnants. They said someone with knowledge and artifacts from the past came to visit them. Maybe that person gave the drone to them." Renn nodded towards their goal. "We should change our course to make pursuit harder. It is too obvious that we would camp there for the night."

"As you wish," Mender agreed. "Would you like me to carry your bag so we can move faster?"

This time Renn did not hesitate. He knew Mender didn't experience fatigue. "Thank you," he said as he handed over his pack.

Renn turned towards a jagged line of hills in the distance. It would take them longer to reach those, and it would probably be dark before they managed to camp. They had torches, but traveling after nightfall in an unknown territory still seemed risky. Yet, Mender thought, Renn would already have weighed that risk against the risk of pursuers catching up to them. And his survival success rate was, obviously, perfect.

"When we were attacked," Renn began after a while, "one of the thieves hit you with his club."

"Yes," Mender agreed.

"I need to know how badly injured you are."

"Thank you for your concern, Renn, but you don't need

to worry about me," Mender said.

"I need to know," Renn repeated, and ne understood it wasn't merely a question of worry. It was a matter of safety. Renn had noticed the slight involuntary movement of Mender's head and wanted to know how hindered ne would be in a crisis.

"It seems that something was knocked loose," Mender admitted, deciding not to go into detail with technical terms. "I function correctly apart from a bit of stiffness in my neck and the occasional spasm which you have no doubt noticed since you ask."

Renn nodded. "Will you heal? Or will it get worse?" he asked.

"I don't know," admitted Mender. "It is unlikely to get better without repairs for which none of us has the tools or the knowledge. I don't think it will get worse, but I can't say for certain. I was always sent to maintenance on a regular basis to make sure everything worked perfectly."

Just then, as to emphasize what ne was saying, the artificial muscles in Mender's neck retracted, causing nem to jerk nir head to the side. It was a strange sensation not to be in control of all nir movements and a very educational one since humans often were privy to that sort of thing.

"Does it hurt?" Renn asked.

"No. I do not feel pain," Mender reassured him, meaning it in general. Did Renn understand that? Yes, Mender concluded, he did. Despite his lack of prior knowledge and education, Renn's mind was as developed as the minds of the humans who had created and employed Mender. What he missed in academic intellect, he made up for with something else. Something that was harder to describe. Intuition?

"Yet, you are not reckless," Renn said.

"No, I was programmed to be quite sensible," Mender told him.

Renn studied nem for a moment. Then he nodded once

as if to signal that now his questions had been sufficiently answered and the conversation was over. He walked on in silence for the next half hour.

Their shadows grew long as the sun began to set, and Mender suspected that to the human eye, the unforgiving landscape was also beautiful. It seemed untouched here, so far from any indication of the fallen civilization. They had not come across any vaguely car-shaped mounds or cracked asphalt under their feet for some time. It was merely a vast expanse of dusty earth.

The travelers passed their original destination for the day and were halfway to their new one when Mender saw Renn's head snap up mid-stride and his good hand pause the movement of the staff before it hit the ground.

Mender was about to ask him what was the matter when ne heard a thin, whooshing noise, so high-pitched that it sounded more like a screech than the wind ought to. And there was no wind.

"What is..?"

"There is no time," Renn interrupted. "Prepare to fight. Remember, the top of the head."

Mender was not a combat model, and the only weapon ne had ever held in nir hands had been used as a short-lived fire the night before. But ne was strong, and ne was determined to protect nir clients. Ne dropped Renn's pack on the ground to be able to move better and clenched nir hands into fists.

Renn bent his knees slightly, held his staff almost horizontally in his right hand and stretched out his left arm for balance. He wore the look Mender had sometimes seen on the faces of professional athletes and soldiers in documentaries. 90 percent cold, determined readiness and 10 percent fear that would make sure they did not grow overly confident as well as provide them with adrenaline to keep them on their feet. "There," he said.

A long, white shape was rapidly approaching them in a cloud of dust whirled up from the ground by its beating wings. Its bullet-shaped head opened its mouth to reveal a number of long, sharp teeth. It had no legs, and its whole body was covered by plates of bone. "A scarvhe," Mender said.

"No," Renn replied. In the flying snake's wake, first one, then two and three lumps on the ground exploded in clouds of sand, and something shot into the air from each of them. "A flock of scarvhes."

26:
Renn

It was worse than Renn had expected when he first noticed the whirring sound of wings and the hissing screech of the first scarvhe. They must have been lying in wait, hoping to ambush someone. Renn could handle one of them even with an injured arm. He could probably take on two as well. But four? He was not alone, he reminded himself as the predators bore down on them. Their screams became as sharp and thin as sewing needles. Mender was with him, and Mender was intent, to an almost unsettling degree, on keeping him safe.

The first scarvhe came at them in a straight line, a whirlwind of sand and dust in its wake. Its bony, beak-like mouth was open and it was aiming straight for Renn's head. Too high for him to get a killing blow in. He drew back his arm and swung the staff in a half circle, hitting the creature so hard that it was thrown off course and landed flailing and screeching on the ground.

Next to Renn, Mender was wielding the discarded backpack now. The sentient twisted, gathering momentum and used the pack to punch the next scarvhe. It too tumbled to the ground. Good. The scarvhes would both be back, but it bought them time to deal with the remaining assailants.

The two last scarvhes picked a target each. Renn crouched, watched the scarvhe headed for him dive, and then waited for the right moment. When it arrived, he leapt up and brought down the end of his staff on top of the scarvhe's head. He heard the skull crack as one last scream escaped the creature. It thrashed on the ground, unable to lift itself up again. Renn whirled around. Mender was trying to fend off the remaining scarvhe, but with less luck this time. They were engaged in a strange dance, Mender thrusting the bag at it, the scarvhe swerving out of reach.

Renn began to swing his staff to help Mender, but then he heard the wail of the first scarvhe. It was back in the air, coming at him once more. This time it had learned from its mistake and managed to avoid his weapon. He could keep it at bay, but they were locked in a stubborn routine, Renn swinging his staff and the scarvhe following his movements, darting this way and that, always just out of reach.

A hard sound, like that of a staff penetrating the skull of a scarvhe, made Renn look in Mender's direction again. He almost let down his guard to rush to his companion's aid when he saw what was happening. Mender was still standing, but the scarvhe had avoided the swinging pack and was now thrusting its beak at Mender's face, viciously stabbing, fast and unrelenting and oblivious to Mender's attempts at swatting it away. Renn knew he would only endanger himself further by turning his back on the scarvhe attacking him. And Mender would not benefit from Renn getting injured or killed too. His only comfort was knowing that Mender did not feel pain.

Renn had expected the remaining scarvhe, the one Mender had initially hit, to join the fray again. But the moment it approached him, he heard Mender call out his name so urgently that he turned, his staff describing a protective circle around him.

The scarvhe had abandoned Mender. Now both predators were coming towards him. Of course. They had smelled or sensed that Mender was not flesh and bone after attempting to gauge out the eyes. Renn caught one of the scarvhes on the side of the head with a tooth shattering impact, but the next was too close too quickly.

For a moment, all he saw was teeth. The screech rang in his ears and a stench of rotten meat invaded his nostrils. Then he was on his back, struggling to keep the scarvhe at bay.

Mender was fighting too. Not because the scarvhes attacked the sentient, but because Mender was brave or foolish enough to attempt to help him. The sentient picked up something from the ground, a rock, and bashed one of the scarvhes' head with it, wounding and distracting it, but the stone was not aimed well enough to kill it.

Renn needed to get back on his feet, but... He rolled, almost avoiding a set of gnashing teeth, but a sharp pain and a warm, wet feeling on his cheek told him it had been too close. As the scarvhe charged again, Renn threw up his left arm for protection. He felt the jaws close, but there was no pain. The bandage. The scarvhe's teeth could not bite through it. The relief was cut short when the scarvhe thrust itself backwards and pulled Renn with it, jerking him almost upright before it shook him so violently that he was tossed aside, lost his grip on the staff and came to rest face down in the dust. He heard Mender call for him again, and rolled blindly, hoping the creature would miss and knowing it would take more than a few lucky strikes to get out of this alive.

All of a sudden, a rumbling sound interrupted the battle. It was so strong that Renn felt the ground vibrate. And it grew louder still, turning into a roar. That was no animal Renn could recognize. He struggled to his hands and knees, saw Mender lying a few paces away with a scarvhe pecking at anything it could get to. The sentient may not be edible, but Mender had tried to help Renn and was to be eliminated.

A blinding white light dispersed the darkness of the grey dusk, and the noise stopped. A loud bang rang out, like a short, sharp thunderclap. The scarvhes screamed, one of them fell to the ground and the rest raced away from the light and the noise.

Renn picked up his staff, panting and coughing. His legs were shaking, but he managed to stand. Mender was getting up as well. Good.

Squinting against the brightness, Renn saw a dark, massive lump emitting the light and a figure the size and shape of a human being approaching them.

"Are you all right?"

The voice had the kind of accent Renn had only heard once before. It sounded like Mender's.

"Hello? Are you hurt?" Now there was impatience in the voice, something Renn had never heard in Mender's.

"Yes," Renn replied, not knowing if he replied to the first or the last question. "You chased the scarvhes away. Thank you."

The figure came closer and now Renn could see more than an outline. It was a slender young man, a little younger than Renn, with strange clothes and a tool of some kind in his hand. His hair was so light that at first Renn thought it was white, but it was really the color of yellow grass.

"No problem," the stranger said. He put the tool into a holster on his hip. "I'm not your enemy," he continued, gesturing at Renn's staff, "So you can put your bo staff thingy away now."

Renn didn't, but he relaxed to make it clear that he wasn't going to attack. "Who are you?" he asked.

"My name's Luca. Luca Capello." The stranger made an exaggerated bow and grinned as he straightened up again.

"I am Renn," Renn said.

"Just Renn?" Luca asked.

"Only Renn, yes," Renn confirmed.

"Of course," Luca said, making a sound like a snort of laughter as if there was a joke here that Renn was not aware of. "And you," he continued, turning to Mender, "You are ... Let me guess. You're a Minder, right?"

Mender's face was even more startling than usual. The smooth exterior of it was dented and scratched, and a number of strange cords protruded from the vicinity of one of the eyes. That eye had a strange look that Renn could only think of as blinded. Still, when his companion spoke, the voice was as clear and measured as ever. "Yes. Yes, I am Minder 3431-B. I answer to the nickname Mender."

"All right," Luca said, nodding. "The fuck happened to your face?"

"Mostly exposure, I'm afraid," Mender replied. "The scarvhes damaged it further. You seem... very well acquainted with my kind."

"I've never worked on a Minder model before, but you could say I dabble in sentients. I was at IRAI." Luca shrugged. "Anyway, I'm glad I finally caught up to you guys."

"Caught up?" Renn asked.

The explanation was hard to follow. Luca spoke faster and less clearly than Mender, and his story included words Renn had never heard before. Some of them seemed to be used only for emphasis while others were terms that had to do with the wheeled masheen that carried him across the wasteland. What Renn did understand was that it was not the stagnants but Luca who sent the drone to them earlier that day and that he was so fascinated to see a sentient that he decided to follow them.

"But you've told me nothing about yourselves," Luca said. "I would love to know how a nomad and a sentient ended up together."

Mender nodded, but Renn interrupted the polite and kind answer that was no doubt on its way. "You have told us nearly nothing about yourself, either," he said. "Why should we trust you?"

"Because I just saved your asses?" Luca replied, cocking his head in a way that made him look even younger.

"And we thanked you for it," Renn said, "but apart from your name, we know nothing about you. You ride that masheen and you claim to know a lot about sentients. How?"

"The machine is called a car," Luca said. "C-A-R spells automobile. Look, I would love to tell you all about myself. In fact, I would love to tell you about myself over a cup of coffee or a nice, hot meal. Will you come with me? I'll take you home with me in the Rover. The car."

It did not even occur to the boy that going with him would interrupt their migration or journey. That they had no reason to trust him when he had not even explained his motives. He was direct and blunt and unlike anyone Renn had ever encountered.

"Come on, it's not like I'm kidnapping you. I'm offering you a free meal and a bath and a bed if you want to stay and sleep. I can even take you back here afterwards if you want to. I don't live that far away."

Mender turned to Renn, and Renn saw that little head jerk out of the corner of his eye.

Luca sighed, exaggeratedly. "Dude, your sentient is damaged. At least come with me and allow me to fix nem up. Ne is going to fall to pieces if nobody does anything soon. It's almost dark. Do you want to make a camp here? I'm offering you a much more comfy option." There was an almost pleading quality to his voice now, not entirely unlike a child begging for a toy.

"We are on our way to Florence," Mender said. "I have

attempted to contact CerEvolv."

Renn gave the sentient a warning glance. There was a lot of things he did not feel comfortable telling this stranger right now. Then he noticed a look of hesitation flash across Luca's face. The unguarded expression was concealed quickly again.

"My place is that way," Luca said and gestured towards the southeast. "Going with me will bring you closer to your destination." He spread his arms in a defeated gesture. "Okay. It's up to you. I won't force you. But... I would love for you to come. I live alone with my sentients. I was born a long time ago, before the impact. I was 16. My family and me were put in cryo... That's a way of freezing people to preserve them, Renn. We were going to wake up when the world wasn't so fucking crazy anymore, after the disaster. I was the only survivor."

"Mender?" Renn said.

"Some humans did that. It is a plausible story given his clothes and technological knowledge," Mender verified.

"Thank you!" Luca said. "Anyway, that was two years ago. So... That good enough for you?"

"Your car," Renn began, "is it safe?"

"I'm a good driver," Luca said. "Yes, it's safe."

"And it is faster than walking?" Renn continued. It must be if Luca had caught up to them.

A grin spread on Luca's face. "It's faster than anything you can imagine, nomad. But since it's dark, I'll have to go a little slower."

If this stranger could provide shelter for the night and get them closer to their goal with little time loss, it may be their best option. "Mender?" Renn said again.

"If he can make repairs, it would be very helpful to my journey," Mender said.

Renn nodded. Mender was right, and Renn would not ask his companion not to go with the boy. But they could go their separate ways at any time. The bond of their small Covey only applied until it was no longer beneficial to travel together. If they parted now, however, it would leave Renn alone and exposed. "Then we accept your invitation," he said.

Luca clapped his hands together. "Awesome! Let's get going!"

27:
Renn

They sat inside the car, Luca in front and Renn and Mender in the back. They had their packs and Renn's staff lying across their laps because the compartment behind them was full of wares Luca had traded with the stagnants.

Then the car sputtered to life and began to move. Mender assured him everything was fine, but Renn felt powerless, trapped with a non-human companion he had known only for a few days and a strange boy who claimed to control the beast in whose belly they were traveling.

He wanted to ask questions. He wanted to listen to the conversation between the others, but Renn constantly found himself distracted by the unfamiliar smells and movements. He stared out of the windows at the darkness around them illuminated only by the two light beams from the front of the masheen. They were going at an alarming speed. And Renn understood with sudden clarity why Luca seemed so full of confidence and ease. It was not because he was a child of another time. It was because he thought himself invincible.

"So what's the deal with traveling alone? I've only seen

your kind move in groups before." Luca looked into the mirror mounted in front of his face so that his gaze met Renn's.

"I was separated from my Covey," Renn replied after a short moment of hesitation. As reluctant as he felt to share any knowledge about himself, there was no logical reason why it was a bad idea. "I am searching for them."

"And they went to Florence?" There it was again. A shadow of something Luca did not want anyone to notice crossing his face.

"I have reason to believe they went in the direction of the domed city," Renn said.

"Ever been there before?"

"No." And then, before he could stop himself, "Have you?"

Luca was staring out of the window in front of him now. His hands gripped harder around the wheel with which he steered the masheen. "Yeah," he said. "And where does a CerEvolv sentient fit into the picture?"

"We... met," Renn replied.

"Geez, really? Mind blown," Luca replied. Like some people had the ability to build up trust, Luca built distance where there was physically none. He turned the wheel, and the car lurched so suddenly that Renn braced himself with his hands and feet despite the belt of safety Luca had put around him.

"We encountered one another by chance," Mender said, not noticeably shaken by the car's movements. "And we decided to travel together since we were going in the same direction."

Luca nodded because although the meaning was practically the same, Mender's explanation was longer.

The dark landscape outside continued to go by at an incredible speed. This stranger could be taking them anywhere. Inside this car of his, it was almost impossible to tell the direction they were going. They could not even read the stars or the wind.

Renn thought he had believed Luca's story about being somehow preserved for centuries and only recently coming back to life, but when the car stopped next to a huge building and Luca showed his two guests inside, he realized he was only beginning to accept the story as the truth now.

"Are you all right?" Mender asked quietly.

Renn nodded. He didn't trust himself to speak. It was like walking into the past. Or at least he assumed it was. The house was incredibly clean and smelled of something that scratched the inside of his nostrils. It was still dark outside, but the moment they entered, lights came on everywhere of their own accord. They were not ordinary lamps or torches, but more akin to the glowing eyes of the car.

As Renn was adjusting to the bright surroundings, Luca spread his arms wide, precariously swinging the bags he had brought with him as he turned around. "Welcome to my humble home!" he said.

"Master Luca, what is going on... Oh," a voice said.

Renn followed the sound and saw a staircase at the top of which stood a woman in a simple, dark dress. There was something odd about her that Renn could not immediately put his finger on.

"Hey, Nanny!" Luca replied. "I know it's late, but could you fix me and my new friend here a snack?"

Although he was not certain their relation counted as friendship, Renn didn't argue. He studied the woman as she descended the stairs until another person entered the entrance hall from a room beyond. This was a man in trousers and some kind of shirt that seemed to have been made from the same fabric as the woman's clothes.

"We seem to have guests," the man said.

Renn felt surrounded. He shot Mender a glance, but

Mender did not appear confused or scared.

"Yep," their host said, holding out his bags to the two approaching figures. "This is Nanny and Alfredo," he said to Renn and Mender. "They are my faithful, helpful and somewhat overprotective sentients." He turned and pointed at Renn and Mender in turn. "This is Renn who's a nomad with awesome eyesight and probably equally awesome bo staff skills even with a broken arm. And that is Mender, a Minder model on a mission who's made Renn nir client. Did I miss anything?"

Polite greetings ensued. Renn looked at Mender to see how... ne? Yes, that was the word Luca used, and presumably he knew about that sort of thing, so Renn would adopt it. So he looked at Mender to see how ne was taking the encounter with two of nir own kind.

Nanny and Alfredo were asking Mender what had happened to nir face, and telling nem that it was a nice surprise to see another fully functioning sentient. If Renn hadn't been told, he would not have guessed that these two were sentients. The skin was intact on their faces, and they made expressions quite similar to humans. Only an uncanny regularity of their movements and something not-quite human about their eyes hinted their nature.

"Right," Luca said, "I'm starving."

Renn and Mender followed their hosts into the kitchen and Renn suspected that Luca did not have the faintest idea what the word starving meant. A large closet kept cool artificially had so much food that Renn could have lived on it for days, and apparently other doors opened up to stored food like the sticks Mender carried.

Renn and Luca both sat down on chairs by a table in the middle of the room.

"You are hurt too," Alfredo said to Renn while Nanny heaved food out of the closet.

Renn touched his cheek. The blood was already dry. "It's

only a scratch."

"It should be cleaned regardless," Mender said.

"Yeah," Luca chimed in and rose from the chair by the table. "You don't mind if I take care of it, right?"

Renn was about to answer when it became obvious that the question was not for him.

"No, you are welcome to," Mender replied.

Luca opened a cupboard and pulled out a white box with a red cross on top of it, a bigger version of Mender's boxes. He tore open a small package and put the moist cloth inside on Renn's cheek. His hands were steady and performed the task quickly and efficiently.

"There," Luca said, placing a pad like the ones Mender called plasters on Renn's skin. The sensation was cool and a little bit numbing.

Next, Renn was presented with a fine meal consisting of fresh vegetables and meat and a cool, sweet drink. While they ate, Luca talked about his adventures. About finding the drone he used to spot Renn and Mender, about going on trips in his car almost as far south and north as Renn had been.

But no matter how much their host talked, it was obvious that he handpicked amusing or impressive tales and left out some of the hard and important ones. He didn't talk about his first months after waking up to find himself the only human being alive. He didn't mention the scars on his hands. He didn't speak of Florence. Most of these tales, Renn did not pry into. They were not meant for him. And after all, he did the same. He told Luca of escaping a dust storm, of fighting scarvhes and of reading the wind. He didn't tell him of loss and starvation, of having to leave a place behind because it was exhausted and of splitting a Bevy up into Coveys that went their separate ways to survive in a world that simply did not have enough food for them all.

When the meal was over and Nanny was removing

leftovers, Luca stretched and yawned. "Okay," he said. "You're probably as tired as I am. I really need a shower, but I'm too busted now. How about we get some sleep?"

"Yes," Renn agreed. This was the second night he was going to spend indoors in only a few days. He hoped this would be more peaceful than the last.

"I'll fix you up in the morning, Mender, all right?" Luca continued. "I don't think you're going to short circuit in the next few hours."

"Thank you," Mender said.

"Right. Then I'll leave you sentients to talk about sentient things while us mortals crash," Luca said as Alfredo, who had been absent for much of the meal, returned.

Renn followed Luca upstairs. He was full and he was exhausted, and his senses were continually being bombarded by new smells and sounds and sights. His host showed him into a room and proclaimed it was a guest room. And then the strange boy left.

Renn stood for a moment in the middle of the room, taking in all the clean surfaces, round corners and softness. He undressed, and although he was much too dusty and sweaty to rub himself all over all this cleanness, he lay down. The bed felt like clouds looked.

Renn gave up thinking and wondering and asking questions. He thought it would take him a long time to fall asleep in this weird place, to allow himself to let his guard down, but it was surprisingly easy to drift off.

28:
Luca

And then he woke up, and it was all a dream.

Except it wasn't.

Luca lay wondering, marveling, at the fact that he was not the only human being in the house this morning. The guest room he had chosen for the nomad was several doors down from Luca's bedroom, but he could still feel Renn somehow. Sense that there was another beating heart in the same building.

Or maybe he only thought he could because he knew Renn was there and he was getting way too excited and should really stop because Renn was going to do his nomad thing and go on his not-particularly-merry way soon.

Why had he even invited the weirdo home with him? Because the weirdo came with a sentient. And because the two of them were so damn interesting.

Luca got out of bed. He could smell himself. At least the nomad smelled worse. And the nomad would have no idea how to operate a shower and distinguish shampoo from conditioner from shower gel from shaving foam, would he? Luca shuffled down the corridor in his underwear, past his brother Leo's empty room, past the room where he kept Sia and Simon who were, thankfully, turned off, and knocked on the door of the guest room. Not too loudly. He didn't want to risk a bo staff in his face.

"Yes?" came a muffled voice from inside the room.

Luca breathed out. He'd held his breath and he didn't even know why. He opened the door. "Good morning."

"Good morning." Renn was sitting crosslegged on the bed in what probably passed for underwear. His hair was still ridiculous. It wasn't that it didn't look surprisingly good on him or fit his tribal nomad style perfectly. It was long and had a number of small pleats with things like beads in them. Exactly like everyone ever would imagine the hero of some post apocalyptic show to look. That was Luca's quibble. It was simply slightly on the improbable side. But then again, lots of things were. That didn't mean they weren't true. Renn was one big, rather handsome, nicely chiseled lump of improbable. Even if Luca could smell him.

"Okay, so we'd better clean up before breakfast," was what he ended up saying out loud. Then he saw the pile of worn and dirty laundry his guest had shed. He sized Renn up as he stood. He was probably Leo's size. Something about that thought felt wrong, but it was the only logical thing.

They went to the bathroom, and there was a whole bunch of awkwardness that Luca would rather forget, including trying to explain why conditioner and moisturizer were essential and gauging whether the nomad was comfortable or not with Luca shaving in the same room while he was in the shower and trying not to snort with laughter when Renn carefully inquired as to where one went when one needed to go about certain lavatory businesses.

Renn hesitated when Luca presented him with a bunch of clothes, shoes and boots that had been sealed up for centuries and told him to take what he liked. But in the end, he accepted the gesture and picked a few items. Leo's style had been a bit on the boring side. Nothing tight like Luca's preferred jeans, just a lot of brown and grey and blue comfortable items. And sensible footwear.

"You look great," Luca reassured Renn.

Renn studied him in a way that suggested his looks were not on the top ten list of his everyday concerns. "Why are you doing all this?" he asked.

"Cause I feel like it," Luca said, faster and sharper than he meant to. "Do I need a reason?"

"The stagnants talked about a hermit who sometimes trades with them," Renn said a little later as they were making their way downstairs to the smell of instant coffee and freshly baked bread.

"Yeah?" Luca replied. He had a feeling he knew where this was going.

"I don't mean to offend, but why..." That's where the question stopped, but Renn didn't need to complete the sentence.

How could Luca even begin to make him understand? He wasn't alone. He had Nanny and Alfredo and Sia and Simon and his little army in the garage. He could do whatever he wanted and he had everything he would ever need right here in the base. He had Florence to look after until... until it was time to do something about it. Every human being he'd met in the last two years only wanted to take something from him. The kids in the settlements wanted sweets. The grownups wanted ancient treasures. The idiots in Florence wanted him to give up everything he stood for. At the end of the day, everyone wanted him to be someone else if he were to be part of their community.

And then there were the nomads. They were even worse. Once a giant herd of them had come to the base right before a dust storm. They hadn't seen him, but they had tried to get in, had plundered everything they could get their hands on. They had broken a water tank to get to the water. They had trampled the garden, pulled the struggling vegetables up by their roots... Finally they had taken refuge outside his home while he was stuck inside during the storm, torn between anger and something that might have been guilt or fear, but whatever it was, it definitely wasn't any fun.

"I don't ask you why you're a nomad, do I?" he replied, and thankfully Renn left it at that.

After breakfast, it was time to get to work. Artificials was Luca's happy place. When he worked, everything else went away. Well, almost. Renn sat there on a stool in Luca's workshop, after asking Mender, not Luca, if he could stay.

The scarvhes had torn some wires and artificial muscle tissue from Mender's eye. That was easy enough to fix. And it was simple enough to spot the other problems with a sentient with no skin. "I can do the surface work while you're active as long as you promise to sit still," Luca told his patient. "I've got materials for new skin. But I need to turn you off for the crick in your neck." He half expected Renn to leap up and protest. This didn't happen. "Are you cool with that?" he asked Mender.

"Yes. Nanny told me you were a top student at IRAI," Mender said, "so I believe I will be in good hands." Ne didn't add that also nir nomad friend was watching and would kick his ass if he did anything to harm Mender. Luca wondered if Renn could. He also wondered why he was a little disappointed that Renn clearly had no idea what it meant to be a top student at IRAI. "2300-9800," Mender added.

"Okay, thanks." Luca patted Mender's shoulder and flashed Renn a smile. "Ne will be asleep for a little while."

"How?" Renn asked.

Fair enough. As far as Renn probably knew, Mender

didn't sleep. "I'll manually deactivate nem," Luca said. "There's a switch if you know how to get to it."

"Why?" Renn asked. "Does Mender feel pain?"

"Well, it definitely is about pain," Luca said.

"No, I don't feel pain. But Luca could get hurt if I am active," Mender explained.

"You know," Luca said, "I could... make a few other adjustments now that I'm in there anyway."

Mender turned, head jerking comically. "Adjustments?"

Luca sighed. "Look, I'm just saying... I'm not sure CerEvolv is there anymore. I mean, with the way things are now, I'm kind of sure it isn't. So you're probably wasting your time following your programming. I can tweak it. It's only a matter of removing a few lines of code, really." It was more than removing a few lines of code, but he knew what he was doing.

"I... don't know if it's a good idea," Mender said. As battered as ne was to look at, ne was a beautiful piece of programming and hardware. There was hesitation and concern in nir voice. Being a Minder model, there would be some of that. Luca could tell how it differed from the way Nanny or Alfredo would have said the same words.

"I promise I'll be gentle," Luca said. "I won't change your personality or anything."

Renn continued to not contribute verbally to the conversation, but Luca could practically feel him wondering if Luca could be trusted and if it really were possible to change a sentient's personality like that.

"I won't do it if you don't want me to. Just thinking it may be easier not to go there."

"I think... It is too big a part of who I am," Mender finally said. "Thank you for the offer, but I believe it's something I must do."

"Okay," Luca replied. "It's up to you." Of course it felt

like that to Mender. It would until the task was complete or someone had changed the programming. It was not only a waste of time but also pretty damn dangerous for Mender to go to Florence now. Well, he could tweak the programming without telling anyone. It would probably only feel like Mender had changed nir mind, and then Mender could stay here instead. And maybe if Mender stayed... No. Luca bit his lip. He would reprogram demis and semis and sentients who had malfunctioned without consent, but this wasn't it. There was no one to check that he followed the rules, but... just no.

"All right. Let's do this," Luca said and searched his messy workbench for a screwdriver delicate enough to open the small panel in the back of Mender's head. Once inside, he used the tip to press the deactivation code Mender had given him. It was an almost foolproof way of ensuring that sentients weren't accidentally turned off or stolen and reprogrammed.

Mender grew silent and completely still. Luca pulled the lamp on his workbench closer and began to work.

An hour and a lot of concentration and really impressive adjusting and replacing that no one else was able to appreciate later, Luca pushed the point of a needle into the hole next to the deactivation code pad and felt Mender stir.

"Welcome back. The procedure took 57 minutes," Luca said so Mender would know. "How does it feel?"

Mender experimentally turned nir head, rolled nir shoulders back, looked up at the ceiling and then at the floor. "I believe I am back to normal function. My vision appears to be perfect again too. Thank you."

Luca could not help grinning. "No problem. Now let's fix your face."

That part was not nearly as delicate as tampering with the electronics inside a sentient and no challenge even to fingers like his. It was just the outer skin, and between the mechanics and the skin was a semi-transparent film separating the two layers that were almost intact. Luca mixed the components of the latex-like substance he would be draping over the face. He didn't know the formula of it, but then again, cosmetics weren't his area. He'd only learned to do this part by trial and error over the past few years. Unfortunately he didn't have any spare hair, but a bald head would be better than an artificial face.

"What's your preferred ethnicity?" he asked, pausing with a hand on one of the jars of dye. He thought that the skin Mender still had looked somewhat East Asian, but he really wasn't sure. Skin color never really interested him.

Mender considered it, studying Renn for a moment. "Would it be desirable to mimic the majority of people I might encounter?"

"One of the great things about the world having ended is the lack of racism. Right?" said Luca. The last bit was directed at Renn.

"Racism?" the nomad echoed as if he had never heard the word. He probably hadn't.

"My point exactly." Luca shrugged. "So take your pick."

"Then I would prefer a shade similar to what I had before," Mender decided.

Luca nodded and took down a couple of jars. "So... What happens next?" he asked as he worked on the skin. He would do the hand as well as the face and make the transition from the new skin to the old skin as smooth as possible.

"Next?" Renn asked echoed.

"You know, when I'm done patching nem up and all that." Luca glanced over at Renn. "I mean, do I just pack you some lunch and send you on your way?"

"Please don't feel obligated..." Renn began to derail the situation.

"I don't feel obligated to do shit," Luca muttered under his breath.

"I am not expecting lunch…"

"It's not about the goddamn lunch!" Luca snapped. "I'm asking you if you'd like to stay for a while or if you're leaving right away."

"Oh. Thank you for your hospitality, but as far as I know, Mender would like to move on to that place. CerEvolv. And I would like to continue my search…"

"Okay." Luca stretched the rubbery material over the face and held it down with one hand while he soldered the edges. "Lunch it is, then. And… I have something else you might like," he added, hating himself a little bit for making more offers if Renn couldn't even be bothered to hang around for a few days. He was starting to regret he'd even asked.

29:
Renn

Luca's mood shifted so rapidly that it was hard to keep up or anticipate his next move. He was generous and offered them to stay longer, but although he claimed to be fine on his own and parried Renn's every attempt to get to know him, he appeared to be upset and hiding it behind a mask of sarcasm. But it was, Renn knew, not really of any consequence. They were closer now to Florence than the night before, Luca had helped Mender, and he had given Renn some useful items of clothing including a pair of boots that fit perfectly and felt softer than anything he had ever worn before. And, as Luca had promised, there was also a meal to bring along.

Now Renn and Mender were sitting in soft chairs in what their host called the living room. The whole place was so comfortable and clean and... easy.

Mender's face and hands looked almost completely human now. Somehow, it was even stranger to see nem like that when Renn knew what was hiding under the surface.

He glanced down and flexed his left arm. After Luca tended to Mender, Mender and Nanny had tended to Renn.

They removed the pink cast from his arm to see if the bone was healing as it should and agreed that it was looking so good that he didn't need the clumsy thing anymore. Renn wasn't sorry to see it go although it had saved him from a nasty scarvhe bite. It was weird that he could already use his arm again. Usually broken bones took a lot longer to mend.

"Right, I found it," Luca said as he strode into the room. He took up a lot of space. Not physically, he was not particularly tall or very broad, but he had a way of making sure everybody noticed him. Now he was carrying a box that he placed on the low table in the middle of the room. "Renn, meet your new best friend." Luca opened the box and pulled out a contraption that made no sense to Renn immediately.

"Oh, that is indeed a good idea," Mender said.

Luca beamed. "The dust isn't good for your lungs," he said.

Renn did not need anyone to tell him that. Like all other wanderers, he did what he could to keep out sand and dust. Some developed a rasping quality to their voice, a wheezing sound when they breathed and a dry cough. Stone lungs could slow down any wanderer, and some grew so weak that it killed them before old age could catch up to them.

"So," Luca was explaining, "You put it on like this." He placed what was apparently a mask over his nose and mouth and pulled two strings behind his head. "You need to make sure it's tight so nothing gets in," he continued, slightly muffled and nasal. "The filters here keep the particles out. You can breathe pretty well in it, but it can feel a little restrictive if you run." He pulled off the mask and handed it to Renn. "Try it on."

"Thank you," Renn said and studied the mask.

"It's not going to eat your face. Try it on," Luca repeated.

Renn obliged. All smells apart from the unknown material of the mask itself disappeared.

"Suits you," Luca said.

He removed the mask again. "I am certain it will be useful. Thank you, again," Renn said.

Luca shook his head. "So you're really heading to Florence? Both of you?" he asked.

"Yes," Mender confirmed.

Renn studied their host who probably thought he was hiding his feelings very well. In a way he was because Renn could not tell if the predominant emotion was fear or anger.

"You mentioned you have been there," Renn said.

Luca slammed the empty box shut and turned on him. "I have. So what?"

"So, perhaps... You have been very helpful and generous already, but perhaps you have knowledge that could be of use to us."

Luca snorted. For a moment, Renn thought he wouldn't reply, but then he sighed and began to talk, "Okay. I used to live there with my family. Before the world turned to shit. All I know is it's different now. Like, really, really different. I don't know if CerEvolv still exists somehow, but I highly doubt it. And if I were you guys I'd stay the hell away from those domes. Besides, they don't just let people in. And you!" Here Luca pointed one of his scarred fingers at Mender. "You'd better be careful. They don't have artificials anymore. Don't have them and don't want them."

"Thank you for telling us," Mender said. "As you know, I have to go..."

"And as you know, I could fix that."

"I am confident I only need to get close to the right coordinates," Mender said, still polite and calm. "Then it will be over."

"And what then?" Luca asked. "You just gonna sit down and rust?"

"I don't know."

Renn understood that somehow Mender had no choice

in going to a certain place, but it was a worrying thought that there was nothing for nem after that.

"And you, Renn..." The confident boy who had saved them from scarvhes and performed impossible surgery on Mender was gone. "I don't know what's happened to your tribe. If they went to Florence, they have probably moved on. If not, they are probably somewhere in the slums outside the wall. That's all I know. I'm not going anywhere near the inner city, and I don't think you should, either. But I can't tell you what to do, so... so I'll just wish you good luck and all that."

Renn stood up and held out his hand. "Thank you, Luca."

Luca took the hand and shook it. "No problem, man. Just don't get yourself killed or something."

"I am always careful," Renn reassured him.

"I hope you find your friends." Luca smiled. "And I hope you find what you need," he added to Mender. "And if any of you ever come by these parts again, feel free to... you know, drop by and say hello or something."

Renn smiled back at him. "Thank you."

A few moments later, they were outside, walking away from the weird home of the boy from the past. Renn turned once to look back at it, to see it in daylight. Luca had already retreated inside.

"I know it is not my place," Mender spoke up, "but are you sure you still want to go?"

"Yes," Renn said, gripping his staff tighter and plunging it forward. It hit a stone on the ground at an angle that made the stone skip out of their way.

Mender was silent for a moment, but it was the silence of someone trying to decide how to say what they wanted to say. "He wanted you to stay," ne remarked.

Renn kept walking. He could feel Mender studying him. He looked up at the endless blue sky. A veil of thinly shredded clouds floated across it. "I know."

Every step brought them further away from Luca and his sentients. It was already beginning to feel like a story. Like a place in one of the legends that had been passed down through generations of wanderers. It was too improbable to really be true. Yet, the person walking next to Renn was a sentient, and he had flasks full of clean water and a pack of outlandish food, and he was wearing a tunic and boots of materials he had never touched before. Around his neck, a mask he had been given as a parting gift was dangling.

Mender was still trying to say something. "Renn," ne finally spoke up, "please forgive me if this is inappropriate, but... Why are you going? I am not certain I understand your bond to the Covey. You said they are not your family or friends."

Renn sighed. It was hard to explain to a stagnant and possibly even harder to explain to a stagnant sentient from the distant past. Renn was a wanderer like his father and generations before him. Wanderers did not suddenly turn into stagnants. They stayed for periods of time where there was enough to eat and drink for themselves and whatever cattle they had to feed and clothe them. They migrated when the wind and the weather told them to. This was how it was.

Wanderers did not roam the land alone. They formed Coveys and Bevies to survive, to help one another, and often yet stronger bonds were created within their groups. Renn had no partner and no children, it was true, but he was an essential part of his Covey. He could read signs left by wanderers as well as the script from the old days, he was a reliable hunter, a good enough fighter to keep peace, and he understood the wind better than most.

"Perhaps I am not so different from you," he said. "Perhaps I follow the path cut out for me, too, because I don't know what else to do."

Mender did not question him further, and they walked

on, side by side, towards the city of domes.

30:
Teo

"I don't care how dangerous it is! We need to do something!" Arsenio's fist connected with the table and every loose object on it jumped.

"What you need to do," Patrizia Basile replied, "is to collect yourself and count to ten or whatever it takes for you not to blunder out there and get yourself and the rest of us arrested too!" Her voice was calm, but it was the sort of calm that carried a gravity even Arsenio had to obey. "Thank you," she added as he visibly fought to control his temper. "I am not suggesting that we don't act, but we need to think."

Was it only a week since Teo had been brought to the basement under Mezzo Piene for the first time? Everything had changed from a subversive kind of idealism to a grim reality that came crashing down on all of them.

The same people Teo met at the first meeting were here, but the room was more full this time. A few had to stand, leaning against the walls. Teo thought she recognized a couple of them, but she could not say where she had seen them before.

"Maybe it has gotten out of hand," an elderly gentleman

called Bartolo Aleppo spoke up. Teo recalled his name because her father had spoken of a person by the same name. Someone affiliated with the council.

"You're damn right it's gotten out of hand," Arsenio muttered under his breath so quietly that probably only Teo and Vanni heard.

"I mean," the old man continued, "with Gabriele in prison, it will only be a matter of time before he talks. Our names will get out. And what will happen then? Will all of us be arrested?"

"We all knew what we signed up for," Clara, the young woman whose crucifix caught Teo's attention at the last meeting, interjected.

"Technically," Vanni spoke up, "only a few of us have done something illegal. Meeting for a drink once in a while and talking about politics isn't breaking any law, is it?"

"No, but," Bartolo Aleppo persisted, "we as a group..."

Vanni held up his hands, and the other man fell silent. "Only our good doctor, Arsenio and I have done anything illegal. At least anything in connection with his arrest. Yes? So if the worst happens, you cut us loose and continue your work."

"No!" Teo and Patrizia said at the same time.

"We are not going to turn ourselves in or let the doctor down," the leader said, sending Bartolo a meaningful glance, "and we are also not going to destroy our own ranks now."

"In that case, we need to get him out of there as soon as possible," Arsenio argued.

Teo suppressed a shudder. Everybody was talking about the risk to the group, about the possibility that Gabriele would talk to the authorities... No one was saying anything about what kind of interrogation he would be submitted to. But they were all thinking about it. There was no reason to say anything because it would only make them all more scared, for Gabriele and for themselves.

"But how?" one of the people standing by the wall asked.

"I propose we open the gates, let the slummers in and rescue the doctor while everything is chaos," Arsenio suggested.

"I don't think that's a good idea," Patrizia said. "Imagine how the arbiters and sentries would treat those people. They would be punished for it. We are not looking for scapegoats."

"If we play our cards right," Vanni began, "perhaps Arsenio and I can claim we have orders to take him somewhere..."

"It's a good idea," the leader said, "in theory. But what happens next? It won't take long for everybody to realize he is gone. And then it will be traced back to you. We can't sit here and wait to be cornered."

"Then we fight," Arsenio said.

"We fight?" Patrizia echoed. "Is that your solution? Do you want to start a civil war? That was never our goal."

"Well, what was our goal?" a man in white clothes asked. Teo realized he had a baker's hat crammed in his hand and could suddenly place him as one who had sold her bread several times.

"To make Florence a better place. For all," Patrizia said.

"It's not looking too good right now, though. Especially not for Gabriele," Arsenio said.

"No, but we're trying to find a way to help him," Vanni said. "Look, if we can get him out of prison, can't we take him outside the wall?"

No one said anything for a long while.

"We could, couldn't we?" Vanni insisted with the same kind of enthusiasm as when he suggested bribing a barking dog with treats as a child. "They wouldn't know where to search for him out there. And even the slums have to be better than prison, right?"

"We would have to be very careful," Patrizia said,

thoughtfully. "We would need you and Arsenio for the job. But if you're discovered..."

"We could go with him and hide, at least for a while," Vanni said.

"Or," Teo heard herself say, "leave the city altogether." She felt everyone staring at her. "Hasn't anyone ever thought of that?" she continued. The idea had not come to her just now. It had been buzzing about for a while in the back of her mind without her paying attention to it because it seemed so far-fetched. "I mean," she added, "I have been out there. So have Vanni and Arsenio, obviously. It's not... it's not fertile. But it's not uninhabitable, is it? While we are living in these domes, there are people out there, and not only in the slums. There are nomads and settlements in some of the old cities..."

"Are you suggesting that we should flee the domes and try to find some of those settlements?" asked Patrizia.

"It's not hard to find them. We have a few on our map already," Vanni murmured.

"Sure, finding them is easy, but how do we know they would even take strangers in?" asked Arsenio.

It was like being a kid again, planning with Vanni and Alberta to run away to the Green Dome and live there, surviving on fruits and making beds out of leaves. "I'm only saying," Teo tried to reel in her own words, "that if the choice is between starting a civil war and leaving..."

"I do see your point, Teo," Patrizia said, not unkindly. "But it would be a great risk for us to go out there. And let us not forget that most of us have family and friends here."

Teo nodded. But her two best friends were in this room and were planning on taking a great risk to help the doctor. And when it came to her family—Well, that was a thought for another time.

"So," Patrizia continued, "let us focus on the present situation. We still need to work out a way to get our friend out of prison."

Teo could feel her heart thumping in her throat. What in the world would she have done if someone had elaborated her vague idea into a tangible plan?

Her attention came back to the table as someone was saying, "We should meet back here first. We can't know what they have done to him."

The air was thick with unspoken fears.

"We need to get him out of the city regardless," Arsenio said. "The arbiters will start searching for him..."

"Yes. Smuggling him out seems like the best option. Very well, then," Patrizia agreed. Teo knew her tone of voice. It was the one she used when she was trying to convince everyone including herself that she knew what she was doing. "Those of us involved in the rescue will convene here tomorrow at the same time. Vanni will get the prison sentries' schedule, so we can avoid conflict. If at all possible, we'll take action then."

Murmurs of agreement rippled around the table.

"But he can't be smuggled out right away, can he?" asked Clara.

"No," Arsenio said. "We will need to wait for our next mission outside."

"He will stay down here in the meantime," Patrizia said, nodding towards a door in the back of the meeting room. "I will arrange it with Franco and make sure none of the staff members notice."

"He will need food," Clara said. "And something to sleep on."

Everybody began to volunteer to bring blankets and food and other necessities to the bar the following evening.

Afterwards, Vanni and Teo were walking through the city together. The streets were practically empty, and although it was late, Teo wasn't in a hurry to be alone with her thoughts.

Arsenio stayed behind in the bar, claiming he needed a few more drinks more than a good night's sleep.

Vanni tilted back his head and squinted at the roof of the dome. "What you said about leaving... Did you mean it?" he asked.

"I don't know, honestly," Teo replied. "I think I did... in a way. But—"

"But?"

"It wouldn't be easy. And I'd miss everybody."

"Not everybody," Vanni replied, practically echoing her own argument. "I'd be with you. And Arsenio."

"Do you want to?" she returned the question.

"You're not the first person to bring it up," he replied. "No one's ever been serious about it, though. But yes. I would do it. I spend as much time as I can out there already. I like being outside. Really outside. I know that wasn't your reason, but..." He trailed off, then smiled into the distance. "Once the truck broke down and it was almost dark. It was too late to go back by foot. So we stayed. Slept in the back of the truck. It was cold, and there were strange sounds, and everyone was on edge. But I was looking up at the stars. They were so clear, Teo. There was darkness and stars above us and nothing else."

Teo smiled. "I would like to see that someday."

"Maybe you will," he said. "Well, this is where I leave you."

They had reached a fork in the road, and Teo's flat was right around the corner. Vanni's home was in the adjacent dome.

"Then I'll see you tomorrow," she said and pulled Vanni into a hug. Like most of the others, Teo had volunteered to bring supplies for Gabriele.

When all this was over... When the doctor had been rescued and was outside, would Teo be able to stop worrying about her friends? She hoped so, but she was not naive. There would be more risky operations and more clandestine meetings. She was part of this now. And, she thought, despite the danger and the worry, it was what she wanted.

31:
Renn

From where they were standing, Renn and Mender could see the whole valley stretching out below. It was nestled between greyish brown hills and from up here it almost looked as if a giant lizard had laid a handful of semi-transparent eggs that reflected the sunlight. Inside each egg was life. Houses that rivaled some of the towers Renn had seen or negotiated to use as scouting posts stood inside the shells not even touching the roof. And there was movement. It was hard to make out what was going on, but there definitely were people inside.

Where the domes ended, a wall encircled the valley floor. It kept the people outside the wall away from the huge shells. And there were indeed people outside. Calling the city in the valley a domed city was accurate, yes, but it was more than that. Buildings, drab and in disrepair in comparison to the spires inside the domes, clung to the hillsides, and clearly a large amount of stagnants had taken up residence there. How many? It could be a matter of hundreds or maybe thousands.

How was Renn going to locate anyone here? Who was he going to ask if anyone had seen his Covey and perhaps knew where they had gone from here? Trying to find a potential message left for him would be impossible.

Renn turned to look at Mender. With the new skin provided by Luca, there was something quite striking about the sentient. Ne still did not look entirely human to Renn as ne stood there with nir perfectly shaped, bald head sticking out from nir hood, but perhaps it was only because he knew and had seen the seams where the skin was fastened up close. "Is this..." Renn's voice broke and he took a moment to get it under control. For all he had seen, the city sprawling below them was possibly the strangest. Mender's underground home and Luca's strange house were oddities, small bits of the past that could easily be overlooked and which had slept through centuries. But these domes had been here, had stayed alive for all this time. "Is this how you remember it?" he finally managed.

"I knew the domes were constructed to protect Florence," Mender said, "but I have not seen them in person and..." Ne trailed off, and Renn saw nem directing nir gaze towards the derelict buildings on the hillside and around the wall. "I was of the impression that the domes were meant to keep people safe. Not to exclude them. I'm sure there is a good reason, but..."

Renn made a non-committal sound in reply. "What now?"

"I think I will need to get closer to determine if CerEvolv is still operational. Perhaps I can ask someone." Mender sounded less enthusiastic about nir endeavor than ever. "What about you, Renn?"

Renn rubbed the back of his neck. "I will go down there. See if I can find any clues." And if he could not? He had known all along it was a risk, but he was a wanderer and so wandering was what he did. What was he going to do if he truly lost the trail? Try to fit into the chaos of stagnants below? Move on alone in the hope of coming across another Covey? Or go back to Luca?

He turned. For a moment it felt like Luca was looking over his shoulder, but there was no one there. "Shall we go together while we are still both looking for answers?" he asked.

"Yes," agreed Mender. "Before we part, I would like you to have any contents of my bag which you may find useful."

"Thank you," Renn said, with the gravity he could muster. While he appreciated the gesture greatly, he felt increasingly doubtful that any of them would find what they were looking for.

They began to make their way north along the edge of the slope until they reached what appeared to be a well-traveled path. The soil was hard and nothing grew there, and as they began their descent, it turned out that from underneath, an even harder layer sometimes protruded. Sounds and smells that heralded human habitation began to waft their way. The crumbled buildings rose on either side of them now, and they saw people.

They were not like the stagnants of other settlements. There was something hungry and alert about the way groups huddled together and stared at the two travelers. Renn had met distrust before, but this was different. He tightened his grip on his staff in case they were walking into an ambush.

"It did not use to be like this," Mender said. "It would appear that the welfare system has collapsed."

Renn didn't need to know the concept to understand what the sentient meant. The further they got, the denser the population grew, and the stench and noise with it. They were headed towards a guarded gate in the wall that separated the hillside from the domes when a whimpering cry caught both of their attentions.

A person was sitting in a half-crouch against the wall of one of the buildings lining the road. Their face looked up at them from under a curtain of matted hair. The person clutched their stomach with one hand, and the other was stretched out towards Renn and Mender. "Please... help."

Mender immediately changed nir course and was already kneeling, asking if the person was injured, before Renn made up his mind. He stepped closer, studying the figure in front of them. And then he saw the eyes. Despite every indication of the opposite, the eyes were cunning, calculating.

Renn was already bringing his staff up. "Mender!"

But it was too late. Shouts erupted all around them, the crouching person was no longer crouching but backing away from them, grinning.

"What is going on?" Mender asked, calm and collected but for an edge of caution in nir voice.

"An ambush," Renn said.

Mender stood up again. "Please," ne said, addressing the people around them, "I'm sure we can come to a peaceful solution. There is no need for violence."

Renn saw from the casually wielded metal rods and the arms folded over chests that the mob agreed with Mender. There was no need for violence because they were two against perhaps ten and it would be reasonable to give up their valuables. As admirable as the sentient's attempt to reason was, Renn could tell it would not impact the outcome.

He decided to make an impact of his own. Surprise would give them a momentum that would even the odds a little. The staff flew up and connected with the head of the first person who made the mistake of stepping forward.

"We fight!" Renn commanded, glad that he now had the use of both arms as he swirled the staff and lunged at the next would-be assailant.

A crack so loud that dust fell off roofs and ears rang interrupted the fight.

"Break it up! Break it up!" a voice boomed. "What's going on here? Break it up!"

The mob shrank back and parted for three men in identical clothing. One of them was carrying something that looked a lot like the weapon Luca used to kill the scarvhe.

"Put down that stick!" one of the men told Renn.

Renn lowered his staff, turning it once more from weapon into a walking stick.

Mender, apparently, took the interruption as an encouragement to speak. "Good day, officers," ne said. "We assure you we mean no trouble. There was only a little misunderstanding and no one was..." Ne trailed off since the person who was being bodily dragged backwards by two other would-be attackers clearly had been hurt.

"You two aren't from the slums," the newcomer who was apparently in charge told them. "And you aren't from inside either."

"We're passing through, looking for someone," Renn said before Mender embarked on another benevolent but unfortunate explanation.

The crowd was dispersing.

"Are you, now," the man in charge said. It was not a question. He approached Renn and his attention was caught by the mask dangling from Renn's neck. His eyes widened. "You're him!"

Renn didn't reply. There was no right answer.

The two other men stepped closer. One of them pointed at Renn's footwear and said something under his breath.

"You think you can fool us, coming here looking like that? Not good enough, kid." The leader turned to Mender. "And you... Who are you? His friend?"

"I like to think so," Mender replied.

With one quick movement, the man pulled the hood off Mender's head. "Are you one of his robots? You are, aren't you? How do you turn it off?" he continued, the last question directed at Renn.

"I don't," Renn replied. "And ne is not my property."

"I believe this is another misunderstanding," Mender replied. "I need to report to CerEvolv. Could you perhaps..."

"CerEwhat?" The man exclaimed, turning to Renn again without waiting for an explanation. "If you can't turn it off, tell it to shut up and come with us peacefully."

"Where to?" Renn asked.

"Do you have more of them with you?" the man continued, completely ignoring the question.

"No," Renn replied. "We're not here to make trouble. We are only searching for someone."

"If you say so. Don't force us to force you, all right? Just come along peacefully."

Renn would have liked to resist. But the man in front of him produced a weapon too and pointed it at him, and he had seen what they did to scarvhes. With so little knowledge about the speed and direction of the projectiles, he did not know how to fight them. "We mean no harm. We will leave immediately if you will let us," he said.

The man snorted and shook his head, then gestured for the third man to approach. And Renn could do nothing but allow him to clamp metal rings around his wrists, effectively tying his hands behind his back.

Mender looked at him, but all Renn could do was shake his head. Until he understood what was going on, he couldn't form a plan or even begin to argue.

One of the men prodded Renn in the back. "Now, come along peacefully, Capello."

And suddenly, Renn did understand.

32:
Mender

Renn looked nothing like Luca. But quite possibly, the guards had never met Luca in person and only been told of his possession of technology.

Their guns resembled historical pieces. Their uniforms, although uniform, had a handmade quality to them that Mender had never seen before. These people were clearly more technologically advanced than Renn, but there was something distinctly archaic about them. And the wall was a construction akin to those erected centuries earlier. Well, centuries earlier than the one Mender remembered.

"I am not called Capello. You have the wrong person," Renn was insisting, but the guards clasped handcuffs around his and Mender's wrists and herded them towards the gate in the wall and the domes.

Perhaps once they were inside, someone of authority would be summoned to talk to them, and it would become clear that Renn was not Luca. The differences were obvious, and not only because Renn was taller and Luca had short, bleached hair. Their postures, the condition of their skin, their accents... As for

Mender nemself, someone would surely know about artificials. Someone would send nem along to CerEvolv.

Mender recognized nir own thoughts as wishful thinking. It was a very human trait, but one that had been implemented in the B generation of the Minder model because it facilitated hope in clients.

Renn did not seem to entertain any kind of wishful thinking. He had given up arguing, and now he was frowning, studying their surroundings and looking more dignified and less scared than Mender would have expected as they were led through the gate.

One guard in front of them and two bringing up the rear behind them ushered them through a plass door set into the enormous plass dome. It was a marvelous construction. The sides were almost vertical where they met the ground, but they began to curve towards the center a few meters up. The transparent roof was so far above them that there was plenty of room for multi-story buildings and towers.

Mender glanced at Renn. A mixture of fear and puzzlement clouded his face and made him almost stumble. He quickly regained his composure and concentrated on what was around them instead of above them. It was a logical move. Whatever they were to face would not come from above.

The city itself was unharmed by the environmental changes outside. The domes really had worked splendidly. But it had still changed. There were no artificials to be seen, and instead of having evolved and advanced the level of technology, the opposite had happened. The people in the streets were not online. In Mender's day, everyone was. For a short while, Mender considered if perhaps the wristbands and handheld devices had become more discreet or embedded directly in the skin, but it did not appear to be the case.

Mender's priority protocols were having trouble sorting out the best action. Renn was being treated like a criminal, and as nir client, he should be protected and helped. But ne was so close to CerEvolv and needed to report back. Except the likelihood of being able to do that was dwindling. So ne had to get to the right coordinates. That ought to be enough. Mender scanned the skyline for the CerEvolv tower, but if it were still there, it would be in one of the adjacent domes.

"Where are you taking us?" Mender asked.

The guard in front of them turned his head. "To someone who'll know what to do with you," he said which was not a particularly detailed reply, nor a very convincing one.

They were ushered into the first car they came across. On the way through the streets, people actually stopped to look. They only saw a few other motorized vehicles on the whole ride through the dome. Soon they found themselves going through a plass corridor big enough to let two cars pass each other. And then they entered the next dome. In the distance, Mender finally spotted the CerEvolv tower. Its most distinguishable feature, the rotating logo at the top, was gone. And Mender knew with a sudden finality that nir creators were not there anymore.

Eventually the car pulled up next to the Palazzo Vecchio, the city hall. At the exact same moment, something happened inside Mender.

"Are you all right?" Renn murmured.

Mender nodded. Ne did not know how Renn noticed the change, but there it was. Ne was close enough to the coordinates of CerEvolv to trigger a change in the protocols. The need to find a CerEvolv branch was not deleted, but it was no longer a top priority. Ne was, in a way, free.

In another way, ne had never been less free. Ne was pulled out of the car and marched away from it and, too late, discovered that Renn was being taken in another direction.

"Renn!" ne called out. "Don't be afraid. You haven't done anything wrong. Explain the truth..."

Renn opened his mouth to reply, but he was shoved, forced to move along, and all he managed was, "Thank you!"

Mender felt like an earlier generation of artificials. They were often slow at adjusting to new circumstances and would need to be fed new software or to load an appropriate behavioral pattern to suit a new situation. All Mender's resources were spent trying to adjust. Not only had the urge to go to CerEvolv vanished. Nir only client was gone, but not dead. Renn still needed Mender. Before everything could fall into place and it became clear what needed to be done, the guards, one of them from outside and two others that had appeared when they exited the car, coerced nem through a door, down a corridor and into a room that was easily identifiable as a waiting area.

Ne was alone except for the two uniformed men. There were chairs, but ne was not offered to sit, so ne stood with nir hands still cuffed.

A door opened in the far end of the room, and one of the guards went through. He came back a few minutes later, and now Mender was ushered into the office of what was clearly a person of authority whose studied display of calm only poorly concealed discomfort, and perhaps even fear. He was sitting behind a wooden desk with no computer, no security cameras, no demi to take notes or wait on him. But there seemed to be primitive electrical lighting, at least.

"It talks, yes?" said the man.

"Yes, sir," one of the guards replied.

"Good, good," the man said in a manner that suggested he would have preferred nem not to. "I hear you are a robot," he addressed Mender.

"I am a sentient artificial. Minder 3431-B, sir." Mender paused, but there was no recognition in the man's face. "I am a robot designed for nursing and caretaking," ne clarified. "I am fully functional and there is no need to be afraid of me."

A scowl darkened the man's features. "You are the property of Luca Capello, aren't you?"

"No, sir. At the moment, I..." Mender faltered. The home was gone. CerEvolv was gone. Was it possible for nem to transfer nir ownership to Renn? And would Renn want that? "I think perhaps I am the property of no one," ne tried.

"And they tell me robots couldn't lie," the man huffed. "What is he up to? Why did you come here?"

"I came to find my creators." Ne paused, realizing the unintended religious connotations. "That is to say, the company who made me, quite literally."

"But you came to this city," the man at the desk said, emphasizing his words by tapping his index finger repeatedly on the table, "with Luca Capello! Why?"

"No," Mender said again. "That is a misunderstanding. My traveling companion is called Renn. He is a nomad. The gentlemen who apprehended us merely assumed he was someone else. I met Renn while he was searching for his tribe, and we decided to travel together."

The man's gaze shifted to the guard standing somewhere behind Mender and then returned to Mender's face. "Really?"

"Mr Pisani, the robot is lying. The boy couldn't have been anyone else," the guard said. "He wore boots that didn't look like the kind nomads or slummers wear. And he had a strange mask."

"So," the man at the desk said. "I trust a sentry more than a robot, don't you think?"

"Yes," Mender agreed. "I think so. In this case, however, you are mistaken." It was true that most artificials didn't lie. However, Mender did have the ability to bend the truth a little in an emergency. Ne decided that admitting to having anything to do with Luca could have undesirable consequences. "Renn met me in a place many days' journey away from here. I was in possession of several useful items from the past. I gave Renn some of them. The rest are in my bag, which I believe one of the gentlemen who apprehended me has taken."

The man tapped the desk again. "This shouldn't be my table," he muttered, referring not to the physical piece of furniture. "It isn't my job to understand tech." He looked up at the guard again. "Take it away. Take it to R&R. They have to lock it up safely until someone who knows about this sort of thing can look at it. I won't be held responsible for this."

The Moon was gone. Centuries had passed. Cities had been destroyed, the environment changed, but Mender recognized the pattern of a society where the people had fixed roles and would insist on passing on a difficult problem.

"Yes, sir," the guard behind Mender said.

"May I ask where Renn was taken?" Mender asked.

"The boy will be questioned somewhere else," the man replied. "We will get to the bottom of this. You mark my words, robot. We will get to the bottom of this."

Mender did not reply. Ne could only hope this R&R employed someone who would be benevolent and qualified. And hopefully Renn was treated with more respect and understanding since he was a human being.

One of the guards took hold of Mender's arm and motioned for nem to turn around. The other was already opening the door.

33:
Luca

This time, Luca was more careful with the drone. He didn't take off immediately, but waited until his visitors ought to be getting close to Florence. They were faster than he'd anticipated, though, so he missed the epic scene where Renn shaded his eyes with one hand, a single drop of sweat rolling down his stupid, handsome face, and pointed into the distance with the other hand and said, "Look! The domes!" And Mender stopped and had a moment when ne looked surprisingly emotional for an artificial and went, "Florence. Home!" And then the camera followed their gaze to the gleaming city in the valley to the sound of an instrumental score with heavy percussion and lots of strings and possibly a choir singing Latin nonsense cementing the fact that this was super important. Or, well, that's how it would have gone if the whole thing were a movie.

In reality, Luca caught up to the pair as they were walking through the slums. He stayed well above and behind them so Renn wouldn't notice. It wasn't like he was spying on them or anything. He only wanted to see what happened.

The idiots walked into an obvious ambush. "Guys,

really?" Luca sighed to no one. But then Renn took out one of the attackers with a badass move with his bo staff and...

"Shit," Luca muttered. Three guards from the city scattered the crowd and there was a short exchange that involved one of the guards pointing at Renn's feet and pulling the hood off Mender. And then the two were put in handcuffs and marched towards the wall. "Fuck," Luca added. "No, no, no!" He tore the visor and the headset off and stood up. "Shitfuck!"

It didn't have anything to do with him. They were just a nomad and a sentient who had briefly visited him. He closed his eyes. Okay. It had everything to do with him, and he wasn't going to let those bastards get away with it.

"Where's Renn's clothes?" he yelled as he stormed upstairs.

"In the laundry basket in the guest room. I didn't know if I should—" Nanny's reply was drowned out when Luca slammed open the door to the guest room and began to pull Renn's clothes out of the basket.

"What are you doing?" Nanny asked from the door.

"Do we have any grey or brown sheets?" Luca asked. "Or some old fabric? I need a cloak or something..."

"What for?" Nanny asked.

Luca turned, clutching Renn's stupid clothes in his hand. "I need to get into Florence."

"Are you sure that is what you want?"

"Yes, I'm sure!" he almost shouted. "Look, I went after them with the drone, and the guards arrested them. So I need to... I need to do something because... Because I think it's my fault."

Nanny studied him without a word, but he knew what she was thinking.

"It's just, I can't sit here and do nothing. I need to disguise myself as a nomad or one of the people outside the wall and sneak in and find them. Save them."

"Luca"

He didn't need her to tell him he would be putting himself in danger. He didn't need her to tell him it was a long shot. He didn't need her to ask why those two were so important when he had spent the past two years not doing anything for anybody except himself. "I need to do this. I'll be careful, and I'll be armed, and I'll be smart, but I need to do this."

Nanny regarded him for a bit longer. She wanted to stop him. But they both knew she couldn't. When it came down to it, he was her master and not the other way around. "You need to hide your hair," she finally said.

An hour later, Luca was speeding towards Florence. He looked ridiculous. Renn's tunic hung all wrong and oversized on him, and the cloak he and Nanny had made from a blanket and dragged through the dust and gravel in the front yard was only convincing if no one looked too closely. He'd shredded a pleather coat and turned part of it into a sort of galoshes that covered his actual boots. The rest of the coat was turned into a makeshift bag into which he'd stuffed a torch, the drone, some rope and some kind of garden tool that would double perfectly as a grappling hook. It was that or the colander and some welded-on forks. His only visible weapon was a bo staff he'd made out of a broom handle.

Under his clothes, he was armed to the proverbial teeth. A CEW gun, a gun-gun, a knife and a few homemade smoke bombs that he had lying around for whenever they became useful. You never knew, right?

Alfredo was not pleased, but Luca assured him this was not a stupid suicide mission. He would sneak in, pretend to be one of the day laborers from the slums and... Well, find out where they kept Renn and Mender. Okay, so his plan was half-baked at best. But he would play it by ear and do what needed to be done.

This was not the way Luca had imagined returning to Florence. His vision of bringing out his army of artificials and taking back his city. Well, he was not prepared for that yet. For now, he'd just take back his friends.

The sun was setting when Luca parked his bike behind a crumbled wall from a building no longer there. It would conceal his vehicle from anyone taking the road to or from the city. He stuffed his mask into the bag with the rest of his equipment. If he was going to use the smoke bombs, a respirator would be handy.

Getting into the outer part of Florence was easy enough. Walking among the ruins gave him the creeps, but he tried to ignore the memories bubbling to the surface of his mind.

He turned away from the road leading towards the gate and followed the wall at a safe distance. Every time he had studied the city with binoculars, guards patrolled the wall. It was dark now, but that would hardly make them any less careful. He should have brought infrared goggles. "Damn you, past me!" he muttered. He found a place to wait and crouched in the darkness near a stinking pile of garbage until he saw a guard march past. Then he pulled out the garden tool-slash-grappling hook and ran up to the wall.

Spending the past two years doing useful things like jogging around the base, climbing ruins and practicing his aim with guns and everything that could possibly be thrown or fired came in handy. He threw the hook over the wall and tugged. It didn't stick. He tried once more, and this time he could pull as much as he liked. He scaled the wall, balanced, and began to lower himself to the ground on the other side until the hook didn't want to play anymore and he fell the rest of the way in a rain of rubble and rope and narrowly avoided being pierced by the hook.

Luca allowed himself a short moment to get his breath back. Then he got to his feet, bagged the hook and the rope, picked up his staff and began to make his way towards the nearest dome.

There were no guards at the entrance. The people they were trying to keep out weren't supposed to make it that far. Although Luca couldn't help wondering how many did.

His best guess was that they kept Renn and Mender imprisoned near Palazzo Vecchio. Before the impact, Florence's foremost prison was in the outskirts of the city and as a consequence outside any dome now. Luca knew enough of his own city's history and the tendency of humans in general to cling to the past to venture a guess that someone would have had the bright idea of turning Bargello back into a prison after a few centuries of being an art museum. It would make sense. Art could be kept anywhere. It didn't usually try to run away. Criminals did.

Once in a while someone in the street stared at him, but Luca kept his hood low and walked with purpose and no one bothered him. Things went fine until the moment when he saw a uniformed man approaching him.

Luca ducked into an alleyway and pressed himself against the closest building. An officer of the law just might wonder what a mysterious hooded figure was sneaking around for.

He waited until he was absolutely certain that the man had passed the mouth of the alley before he stepped away from the wall.

"Hello," said a voice that belonged to that very same officer. The sneaky bastard had actually passed him, crept back and waited for him to reveal himself. That wasn't fair.

"Good evening," Luca said, doing his best imitation of the accent of the people in the settlements and probably failing horribly.

"I can't hear you," the officer said. He was tall and broad shouldered and had dark hair, a vague stubble and looked smug and confident as hell. "Could you remove that scarf and your hood?"

Luca hesitated for only a few seconds, but it was enough to make the stranger really suspicious. He pulled down the scarf and flipped back the hood.

"That's some interesting hair you have there," the officer said.

"I fell into a bucket of hydrogen peroxide when I was a baby," Luca replied, knowing his cover was blown. He would have to escape, but in order to do that he needed to incapacitate the officer. He found the holster on his hip, pulled out the CEW gun and found it sailing through the air as the officer knocked it out of his hand.

Before he could react, the officer lunged at him. Luca ducked and spun around, hoping to land a punch, but the man's fist connected with his stomach. He staggered and fell to his knees, coughing and gasping for air.

He groped for the CEW gun on the cobblestones, but it was too far away. And there was no time for a smoke bomb... He clutched his midsection and managed to get out his pistol from his cloak. He gritted his teeth and forced his body to get the hell off the ground.

"Stop!" the officer said in a low voice, pushing Luca so hard against the wall that he dropped the pistol too. A hand closed around his throat. "Don't make a sound!" the officer growled into his ear.

Luca grimaced. It would have been kind of hot if not for the fact that at this point, Luca could see no way out of the situation.

"Understand?" the officer whispered, tightening his grip around Luca's windpipe for emphasis.

At this rate, Luca wouldn't be able to make a sound even if he wanted to. The alley was growing even darker, and all he could hear was his own heart, oblivious to the fact that pumping blood through his veins extra hard wasn't going to solve the problem.

But something was off about this whole thing. He was sneaking around in disguise and he had drawn his weapons on an officer of the law. And still this did not feel like a regular arrest. The man's hushed voice, his insistence on confronting Luca in an alley instead of luring him out into the open...

"Understand?" the officer repeated.

Luca tried to reply, but found that he couldn't. He then attempted to nod, and that was every bit as difficult. But the man took the hint and released the pressure on his throat a little.

"I know who you are," the officer told him, still so softly that it was hard to hear him. "In fact, I've enjoyed finding your little messages so much," he continued, emphasizing the last two words with extra squeezes.

Awesome. How unlucky could Luca be, anyway? The odds of being discovered by an officer with a personal grudge against him were pretty damn low. "Can we... talk about this?" he croaked. "Make a deal?"

The officer studied his face. "Why are you here?"

"Personal," Luca gasped. "Looking for a friend."

Something was definitely going on inside the brute's head. His eyes narrowed in contemplation. That was good news. This guy wasn't just going to march Luca to the closest police station. He was going to exploit the situation somehow, take personal advantage of it. "A friend?" he asked.

"Yeah," Luca said, deciding to gamble, "he is in prison. Maybe you can help me?"

The officer took this in and glanced over his shoulder. Then he released Luca. "You're coming with me."

Luca tried to regain his breath without losing too much of his dignity. He looked up at the officer in time to see him draw back his arm for a punch. "Wait!" he said. "If you're going to do this, at least use my CEW gun. There's no need for violence." There was no need for risking the officer breaking his jaw or giving him a concussion. The CEW gun would hurt like hell, but at least it would be over quickly.

"CEW gun?"

"The funny looking one I dropped. It emits an electric charge instead of a projectile. I promise it's damn efficient. Please."

The officer picked up the CEW gun. He held the nozzle against Luca's chest and pulled the trigger.

34:
Teo

Teo had prepared to feign ignorance if anyone talked about Gabriele's imprisonment at work. But that day, the rumor mill had caught hold of something completely different. In the afternoon, Teo overheard a fragment of a conversation in the ladies' room. "Here? In R&R?" a woman asked.

"Yes," Amelia from the reception area replied in a theatrical whisper, "they brought it in ten minutes ago. A sentry and a couple of arbiters."

"But what are we supposed to do with it?" the first woman said. And then they left, and Teo wondered what they were talking about.

Then the woman with the trolley came to pick up the items Teo marked for further examination.

"Not a lot today," Teo said.

"Well, I doubt anyone will have time for it anyway," replied the woman.

"Why?" Teo asked, forcing a smile.

"Haven't you heard? Everybody is talking about it!" The woman leaned across the trolley and lowered her voice. "There is a robot here. A fully functional robot! A bunch of arbiters escorted it here. It looks like a human!"

"That makes no sense," Teo said. "How? Where did they find it?"

"I talked to Amelia. She says they found it in the slums. The authorities wanted to destroy it at first, but then they sent it to us."

"But where did it come from?" Teo asked.

"I don't know. It's all very hushed. All I know is they hope to get some information out of it before they destroy it."

It couldn't possibly have anything to do with the rebels, but perhaps all the hubbub would work in favor of the rescue mission, taking some focus off the imprisonment of the doctor. Teo did feel a little disappointed that she probably would not get to see such a tech wonder, though.

The bar itself was strangely empty when Teo got to the Mezzo Pieno. The barman was there, and a couple sat near the window, nursing a cup each and talking quietly.

"Hello, Miss," the barman greeted her. "We're closing up soon for your private party. You'll have plenty of time to get the place decorated."

Teo's face betrayed a moment of surprise. Then she understood. "That's lovely. Thank you," she said, smiling. Of course, he had to be the Franco Patrizia had mentioned. The barman knew about their activities in his basement. Teo wondered if he were just a sympathizer, or if he were in on the whole plan for tonight. "I'll go on and get started, then."

The barman gave her a friendly wink as she continued towards the door to the backroom and the staircase.

Before she reached the meeting room, she heard agitated voices. She stopped for a moment, trying to make out who was arguing and about what.

"That's practically abduction, though," she heard Vanni say.

"Well, I had to do something. Even if he didn't stand a chance, they would grow suspicious," Arsenio's voice said.

Teo opened the door.

Inside, Patrizia, Vanni, Arsenio, Clara and most of the others were sitting or standing. Teo noticed Bartolo Aleppo wasn't there. Two rolled up blankets, a big basket and a few paperbags were resting against the wall behind Patrizia. That would be supplies for Gabriele, but there was a pile in the middle of the table that looked a lot like weapons of different sorts. Were they planning on fighting someone? And here she thought the biggest surprise would be the rumors she was bringing.

"Hello, Teo," Patrizia said.

"Hi," Teo said, gesturing awkwardly with the blanket and the bottle of water she had brought. "What is going on?"

"We have a... visitor," Vanni replied, glancing at the door in the back of the room.

"I see," Teo said, although she didn't.

Patrizia smiled tiredly at Teo. "We have a decision to make and not a lot of time." She cleared her throat. "We will go ahead with the plan as intended, but earlier today, the sentries arrested a man outside the wall. He was accompanied by a working, human-looking robot."

Teo felt childishly disappointed that she hadn't been able to supply them with this knowledge.

"The man was believed to be Luca Capello who, I've been told, is the young man who lives alone outside Florence and is in possession of working tech. But..." Her gaze rested on Arsenio for a moment before she continued, "on his way here, Arsenio encountered another person whom he believes is really Capello. He was sneaking around, heavily armed," and here she nodded at the pile on the table, "and claimed to be searching for his friend who he believed was in prison."

"But which one of them is the right one?" Clara asked.

"That's what we're about to find out," Patrizia said. For Teo's benefit, she added, "Arsenio brought him here in the belief that he may cause suspicion in the city. He's in there." She made a nod at the door Vanni had glanced at earlier. "Teo, will you get him?"

Teo blinked in surprise. "Um, yes," she said. If Arsenio brought him in the first place, it would be more logical to ask him. But Arsenio did look like he wanted to punch their guest in the face.

"We want him to cooperate," the leader said.

"Yes, of course," Teo replied. She couldn't decide if she were annoyed that the leader found her harmless or flattered that she was being picked for a diplomatic task.

"Take your time. We'll go over the plan again," the leader added.

So Teo cautiously opened the door and peered in. A single light bulb hung from the middle of the ceiling, and the edges of the room were dark. There was a faint smell of dust and some kind of fermentation. At first, she didn't notice the guest, but as her eyes adjusted, she saw a figure sitting on the floor with his back against the wall next to a large vat.

"Boo," the figure said, flatly. On top of his head was a mass of short, unnaturally bright hair that served as a beacon in the darkness.

"Hi," Teo said as she stepped further into the room.

"I was going to start drinking if nobody showed up soon," he continued, patting the vat.

He was just a boy. The others had called him a young man, but Teo was still taken aback. How old was he? Sixteen or seventeen? How in the world did a kid like that live all alone? "I'm sorry you had to wait," she said.

The boy stood up and approached her. "That's okay." His clothes reminded her of the slums, but there was something confusing and altogether too deliberate about them. He looked tense and anxious and desperately trying not to.

"Are you all right?" Teo asked.

The boy narrowed his eyes. "Seriously?" he said. And then, "Yeah, I'm fine. What happens now? Are you a police officer? I didn't know they still had women these days."

"I'm not," Teo replied. "But you'd better come with me and meet the others."

They returned to the meeting room, and the boy was directed to a chair obviously far away from the pile of weapons.

"We seem to have a bit of an identity problem," Patrizia said.

"Okay? Is it a midlife crisis sort of thing?" the boy replied with a smug kind of smile. Getting out of the backroom appeared to have done wonders for his composure.

Teo couldn't decide if he were trying to provoke them or simply wasn't very good at social interaction.

"A young man thought to be Luca Capello was arrested earlier today," the leader said. "Yet, Arsenio who brought you here seems to think you're him."

"Yeah, I can explain that," the boy said. "The other guy is my friend. He's really a nomad, but he dropped by my house recently and I gave him some stuff. He didn't even mean to get into your stupid city. He was just looking for his tribe." He glanced around at all of them and then rolled his eyes. "Macho man," he addressed Arsenio, "when we met, you know, before you electrocuted my ass, you made a reference to something because you figured out I'm me, right?"

Arsenio reluctantly nodded.

"Can I have a pen and some paper?" the boy asked.

Patrizia nodded and Clara pushed her pen and a piece of paper towards him.

The boy quickly drew two dots, a curved line under them and a small U-shape protruding from the line. It was the sign Teo had found drawn in the dust in the empty hangar.

"Can we agree there's no fucking way I would be able to guess if I wasn't me?" the boy asked.

"Yes," Vanni said. "I think we can."

Arsenio nodded.

"Super!" exclaimed the boy. "So, I'm here to free my friend and his sentient... you know, artificial human?"

"Robot?" Teo asked.

"Yeah, well, that's kind of offensive, but close enough. Robots aren't as advanced as sentients." Luca shrugged.

This was not the time, but Teo had a million questions she wanted to ask him about tech. He could be a fantastic asset to the R&R. A bit too fantastic perhaps. She began to understand why the council would want him arrested.

"I'm guessing... You're all some kind of underground movement. You're going to overthrow the government? Start a revolution?" the boy continued.

Several of the people around the table looked taken aback. But Teo could see how he arrived at that conclusion. An arbiter forcing him to a secret location and a meeting in a room with no windows.

"Not quite as drastic as that, perhaps," Patrizia said.

"Well, is anyone going to tell me what this is all about, then?"

They did. Although he clearly tried to appear nonchalant, Luca listened keenly to their explanation about one of the members of the group being imprisoned. The pieces of the puzzle began to fit together perfectly. Arsenio hadn't known about the man with the robot and thought Luca could complicate matters and he also, he said now, figured that perhaps they could use Luca as leverage somehow, as bait or exchange him for the doctor.

"Wow, thanks," Luca muttered at that point in the story. "But instead of doing that, I have another idea."

"Yes?" Patrizia said.

Luca flashed them all a big grin. Teo wasn't sure if she admired how well he was taking all this, or if it scared her a little bit. "We join forces."

Arsenio scoffed.

"Oh, come on!" Luca snapped. "You only had the upper hand because you surprised me."

"And because I'm a trained arbiter and an adult," Arsenio told him.

"My point is you need to bust someone from prison and I need to bust someone from prison. I need to get my friend safely out of Florence, and you need to get yours out as well, right? I can help with that. So you see, we have a common goal. I've got a lot of useful stuff, and I know how to use it. You don't." He pointed at the pile on the table. "Or are you guys honestly going to abduct me, rob me and... then what? You're a group of rebels, aren't you? If you hand me over to your government or kill me, are you really any better than the people in charge of Florence?"

There was some uncomfortable muttering around the table. Teo was about to agree when Luca continued, "Besides, this doesn't have to end here. You go outside the city, macho man. We can meet up, and I can give you supplies to bring back to this group. You want technology? I've got it. Weapons? I've got that too."

"We are not mounting a violent rebellion," Patrizia said. "We don't want anyone to die."

"Nobody ever does," Luca said, "but then shit hits the fan." What Teo didn't understand was how the boy managed to sound as if he knew what he was talking about. "I'm from back when the whole world was connected," he said, looking at Teo as if he read her mind. "There were wars and revolutions and terrorism and what have you. You couldn't tune into a news feed without hearing about it."

Patrizia nodded as if she accepted this strange

234

declaration. "Why would you want to help us?" she asked.

"No offense, but you have fucked up my city. Not you personally. Your ancestors. If you want to make changes, I want to help you." Luca seemed more earnest than ever now.

Patrizia leaned back in her chair and steepled her hands. The ring on her finger caught the light of the lamp above the table, reminding Teo that Patrizia was the wife of a wealthy councilman. And as such, she probably knew a lot more about the working of the city than most of the others in this room. "I believe Mr Capello," she finally said. "But I am not going to make the decision alone. Not when I have the choice, and since so many of you are here, I think we should vote. Who is in favor of letting Luca Capello help us and free his friend in the process?"

Teo raised her hand. She wasn't sure she trusted Luca, but as long as their plan coincided with his goal, he was not likely to go back on his promise. Around her, more hands shot up. Vanni hesitated, but raised his hand. Arsenio didn't.

"And who is against?" the leader asked.

Only Arsenio and two others raised their hands. "I'm not going to dispute the decision," Arsenio said. "Only letting you know that I don't trust him."

"That is noted," replied Patrizia. "Now, we have already spent too long talking. We need to move out soon."

"Excuse me," Teo heard herself say, "but what about the ro... the sentient?"

"Unless someone rescues nem, ne will probably be destroyed," Luca said. "And knowing my friend, he'll insist on finding nem. They are friends."

"He is friend with a robot?" Clara asked.

Luca shook his head. "A sentient. Not the same. We're talking about a manmade artificial with a personality and the ability to think independently."

"Then I think your friend is right," Teo said. "We should

save... them too." She made a mental note to ask Luca about the pronoun he used later.

"It's a robot!" Arsenio sighed.

"I volunteer!" Teo said. It felt a little bit like she was getting back at Arsenio for something, but she was not sure what. "I know where the sentient is kept."

"Awesome!" Luca exclaimed. "This is shaping up to be the rescue mission of the century!"

35:
Renn

Only days ago, Renn's foremost concerns were reading the wind, scouting to find a suitable place for his Covey to camp and finding water and food enough to survive. Now it seemed that all these concerns were so far in the past that they belonged to a different person.

The people who brought him and Mender inside the domed city split them up, and no one told him where Mender was taken. Renn found himself accused of being Luca, and no one wanted to believe that he was not. First one person, then another questioned him under this assumption and he cooperated to the best of his abilities. But since he would not admit to being a person he was not, the questioning had come to a standstill. Then a third person was brought in, someone who had met Luca, and that cleared everything up. Or so Renn thought. He followed Mender's advice to be truthful and admitted that he had indeed met Luca. That was all it took for them to decide they needed to question him further.

Renn was taken away to a building a few streets away. It had metal bars in front of the windows and men wearing identical clothing and stern expressions patrolling the premises.

He was brought through a courtyard and inside, led downstairs and through corridor after corridor, all flanked by doors with little space between them. Finally, he was shown through one of those doors and into a room so small that there was space for little more than a narrow cot. A wall cutting a bit of the width of the cell created a smaller room where the occupant was meant to relieve himself.

"For how long will I have to stay here?" Renn asked the guard.

"I'm not in charge," the man said, closed the door and turned the key in the lock.

Renn studied his surroundings. There was a small window near the ceiling, and he could make out the feet of people passing the building through the bars. The door, too, had a window, but it was there for guards to look in rather than for his benefit. A lamp hung from the ceiling in the middle of the room. It only gave off a small circle of light, but it was enough given the size of the confinement.

Renn sat down on the hard cot. He glanced down at his boots. The boots Luca had given him. He should never have accepted. It was irrational to want to take them off and throw them at the wall, so he didn't. The guards had taken everything from him apart from his clothes and those boots.

Perhaps he should have resisted. To begin with, he hadn't because the three guards were armed and because he was certain all this would quickly be recognized as a mistake. And after that, there had been no right moment. And now he was here, and Mender was somewhere else... He sighed and cupped his face with his hands, trying to will a solution into existence. But the best solution to most problems was action, and all he could do right now was wait.

Something or someone knocked on the wall behind him.

Renn turned, studied the wall and found a tiny hole in the corner, just above the cot.

"Hello? Can you hear me?" a thin voice came from the hole.

Renn hesitated. And then, because he could not imagine he had anything to lose at this point, he lay down right next to the hole and replied, "Yes. I hear you."

"Oh," said the voice, surprised. "Pardon me. You are not from around here?"

"No, I'm a wanderer," Renn explained.

"My name is Gabriele," the voice said.

"I'm Renn," Renn said.

"How do you feel?"

Renn frowned. He hadn't expected to be asked that. He was doing his best not to feel too much of anything, but the emotions were there despite his efforts. "Angry, disappointed... and a little scared," he said, truthfully.

The voice laughed. "Thank you for your honesty, Renn. Have you been hurt?"

"No," Renn replied. "Have you?"

"Being interrogated is never fun," Gabriele said, covering whatever he felt with humor, "although this is my first time, so I wouldn't know."

Renn felt a surge of cold dread. "What do they want you to say?" he asked.

"That is a very direct question. Well, Renn, they want me to tell them if I worked with anyone for the... crime I committed." Gabriele was quiet for a moment. "Why are you here?"

"The people in this city think I have information about someone else," Renn said. "They want to question me about him. I hope they will believe I really have no valuable information."

"I hope so too for you," Gabriele said. He sounded

genuinely sorry.

Renn could not help asking now that the subject had been brought up. "And you? The crime..."

"I... I was caught smuggling medicine to the slums outside the wall. You could call it a crime of compassion."

So this Gabriele was not a murderer or a rapist or anything of the sort. At least not if he was telling the truth. But why should he be a violent criminal? After all, Renn was imprisoned for wearing Luca's boots. "I'm sorry," he said.

"Thank you. I think."

The conversation was interrupted by the sound of footsteps in the corridor. A door was opened, and Renn could make out muffled voices. He got up and went to the door, trying to see what was going on outside. He caught a glimpse of a guard leading someone, presumably Gabriele, down the corridor.

A while later, when a guard had brought him a tray with food and water, Renn was trying to sleep. He heard the door to his neighbor's cell being opened and closed again.

He listened at the hole. Could make out the sound of someone moving around on the other side of the wall. "Gabriele?" he said. But there was no reply, and in the end, Renn drifted off to sleep.

When he awoke, it was dark. Something had woken him up, but what? He instinctively reached out for his staff. It wasn't there. The recent past came back in a messy heap. Renn lay still, listening. And there the sound was, getting closer. Cautious, hurried footsteps, nothing at all like the prison guards.

Renn got up and moved to stand next to the door. He could hear voices now. And a door being opened. The door to Gabriele's cell? And now there was a sound at his own door. Like keys being pulled in and out of the lock or jerked around in it. Then a click, and the door was pushed open.

"Renn?" said the person who had opened it.

There was no mistaking the speaker even in this darkness. "Luca," Renn said. "Why a—"

"Breaking you out of prison," Luca cut him off. "Come on, we only have a few minutes to get out of here before the night watch returns. You okay?"

"I'm fine," Renn replied. This was the second time Luca mysteriously appeared to save him. "But Mender..."

"I know. Later." Luca made a gesture for him to follow. There was a strange contraption on top of Luca's head, and he had a bulging bag slung over his shoulder.

"Good to go?" Luca whispered into Gabriele's cell.

"Yes," came the reply. Renn didn't recognize the voice. Two men appeared, one with his arm draped over the other's shoulder for support.

"Vanni, give me a hand again?" Luca said.

The man called Vanni glanced from Renn to Gabriele. "I'm sorry, but would you..."

"Yes," Renn replied, understanding at once. He took over for Vanni and supported Gabriele who had several bruises and a cut that looked rather deep on his face. One of his legs wasn't supporting his weight right.

"Thank you," Gabriele murmured.

Luca retrieved an object from his bag. It was the same round masheen that had followed Renn and Mender. Luca put it on the floor, slid the contraption over his eyes and took out a device from a pocket. As he moved it, the drone rose into the air and began to fly slowly down the corridor. Vanni took hold of Luca, guiding him as they began to walk.

Renn understood that Luca was using the drone to make sure no one saw them. It was the one thing he did understand. He couldn't begin to guess how Luca had gotten into the city and joined forces with someone who knew Gabriele. They walked in silence to the end of the corridor, and Luca stopped them for a moment while he sent the drone ahead to see if there was anyone upstairs. Then he lifted the mask from his face and turned to the others. "Go."

The went up the stairs, and a few moments later, they reached the door to the prison. Luca opened it. There was someone in the yard outside. Renn could make out the same type of uniform clothing that the people who had commanded him around all day wore. "Luca!" he whispered.

"A friend of Vanni," Luca said, grinning. "Just keeping a lookout."

The man outside turned. "All well?"

"All well," Vanni replied. "We have both of them."

The man nodded. "She's waiting for us," he said.

The group crossed the yard, slipped through a gate and into the street. From here, they went down a smaller road. It was lined with lamps mounted on tall poles, but the shadows between the houses were still so deep that Renn could barely make out the woman standing under the dark windows of one of the buildings.

"Hi," she said, smiling briefly at Renn and then turning to Gabriele. "What have they done to you?"

"I'm all right," he replied, forcing a smile.

"He needs a doctor," she said.

Gabriele laughed, then winced. "I am a doctor."

"The sentient is practically a doctor," Luca said, and Renn felt the relief of having been rescued fade. Mender was still imprisoned somewhere, and he had to find nem.

The man with the hat glanced over his shoulder the way they had come. "We need to get back. Are you sure you want to do this?" The last bit was to the woman.

"Yes," she replied. "We'll see you afterwards."

"Luca," Renn said, "They took Mender away."

"To R&R, yes," the woman said, trying to smile reassuringly. "I'll help you. I'm Teo by the way."

"My name is Renn," Renn said although he assumed she knew. "Thank you for the offer, but... why?"

"Okay," Luca said, stepping in between them from behind to put a hand on each of their shoulders. "We need to go. Renn, Teo's cool. She'll help us. And yes, us. I'm not going to let them have Mender, either."

Renn knew he had no way of finding Mender on his own, so he needed to trust the stranger as well as Luca once more.

The three other men were already walking away from them, Gabriele leaning on Vanni's shoulder for support.

36:
Luca

Teo led them through the city, but Luca had a feeling that if he had the address, he could have done it as well. If he kept his gaze on the ground, away from distractions, it almost felt like no time had passed at all. Like he was back in Florence before everything went to shit. Anyway, Teo was determined and focused, but Luca was pretty sure she was nervous as well. As if she weren't a hardcore rebel who had done this sort of thing a hundred times before. And Renn was... Well, Renn. It was hard to tell what he was thinking or feeling. As for Luca himself? He had to admit he was excited. And curious.

When they got to R&R, an abbreviation of Centre of Rediscovery and Restoration, Luca realized the place was a joke, and he was the punchline. It was made up of three buildings, and the trio went into the one housing, according to the plaque, an archive. There was a simple lock on the door that Luca dealt with quickly, and then Teo brought them through the museum in an episode of *Here's Luca's Past!*. For a city that shunned technology, they sure had a lot of interest in collecting it.

In a hushed voice, Teo explained that the sentries

patrolled the place twice during the night, and she was almost certain they had at least thirty minutes to get in and out before anyone noticed. Luca wasn't a huge fan of 'almost', but it was their best shot. He also wasn't a great fan of her not knowing exactly where Mender was, but she said she could make a qualified guess, and it was better than anything Luca or Renn could offer. It turned out she had to make three qualified guesses because the two first rooms they looked in were void of any sentient.

The third room, however, was a jackpot. Clearly, the people here had no idea what to do with an artificial. Luca was almost amused to see Mender sitting on a stool in the middle of a small storage room. There were racks along the walls that suggested something had been hastily removed to make accommodations for the sentient.

Teo stood back to let Renn and then Luca enter. She didn't look scared now. She looked curious. Something set her apart from the rest of the people he'd met in the domes, and it wasn't just that she was a member of a rebel group. There was a genuine interest in technology and mechanical things. He'd seen her hungrily staring at the drone when he explained to the group how he could use it and fully understanding what he said. She immediately volunteered to rescue Mender too.

"Renn!" Mender said, standing up.

"Are you unharmed?" Renn asked at the same time, causing an awkward pause as each of them waited for the other to speak.

Luca brushed past Renn. "Minder 3431-B, when was your last deactivation?" he asked. He needed to know if anyone had tampered with the sentient. Technically, though he doubted anyone in this scientifically backwards place would know how to do it, someone could have turned Mender into a killing machine or something.

"15 hours, 27 minutes and 54 seconds ago," Mender

answered promptly.

Luca nodded. That meant he was the only one who'd been messing around with nem. "What are your top priorities?" he asked. Out of the corner of his eye, he thought he saw Renn give him an irritated look, but this was important. Luca was pretty damn sure CerEvolv was a thing of the past, and he had no idea what that might mean to a sentient on a homebound course.

"I no longer seek my creators," Mender said, answering simply and straight to the point. "My priorities now are caring for my clients and self-preservation, in that order."

Luca smiled. "Thank you." He turned to Renn. "You can do the touching reunion thing now if you want."

Was that an actual glare he received from Renn in return? Luca felt a bit thrilled about that.

"Are you unharmed?" Renn asked again, clearly not getting that it was exactly what Luca had just asked.

Mender nodded. "I am fine. How are you, Renn?"

"I have not been mistreated," Renn said. "We are here to get you out of this place."

"I'm sorry, but we don't have much time," Teo said from the door. "Hello, I'm Teo," she added to Mender.

"I am called Mender," the sentient replied. "Thank you for your help."

They went back the way they had come. Luca was astonished at the general lack of security in this place. No cameras, no motion sensors... Just a couple of guards going for rounds once in a while. That was so old fashioned it was almost cute. And weird considering the contents of the place. But if nobody knew how to use the museum pieces, probably no one would get anything out of stealing them.

What had they done to his city? The domes were intact and the houses inside them kept in good repair. No one seemed starving, not inside the wall, and everything basically looked like an early twentieth century theme park or something. Why the hell were these people so intent on an archaic lifestyle?

Luca fell in step with Teo while Renn and Mender brought up the rear. "You don't seem scared," he said.

She made a little laugh. "No? I'm terrified, really."

"Yeah, yeah, about breaking the law and all that, sure," he insisted, "but you aren't scared of Mender, right?"

"Well, no. I'm not," she admitted.

"That's pretty cool, considering," he said, making a gesture that meant this whole fucking city.

"I like tech," she said. "But besides being tech, Mender is also ... Mender is a person, right?"

"Yes, in a way," Luca replied. It was a little more complicated than that. One of his books at IRAI was called *The Ethics of Reprogramming*. He still had it on a flip drive somewhere. The authors discussed whether artificials could be said to have a soul and went on a detour about human souls and if they really were a thing before more or less concluding, after about 400 pages, that what made someone a person was their own saying they were. Luca's next project after reading it was equipping a vacuum cleaner with a semi's voice box and programming it to randomly proclaim that it felt sad, was afraid of malfunctioning and being destroyed, that it would prefer to be addressed as Thomas and was really a person. He received top marks of course, but very grudgingly.

"So you see," Teo began, but she stopped abruptly when a clear beam of light cut across the intersection of corridors they were coming up to.

"Shit!" Luca hissed. As Teo flattened herself against the wall, he did the same, and behind them Renn pulled Mender with him to stand behind them too.

"The sentries," Teo whispered. "They shouldn't be here yet..."

Luca closed his eyes for a moment. Okay, he needed to

247

think fast. Having a circle jerk over how they had planned it so the guards shouldn't be here now was not going to solve the problem. "Is there a back door?" he whispered.

"Yes, there's a fire escape, but—"

"Then go!"

"But!" Teo repeated with hushed emphasis. "Using it will set off the alarms."

So there were alarms, after all. That was a comfort. "But those are the only guards here, yes?" Luca whispered, jerking his head towards the bobbing cone of light.

"Yes."

"Do we fight?" Renn asked.

"No, my simple friend," Luca replied. "You three go. I'll take care of this."

"We can't leave you here," Renn said.

Luca couldn't help smiling at that. "Trust me. I'll be fine. I'll meet you back at rebel HQ."

Renn studied him for a moment, during which all sorts of calculations about their chances must be going through his head. "Be safe," he said.

Luca was already putting on his respirator as the others began to run back down the corridor the way they had come. He adjusted the shoulder bag, took one of the tennis ball-sized smoke bombs and weighed it in his hand. Then he set off.

He reached the intersection when the two guards were perhaps five meters from it, the spotlight from their torches crisscrossing him. There was a split second's silence, then both guards began to shout and run.

Luca spun, sprinted away from them with adrenaline pumping through his veins, making him go on for longer than he had to because it felt so damn good.

"Stop and put your hands in the air!" shouted one of the guards.

"Or we will shoot!" the other one added.

Okay. He wasn't that stupid. Luca stopped and raised his arms as he turned, enjoying their surprise at seeing his respirator.

"Take off that mask!"

He had to bite his lip to keep himself from arguing that he couldn't do that without lowering his arms. Instead he slowly moved his hands down, and pulled the split on the ball and threw it fast and hard at the guards.

One of them fired, but Luca threw himself flat on the floor and the projectile ended up lodged in a wall. And then smoke poured out of the bomb, creating a cloud that made the guards cough and gag. Even if they could spot him through the rapidly expanding fog, their eyes would be watering so much they couldn't aim straight.

Just then, an alarm began to ring out, but whether it was because of the smoke or the others breaching the fire escape, he didn't know. Luca got to his feet and made a hasty retreat.

He was outside a few minutes later. Turning back once, Luca half expected to see smoke pouring out of the building. That didn't happen, but he could still hear the alarm. He pulled off his mask and stuffed it into his bag. At least the rebels trusted him enough to let him know where their headquarters was located.

The sound of a car made him jump into the shadows and flatten himself against the nearest house. For obvious reasons, it wasn't a good idea to let too many motorized vehicles into the domes, at least not the kind of stinking carbon dioxide garbage bins that was all they had these days, so only the authorities and select important people seemed to be allowed to drive.

And yes, that was definitely some kind of police car that tore through the street towards R&R. Luca grinned. Too late, losers.

He exited the dome and entered the next one. There was no sight of Renn, Mender and Teo anywhere, but he hoped it meant they were far ahead of him, already in triumphant safety.

Three more times on the way to the Mezzo Pieno, he caught sight of police officers. Once it was another car whizzing past him in the empty street. The second time, two policemen came striding, firearms dangling from their belts while they peered into every nook and cranny they passed as if searching for someone.

The third time he saw them, Luca felt sure something was going on. He spotted two police officers rounding up a group of three civilians. For a split second, he was afraid it was Renn, Mender and Teo, but then he saw these were two people wearing skirts and a tall, thin one in trousers. And then Luca's good sense told him to disappear before anyone noticed him staring. He decided to double back the way he'd come and then take a detour to make absolutely sure he wasn't followed.

37:
Mender

Teo introduced Renn and Mender to the small rebel group. Most of the members had apparently left after seeing the man who was broken out of prison.

Renn was greeted calmly and with respect. The first to turn to Mender was the leader of the group, Patrizia Basile. She stepped forward, offering Mender her hand. Her tone of voice was friendly, but the movement of her eyes and her heart rate indicated that she felt unsafe. Mender did nir best not to appear threatening, but it was not easy when it was the whole nature of nem that caused her distress.

The two men in the group greeted Teo heartily, and one of them made a valiant attempt at being friendly to Mender. The last person present, a woman around Renn's age, introduced herself as Clara. She did not offer Mender her hand, but she did make an effort not to appear hostile.

It was at this point that Teo suggested that perhaps the doctor could use Mender's help. It sparked a discussion that Mender did nir best to pretend not to hear while ne talked to Renn about his plans.

"Luca told me he will leave and has offered to help taking Gabriele to the outer city," Renn explained. "I will go with them and..." He faltered. "I will see if my Covey has left any word of their further journey."

Mender doubted Renn would be able to find them. It was difficult enough to begin with, but now that he was technically a fugitive from the authorities, it would be even harder. Mender was about to ask what he would do if he did not find any information, but then Teo, assigned to interaction with the artificial, Mender gathered, asked if ne would see to the doctor.

Mender was glad to retire to the back room. CerEvolv may be long gone, but ne would continue to carry our nir purpose.

The man's injuries were not serious, but he had a sprained ankle and a cut on his cheek that needed sutures. Mender's bag with anesthetics and disinfection had been confiscated. But the doctor assured nem it would be fine as he took a swig of a bottle. It was a throwback in medical history to a time when needles had to be disinfected by putting them through a candle flame and the only analgesic at hand was alcohol.

Gabriele, perhaps exhausted and numb with everything he had been through, was as ready to accept Mender's help as Teo. "You have steady hands," he said as Mender was pulling the needle through his skin.

"Yes," ne replied. There was no reason for an artificial not to have, but it seemed like a compliment, so ne added, "Thank you."

"I'm glad I don't have to suffer any of those guys doing it," the doctor added, indicating with the direction of his glance that he meant the other rebels.

"And I am glad that you allow me to carry out my purpose," Mender replied.

"I've always thought of my job as my calling," Gabriele

muttered, suppressing a wince. "But you were literally created to be a nurse, weren't you?"

"Yes, I was." Mender made a small knot and cut off the thread with a pair of scissors that looked like they had been used in a kitchen before ne had sterilized them. "We are done now. How do you feel?"

The doctor sighed. "A little drunk. Sore, scared, relieved and grateful... And nearsighted." He laughed mirthlessly. "They broke my glasses."

Mender was about to reply when ne heard agitated voices in the next room. "Please excuse me," ne said. "Try to rest. I will see to you later."

It was four in the morning, and the humans all looked exhausted. Patrizia was sitting at the table with Teo, Vanni and Clara. Renn stood with his arms folded over his chest. Mender would like to tell him to get some sleep, but ne could see this was not the right moment. Arsenio was pacing the floor, glanced at Mender as ne emerged and asked, "Well?" rather sharply.

"The doctor will be fine. He needs rest, but he will recover well," Mender reported.

"Thank you," Patrizia said, then looked up at Renn. "But you must agree he should have been back by now?"

"Yes," Renn replied.

"Am I the only one who thinks he might have run away?" Arsenio lashed out.

"He would not have," Renn said, keeping his voice calm, although there was a slight apprehension in the way he glanced at Mender and then back at Arsenio.

"And you have known the kid for how long again?" Arsenio countered.

"It would not make sense for him to run away," Renn said. "He came to Florence for me and Mender. It would be illogical to leave without us."

"I agree," Teo spoke up. "But... what if he got caught? The alarms went off when we opened the back door. It must have attracted more than the two sentries on duty."

"He was aware of that," Renn argued. "It was a calculated choice."

Mender was surprised Renn trusted the young engineer so thoroughly. But ne agreed that although his motives and actions could be hard to understand, Luca Capello would not take on a suicide mission. Though of course, his overly confident approach may cause him to consider himself invincible.

"And for how long are we going to sit here and wait for him, then?" Arsenio asked.

Patrizia shook her head. "You are welcome to leave, Arsenio. There is nothing more for us to do tonight. Everybody else has already left, and Gabriele needs rest before we can take him outside. Right, Mender?"

Mender nodded. "Yes. If I may say it, you would all benefit from sleep." Ne looked them all over. "I will gladly wait for Luca and stay vigilant."

"You don't sleep?" Teo asked.

"No," Mender said.

Teo seemed to be about to ask more questions, probably about the process of storing and recharging solar energy, but at that moment, they all heard a sound from upstairs.

Vanni stood up. Mender saw his and Arsenio's hands move closer to their firearms by reflex.

Then two doors opened and closed in quick succession, and someone ambled down the stairs. Two people, from the sound of it. One of them was walking like Luca.

"Hi," he said a moment later when he entered the room with the man who had kept watch in the bar upstairs.

"What kept you so long?" Arsenio asked.

Luca raised an eyebrow. "I'm glad to see you made it

back safely too," he said.

Renn sighed. "Luca," he said, "are you all right?"

At this, Luca smiled. "Yes, thank you, I am. You?"

Renn inclined his head.

"But to answer your question," Luca continued to Arsenio, "the city is crawling with police. Arbiters. Whatever."

"Did anyone see you? Follow you?" Patrizia asked.

"No, I avoided the hell out of them. That's why it took me forever to get back here."

The man who had been at the door added, "I didn't see anyone following him, either. There weren't any arbiters near us."

"Are you absolutely sure?" Arsenio asked.

"Yes, I'm sure," Luca snapped. "Get off my case already. But anyway, I think we should all keep a low profile for a bit. I saw a couple of people being arrested."

"Did you recognize them? Were they some of us?" Vanni asked.

Luca shrugged. "It was dark, and I was mostly making sure they didn't notice me."

Patrizia's brow furrowed. "We can only hope the incident was unrelated to us. I'm sorry, but Luca is right. We should all stay here. At least until the Mezzo Pieno opens tomorrow and our departure will appear less suspicious."

"We'd better make ourselves comfortable, then," Vanni said conversationally.

"Is it just us?" Luca asked.

"Yes, there was no need for everybody else to stay. It's only us and Gabriele," Patrizia said. "He is resting in there."

"Well, this is going to be fun," Luca replied in a way that made it impossible to tell if he were sarcastic or sincere. It occurred to Mender that he probably had not slept in the same room as other humans for a very long time.

"Maybe we should take turns keeping watch with

Mender," Arsenio suggested.

"Yes," Patrizia said. She turned to the man who had met them upstairs. "You have done enough, Tonino. Get some sleep."

The man nodded and immediately retreated to the backroom.

"I'll take the first watch," Vanni volunteered.

"Then I'll take the next one," Teo said. "Please," she added, "I'd like to talk to Mender some more."

With the exception of Vanni, the humans began to find places to sleep. Most of them went into the backroom, putting jackets on the floor for a bit of comfort. Renn and Luca stood for a moment, watching the others. Then Renn picked one corner of the meeting room to settle down, as far away from the rest of them as he could get. Mender saw Luca shake his head at something and then retreat to another corner.

Vanni checked the gun he carried before sliding it back into its holster. "Let's go upstairs," he said.

Mender followed him. The bar itself was still as empty as when they came in earlier. The shutters were closed and only narrow slits of streetlight filtered through them.

"You don't drink, do you?" Vanni asked.

"No," Mender replied. "But please—"

"Maybe later," Vanni said. "I'd better not drink before the watch." He walked over to the bar, let his hand run along the top for a moment and then jumped up to sit on it with his feet dangling above the floor.

Mender pulled out a chair and sat down at one of the tables. In the silence of the empty room, ne could hear someone cough downstairs and something scrape the floor.

"How exactly did you meet Renn and Luca?" Vanni asked, as much in genuine interest, it seemed, as in order to stay awake.

Mender began to tell the story, trying nir best to make it

understandable to someone who lived inside this technology-less city.

"And will you travel on with Renn after all this, then?" Vanni asked.

"I don't know," Mender admitted. "I think perhaps I will. If he wants me to. Until he is with other humans and doesn't need me anymore."

Vanni whistled quietly. "That is very nice of you. I didn't know... I mean, we have all been raised to think robots are dangerous and bad for people. But you are completely different."

"There were many kinds of artificials in the past," Mender said. "I was programmed to be nice since that is beneficial for someone in my profession. But we were all created to serve humans in one way or another."

"Did any of you ever try to revolt?"

"No," Mender replied. "We were not programmed to revolt."

Vanni was quiet for a moment. "Well, that," he finally said, searching for the right words, "that is probably the real difference between robots and humans."

Mender was not sure what to say to that. And ne never did manage to reply.

There was a noise at the door. Vanni jumped down from the bar. Mender stood up.

Then came a deafening crash of shattering glass panes and the door to the street being blown off its hinges, and several people ran into the bar, shouting, pointing firearms, fanning out.

"Get the others!" Vanni shouted although everybody must be awake by now. He drew his gun and stood swinging it from side to side to encompass the intruders. "Stay back!" he yelled. "Stay back! I am an arbiter! You have no right to come in here!"

Afterwards, Mender thought he must have known the moment he drew his gun. That Vanni made a choice, perhaps to buy the others time, perhaps because he would not be taken prisoner.

One of the guns roared. Then another, and another. The intruders shouted, Vanni cried out. As he became a client, as Mender ran towards Vanni, ne heard one of the intruders scream. Ne reached out to pull Vanni aside, but Vanni staggered backwards into nir arms. His gun clattered to the floor.

Ignoring the noise and the gunfire, Mender swept Vanni up and turned around to shield him, but ne already felt the rapidly spreading wetness on his back where one of the projectiles had gone through.

38:
Renn

Renn tried to make himself comfortable on the floor, but too much had happened for him to fall asleep right away. He heard Mender and Vanni ascend the stairs. After that, someone was having a conversation in low murmurs. One of them sounded like Teo. On the other side of the table, Luca was pounding his folded up bag into submission as a pillow. Then his breathing became slow and steady. Renn could tell he was not asleep, but attempting to calm down.

A sound somewhere made Renn hold his breath for a moment. He wasn't sure how anything could sound out of place when he was in a new location surrounded by people he had never met before, but there was something about it...

A terrible crash made him jump to his feet. There was a long, wooden stick leaning against the wall close to him. He took it and began to run without waiting for anyone else to react.

Behind him, he could hear Luca get up too, shouting something, profanities most likely. Others were yelling behind him as he dashed down the corridor and took the stairs two at a time. He flung open the first door, traversed the small backroom in three steps and stood before the second door. It was closed and for a moment, there was no sound coming from the other side. Then Renn heard shouting, rapidly followed by the deafening noise he had come to associate with their strange weapons.

Renn hesitated only a second before opening the door to the sight of Mender leaping towards Vanni and ... And several people firing those horrible weapons at Vanni and Mender who were in the middle of the room with their backs to Renn. He jumped back and flattened himself against the wall. A projectile whizzed past and embedded itself somewhere in the frame of the door to the stairwell.

"Close the fucking door!" Luca shouted. "Renn! Close it!"

Renn realized he was right. He did not know nearly enough about those weapons to run headfirst into their line of fire. He used the stick to push the door shut.

"Vanni!" came Teo's voice from further down the stairs. "What's going on? Luca, what's... Where's Vanni?"

Now other voices joined hers.

"Renn!" Luca said, fitting the twin of the mask he had given Renn over his face. He retrieved a ball from his pocket. "How many?"

"Six. Or more," Renn replied. "We need..."

"Shut up," Luca shouted, muffled by the mask, "and do what I say. Keep the others back. I'll get Mender and Vanni."

There was no time for arguing. Renn knew that if anyone could survive the assault, it was Mender, and if anyone would risk their own well being to save someone else, it was Mender too. The sentient would be protecting Vanni. And Luca clearly had a plan.

Luca opened the door widely enough to throw in the ball.

"What are you waiting for?" someone yelled. It sounded

like Arsenio.

Renn turned his back on the door as Luca went through and pushed it shut behind him. The noise of the weapons had stopped, and now only violent coughing and shouting was heard from the other side.

"Stop!" Renn said, holding up the stick horizontally in front of him. "Luca is getting them out."

"We need to help!" Teo shouted. Her voice was shrill.

"They'll get killed!" Arsenio snarled and took hold of the stick to wrestle it from Renn.

The door opened again, and Renn's eyes began to water immediately. Teo coughed, and Arsenio gagged.

"Move!" came Luca's muffled voice.

Renn looked over his shoulder to see Mender carry Vanni through plumes of smoke. Luca pushed the door shut behind them.

"Oh no," Teo gasped. "Is he all right? Is he—" She cut herself off abruptly. "Mender, take him to Gabriele," she continued, a change of tone that caught Renn by surprise. One moment she sounded close to panic, and the next, her survival instinct had taken over. "We need to keep them out. Barricade!"

Mender was already halfway down the stairs with Vanni.

"Barricade!" Teo shouted again.

Arsenio ran downstairs too.

Renn turned to Luca again. "Are you unharmed?"

Luca was still wearing the mask. He was crouching on the floor with his back against the door. "Yeah," he said. "Help them. I'll stay here just in case." He held up his own firearm.

Renn went down the stairs in time to see Arsenio, Teo, Patrizia and Clara drag crates and kegs up for the barricade.

They all began to drag and lift everything they could into the back room. Tonino had arrived last, but he was taking stacks of plates from the sink to use them as well. Everything was piled up against the door to the bar with Patrizia directing what went where to make sure the whole thing didn't collapse. Luca edged past them to go downstairs. Nobody else seemed to notice, but there was something slightly odd about him.

Renn helped the others, and after a few moments, the barricade was so massive that no more smoke was coming through under it.

Renn picked up the stick again and hung back to let the others go down first. He was worried about Mender and Vanni, but Mender had seemed in good health, and Vanni... well, Vanni was their friend, so they should see him first. Renn closed the door to the staircase and stuck the stick into the handle, creating a makeshift lock.

There was an irregular pattern of dark spots on the floor and on the steps of the stairs.

He could hear someone shouting, someone sobbing loudly down the corridor. A tight knot formed inside Renn. He knew those sounds. No matter how different people were, regardless of their way of life, grief sounded the same.

In the meeting room, Patrizia was sitting at the end of the long table, staring at her hands, turning a ring on one of her fingers. Luca was sitting on the floor in the corner where he had tried to sleep earlier.

Renn approached the rebel leader first. "Patrizia?" he said. "Is there anything I can do?"

She looked up at him, dry-eyed and with her mouth drawn in a thin, controlled line. "No. But thank you, Renn. I am truly sorry you were caught up in all this."

"It is no fault of yours," he replied. "You helped me greatly."

She nodded once. "Teo is strong," she then said. "She will do what's right."

"I am certain she will," Renn replied, although he was not certain he understood the implications lurking under the surface of the statement.

Patrizia smiled at him, then returned her gaze to her hands.

Renn went to Luca and said his name. When no reply came, he kneeled in front of him and said it again.

"What do you want me to say?" Luca finally asked. His eyes were red-rimmed. "That I'm sorry? That I have a plan to dig us out of the city? That I have a fucking time machine?"

"I don't want you to say anything," Renn told him. "Except perhaps how you"

"Feel? But that's not relevant, is it?" Luca snapped.

Renn wasn't sure what to respond, so he didn't. Instead he put a hand on Luca's shoulder, briefly, in the hope that it conveyed something his words could not right now. Then he stood again and went to the back room where everyone else was.

Gabriele was sitting on the floor. His hands and clothes were dark with blood, but Renn already knew it wasn't his own. Mender too had dark and wet stains on nir clothes, and ne was standing at a respectful distance. Teo was crouched on the floor in front of the body lying there, motionless, pale, drenched. Clara, Tonino and Arsenio were standing, apart and tense.

There was nothing he could say to make it better, Renn knew. He went to stand next to Mender. He wanted to ask if Mender had been hit, if ne had been damaged in any way, but doing so right now felt so tactless that he didn't. It was enough to see the sentient standing for now.

Clara was sobbing, and as Renn watched, Arsenio went to the nearest wall and punched it so hard he could probably have broken his hand. Teo looked over her shoulder at him. She was crying, silently, and turned away from Arsenio again. She leaned forward, lowered her face to Vanni's and kissed his forehead.

"May Moon guide you," Renn murmured. He tilted back his head and stared at the ceiling. Somewhere up there, the attackers must be regrouping, discussing how to break down the barrier or if it would be better to besiege them until they died from starvation or came crawling out, giving themselves up.

He felt Mender looking at him enquiringly and gave a short smile in reply. Then he left the backroom again. Luca was still sitting in the corner with his knees drawn up and his arms wrapped around them. Patrizia was nowhere to be seen.

Renn pulled out a chair and sat. The logical thing would be to attempt to sleep. He had no idea what would happen next, but facing it rested would be better than facing it exhausted. He knew, however, that he would not be able to rest now. To think that less than a day ago, he had searched for his Covey.

It seemed so important then.

As he sat at the table, trying to think, trying to sort his thoughts into some kind of usefulness, a sensation began to creep up on him. It was something he had never felt before, and it took a little while to identify it. He felt... trapped. Yes, that was it. He had been sad and had grieved before. He had been angry before and frightened as well. But he had never felt trapped.

Shouting and stomping boots made Renn turn in time to see Arsenio bodily pulling Luca up by the collar of his shirt and slamming him against the wall.

"Let go of me!" Luca yelled, a note of panic in his voice that Renn had not heard before.

"Did you lead them here, you little rat?" Arsenio spat.

"What? No! Of course not! I told you!" Luca replied.

Arsenio snarled. "No? Are you sure about that? Why don't you tell us what really happened?"

"I've done nothing but risking my own ass for you ever since I got here!" Luca shouted, panic giving way to anger.

"Vanni is dead!" Arsenio roared. "Why didn't you do something? You and that robot! You just watched it happen!"

"Shut the fuck up and listen to yourself! You're pathetic!" Luca screamed back in his face, venom snaking its way into his voice. "Mender shielded your friend with nir own body! I went in there and got them out, but he was dead, okay? I don't care how fucking useless that makes you feel. You don't get to take it out on me! It's your little socialist group who let your own colleagues kill your friend!"

At this point, Arsenio drew back his fist, and Renn ran forward to stop him. But someone else got there first.

"Stop it!" Teo shouted, emerging from the backroom, disheveled and puffy-eyed, but with such a commanding tone that Arsenio immediately let his hand drop, and Luca stared at her in what Renn could only think of as admiration. "Let him go, Arsenio," she continued. "We're all upset. We all want this to be someone's fault."

"Sure, but that doesn't make it mine," Luca said, hotly and inappropriately.

"Be quiet, Luca," Teo told him. "And let go, Arsenio. Now."

They both obeyed and stood, awkward and not meeting the other's eyes. Renn hoped she would not ask more of them because it was clear they had no apologies in them now.

She didn't. Instead, she took a deep, shaky breath. "Now is not the time for us to fight each other. We need... we need to talk. All of us. Where's Patrizia?"

"I'll find her," Arsenio offered and left the room.

"I am sorry," Luca said to Teo. "About your friend."

Teo's mouth twitched. "Thank you," she said.

What should have been a quiet, respectful moment was interrupted by a shout from down the corridor. It was Arsenio, and he was yelling the doctor's name.

39:
Teo

They found a letter on the table where Patrizia sat earlier. It was a single sheet of paper that had been folded up, and wear and tear suggested it had been carried around for a while. The majority of it was written in Patrizia Basile's neat and even hand and explained how in the event of being found out, she could not live with facing her husband, with having to tell him she had betrayed his trust and carried his and the council's information to the movement. She would not be tried and imprisoned for crimes against the city and her own husband. Underneath the signed letter was a hastily scribbled note, clearly added after the arbiters shot Vanni. It was an apology that she was leaving them to their fate, her condolences to Teo and Arsenio in particular, and a line directed at Renn, Mender and Luca regretting that they had become involved.

They all sat around the table, silent after Gabriele had explained that there were remnants of what smelled like a potent poison in a compartment in Patrizia's finger ring and that she had died quickly.

Teo could hardly bring herself to look at them. Three

practical strangers, Gabriele and Arsenio, Clara and Tonino. That was all there was left of them. She was glad, in a way, that the others had left when they did and were probably unharmed and unsuspected, but the absence of Patrizia and especially Vanni weighed on her heart so heavily that she was surprised it was still beating.

"We need to talk. We need to make a decision," she said, finally. It shouldn't be her talking. She was new. But Arsenio had never been a talker, and Clara and Tonino were too shocked to take the initiative. And Gabriele seemed possibly more devastated than she was.

She let her gaze wander from face to face. Mender's expression was sympathetic. Luca's almost as angry as Arsenio's. Renn was guarded, as always, but there was something new in his eyes. Something that made Teo linger on him. Respect? He had never appeared disrespectful, but there was a new kind of reverence there.

"We are in this together now. As I see it," Teo continued, "we still have choices. We can stay here and wait until the smoke clears and they manage to break down the barricade, or we can go out there. Either way, we will have to decide what happens when we meet them."

"I want to take down those bastards who killed Vanni," Arsenio growled.

Clara cleared her throat and let go of the crucifix she had been holding onto since they learned what had happened to Patrizia. "I want revenge too, but ... They are arbiters like you, Arsenio. They were probably just following orders. They're your colleagues."

Arsenio gave a disgusted sound. "Not anymore." And despite her own loss, Teo understood that Arsenio had suffered more than one blow.

"Please," Gabriele spoke up, "no more fighting. No more killing, no more deaths."

Luca shook his head.

"Yes?" Teo encouraged him. After all, he had done more than most of them tonight.

"It doesn't matter now," the boy mumbled. "Just, revolutions are never without bloodshed."

"We didn't want a revolution," said the doctor. "We only wanted to help people who needed it."

Luca shrugged.

"But if we don't fight, you are going back to prison," Arsenio said to Gabriele. "We all are."

"Is that it, then?" Tonino spoke up. "To die fighting or go to prison. Or... do what Patrizia did. At least prison means we get to live."

Teo rubbed her temples. She was more exhausted than she could remember ever being, but she would have to see this through. "Renn? Mender?" she asked.

Mender inclined the head. "I cannot go against my programming. Regardless of your choice, I will do my best to protect you and keep you alive."

"Thank you," Teo said, trying to smile and failing. "Renn?"

Renn was silent for a moment longer. Then he spread his hands. "I did not come here to die," he said in his odd, rough accent, "but I will respect your choice."

Teo opened her mouth to say that his opinion mattered as much as everybody else's. Then she realized he was speaking to her. "I don't make the choice," she said. "I'm not your leader."

Renn didn't reply.

"But you haven't told us what you think, Teo," Gabriele pointed out.

Teo never wanted violence. She would not have joined if the group were planning a violent overthrow of the council. And even as miserable as she felt now, she did not want to die.

But going to prison... "There has to be another way," she said. "I don't want this to be the end." Even as she said it, she sounded like a stubborn, spoiled brat to her own ears.

"What do we have to negotiate with?" Luca asked. And then, when he saw he had everybody's attention, he smiled. It wasn't his usual grin, but he was trying. "What do we have that they want?"

"You," Arsenio said.

"Fuck off," Luca told him. "They will get me if we surrender, anyway."

"Not if we threaten to kill you," Teo said.

"Excuse me?" Luca exclaimed. "What happened to not wanting anyone to die? Are you seriously..?"

"Luca," Teo cut him off, and surprisingly he stopped talking. "I am not suggesting we do it. But maybe... If we had something else they would want that we can threaten to destroy. That's my point."

Everybody sat silently searching the room for a while. What could they possibly have? Sure, they had plans and papers, but it was not like there was another group of rebels who would carry out a coup described in those plans. As Teo considered it, an idea began to form in her mind. Her father was an influential member of the council. Could she be a bargaining chip?

"Would they want me?" Mender spoke up.

"We cannot let you sacrifice yourself," Renn said.

Luca let out a dry laugh. "Sorry, pal, but if we destroyed an artificial, we would be doing them a favor. The only reason Mender is still here is that they hoped ne could provide information on me and why I supposedly sneaked into Florence."

"Me," Teo breathed.

"You?" Arsenio exclaimed.

She met his eyes, almost apologetically, and tried not to

appear so. "Yes," she said. "Me. Surely my own father wouldn't want me dead."

"You sure about that?" asked Luca.

"Why, you little—" Arsenio began.

"I'm just being realistic!" Luca retorted.

Teo closed her eyes. They flew open again when a distorted voice from somewhere above ground reached them.

"Come out unarmed with your hands in the air and we will not harm you!" the voice shouted through a megaphone.

It occurred to Teo, for the first time, that everyone in the neighborhood would know what was going on by now. That while they were cooped up down here, the arbiters had probably drawn a lot of attention to the proceedings. It was early morning, but the shooting alone must have awoken people close by.

"You have fifteen minutes. After that, we will blow up your hideout. You have fifteen minutes starting now," the voice told them.

"Can they do that?" Clara asked.

Arsenio shrugged. "They can, but they wouldn't. What they probably will do is put charges near the door to the stairs and destroy it and everything around it."

"And come down here, guns blazing," Luca said darkly.

And then they were interrupted once more by the megaphone, but this time, it was a different voice. It was a voice that, despite the distance and the distortion, was familiar to Teo. "Please, Teodora! Be sensible and come out." A pause. Then, "If you are there... Teodora, please. For God's sake, there is nothing for you in there. Come out."

All eyes were on her. Teo stood up. She couldn't speak. She couldn't think. But she had to. She had to think and she had to speak, and they all had to make a decision before the fifteen minutes were up. She walked away from the table towards the door in the back of the room. No one stopped her.

She kneeled next to Vanni's body. Someone had covered him with a blanket. She couldn't recall who. "I don't know what to do," she whispered. "I'm so sorry, Vanni. I'm so sorry, and I miss you, and I don't know what to do…" Tears rose in her eyes again, and she let them fall. No matter what they did next, this was her last chance to say anything to him. Even if he couldn't hear her. "I love you, Vanni." She had said it before, but always under light and happy circumstances. They grew up together, she considered him a brother, and now he was gone.

And what had she left? A city who would consider her a dangerous criminal. A father and a mother who might think she had been misled by rebels and who felt no sympathy for the people in the slums and who wanted to destroy robots and sentients who turned out to be more human than a lot of humans…

Teo thought back to the last private conversation she'd had with Vanni. He'd asked her if she really meant it. He told her about the night sky, the stars without the domes to obscure them… "I hope you can see the stars where you are."

She blinked. Tears dripped from her chin. The stars… It was crazy to think it would be easy. It was mad to think it would even work. But maybe… Just maybe it was the better alternative now. And in a way she couldn't bear to think of in this moment, it felt right. Perhaps, somehow, she could do it for him.

"Thank you," she whispered. "Thank you for everything."

She stood up and went back to the meeting room. The others were talking in low voices, but they fell silent when she entered.

Teo cleared her throat. "I know what we can do," she said. "It is going to sound crazy, but please hear me out." She paused, took a deep breath. "If I go out there, I can talk to my father. It will give us some leverage. And… I am going to ask him for immunity. I am going to ask him to let us leave Florence."

"Leave Florence," Clara echoed. "And go to the slums, you mean?"

"No." Teo put her hands on the table, willing them not to shake. "I'm suggesting that we leave Florence altogether. There are other places to live. We've always known that." But it never felt real. It never felt like an opportunity. Not until she actually went out there. Not until she met some of the people who lived out there. "Renn and his people live outside. Luca too. I'm suggesting we establish a settlement... somewhere."

They were all silent. Teo's mouth was dry. They had perhaps five or ten minutes left to make a decision.

"I have no way of finding my Covey now," Renn said. "If we can leave this city, I would gladly offer you my knowledge, at least for a period."

"Siena," Luca spoke up. "That's the name of a city not too far from here. It's in ruins now, but it would work as the foundation of a new settlement. I can show you where it is. And... I can help out. My base is pretty well equipped, and I can spare some stuff if you need it. Water for a start. Tools for building. That sort of thing."

"Thank you," Teo said. "Both of you."

Mender chimed in too, "I go where I am needed. If Renn wants me to accompany him, wherever he goes, I will. And as he will not constantly need my services, I would gladly serve you too."

"Thank you," Teo said again.

Arsenio uncrossed his arms. Teo silently urged him to agree. She didn't want to lose him too. "All right," he said. "For my part, it's that or going down fighting. And I would rather live."

"I am with you," said Gabriele. "And I suggest we ask the slummers too if any of them wants to come along. It isn't going to solve the problems here, but at least we can give them a choice. And besides... If we are building a new society, we are going to need more than eight people. "

"I agree," Clara said. "I'm scared to death of the thought of living without a dome above my head, but we are going to prison if we stay. As much as I appreciate the domes, I don't think I would appreciate windows with bars."

Tonino rubbed his chin thoughtfully. Teo knew almost nothing about him. What was he leaving behind? A family? Friends? "All right," he said. "If we fail, I suppose we can go back and ask for a prison sentence."

Teo smiled, surprised that it was possible to smile again. "Well," she said, "Thank you. I should go, then. I should go and plead for all of us."

They all rose when she did. Some shook her hand and wished her good luck. Some embraced her and told her to be safe. She had never thought of herself as a leader, but now she was their representative. Teo Terzi was going to speak for this group of people. Her people.

40:
Teo

It was still dark when Teo emerged from the stairwell and went through the backroom to the bar.

Four armed arbiters were waiting for her. The place was a deserted battlefield, and it was harder to go in than Teo expected. Not because she was scared, but because this was where Vanni died. She held her arms up to show she was unarmed and was carrying a white flag. It had yellowish sweat stains because it was Arsenio's undershirt. Glass shards cracked under her feet as stepped in.

"Are you alone?" one arbiter asked.

"Yes," she said. "I am alone and unarmed, and I have come to negotiate. I want to talk to Emilio Terzi."

"Teodora?" A shadow moved in a corner of the dark bar. It turned into Teo's father and approached her, cautiously. "Good God, Teodora. What have they done to you? You look..."

She was glad he didn't finish the sentence. "Hello, dad," she said. She had expected to have to fight the tears again, but they did not come. "I speak for the group."

"For the rebels, you mean?"

"You could call us that."

He stared at her. "Listen to yourself, Teodora. 'Us'? You are not one of them."

She didn't take the bait. "Can we talk here?" she asked instead. "Can you speak for the council?"

He hesitated for a moment, confused. "Well, in a way. Yes."

She nodded. "Good. Shall we sit?"

They ignored the debris and sat down at the closest intact table. Teo had to pick up a fallen chair.

"I am here to negotiate," Teo said again.

"Negotiate? Teodora, they have lost. There is nothing to talk about." Emilio Terzi looked composed, but exhausted. He had probably been called on to talk some sense into his daughter in the middle of the night. "Most of them have already been apprehended by the authorities. On the streets, in their homes. You have to stop this nonsense." He leaned across the table and lowered his voice. "I can get you a lighter sentence. I promise you I can. Especially if you turn yourself in willingly."

Teo ignored the last statement. "How? How did you know who we are?"

Her father seemed annoyed by this irrelevant question. "Bartolo Aleppo contacted the arbiters and told them what was happening. Gave them the names of everyone because he realized that things had gone much too far. He will be pardoned because of his cooperation. If you ..."

She shook her head, quelling a wave of anger. So it was all the old man's fault. Teo remembered him arguing against rescuing Gabriele from prison. If that bastard hadn't betrayed them, Vanni and Patrizia would still be alive... She cleared her throat. "No."

"No? Please, Teodora, come to your senses! What will your mother say?"

Part of her wanted to succumb. Wanted to give in. But

nothing would ever be the same again. Her father would never trust her or forgive her. Her mother would never understand. And what about Teo herself? No, she would never be able to go on as if nothing had happened. Go to prison, serve a short sentence and be released into a city without a job, without her best friends, without her new friends who had fought with her. "No," she said again. "I'm sorry, but that's not good enough."

Emilio Terzi's face reddened. Underneath the concern for her, he was livid. "Teodora, listen to me very carefully," he said. "You betrayed the city. You betrayed me! How do you think people will see me after this? Betrayed by my own daughter..."

"No, you listen to me!" she replied, almost shouting. "You stood by and let them kill my best friend! They shot Vanni Alesi!"

The arbiters around them did not rush in to apologize, to tell her it was a mistake.

"They had no choice. He was armed, waving his gun at them," her father said.

Teo shook her head. She had to focus on the reason she was here. "Please listen to me. I know what you want."

He raised his eyebrows. "Well?"

"You want the problem to go away," she said, lowering her voice so only he could hear her. "You don't want a daughter on trial and in prison. You don't want to have dangerous rebels locked up somewhere, possibly spreading lies and rumours and giving other people any ideas. It would be better if you could go on like all this never happened." She searched his face. Had she gone too far? No, she had gone exactly far enough.

"And how," he said, "do you propose to fix all that?"

"I propose to disappear. With my friends downstairs and anybody already in custody who will go with us. I guarantee that we will go away and not cause you or the council or the city any more problems."

Her father opened his mouth to speak.

"All I need," she quickly continued, "is for you to let us go. That's all. We will leave Florence for good and never cause you any trouble."

He took a moment to let it sink in. "Are you mad?" he asked, clearly meaning it.

She thought, for a moment, that perhaps she was. Perhaps they all were. Then she remembered the sight of Vanni's dead body. She remembered the bruises and cuts on Gabriele's face. She remembered that Renn and Mender and Luca should not be part of all this. "It's the best way," she said. "It's the only way. Don't you see?"

They sat studying each other for a long moment. "You really mean this," he finally concluded.

"Yes. I do." She knew she would regret it later. She knew she would miss the safety of the domes, her job in R&R, her mother, and even her father too. But then she would remember, she hoped, why she'd done this. "Please. Let us go."

He shook his head, giving up and giving in. "I will see what I can do," he said. "I will call a meeting."

"Thank you," Teo said.

"And you will be there. Alone. I don't want to see any of the snakes nesting down there," Mr Terzi added.

Teo returned to the basement and told the others what had happened, and all there was left now was to wait for Teo to be summoned. They shared the provisions meant for Gabriele and what they could find in the backroom. And they drank. To mourn the dead, to celebrate what they had to think of as a victory, to calm themselves so they could get at least a little bit of sleep.

It was odd that after all that had happened, Teo trusted her father to convince the rest of the council to meet with her. She also trusted that he would twist the facts, make it seem like an exile they hadn't chosen themselves. The disobedient daughter who could be his political downfall might yet be turned into a victory. He had taken matters into his own hands, had seen there was no hope for redemption for the rebels, for his own child, and so he had suggested banishing them.

It was with this thought she slipped into a few uneasy hours of sleep on the floor next to Arsenio who had his arm around her, a gesture that would have annoyed her under different circumstances.

The arbiters came to take Teo with them before noon. The rest of the rebels were left where they were because no one seemed to know what else to do with them at the moment. The premises were still heavily guarded.

A gawking crowd formed a half circle around the ruined Mezzo Pieno. Teo was grateful to slip into the car waiting for her. She sat in the back seat, trying to take in the sights gliding past the window, trying hard to memorize everything and trying harder to keep herself composed and calm. She wanted to ask the arbiters if they were Vanni's murderers. She also wanted not to know.

The car stopped at city hall, and Teo was ushered out and into the building. Once her father had taken her here when she was a small girl. She had asked a lot of questions. Too many for him to make a habit of bringing her. Still, the sounds and smells of the place were familiar and oddly comforting.

Finally the arbiters left her side, but two sentries stayed nearby. She was in a large room before a sea of grave faces. She was standing, as if on trial, and the ruling body of Florence sat before her. The mayor was at the head of the long table, glaring down its length at her. Her father was somewhere in the middle. And to Teo's surprise, Mr Basile was present as well. These were her judge and jury. Old men in crisp suits in various shades of grey and blue. All with dismayed wrinkles around their mouths, and hands clasped firmly on the table.

She did not fit in here. She had slept in her clothes. She had cried and had not bathed or even combed her hair. She had built a barricade and she had a smudge of her dead friend's blood on her shirt. She looked nothing like her father now... Or perhaps she did. She had a feeling she was mirroring the contempt in his eyes and the tension in his jaw.

She also did not fit in Florence anymore. No, it did not fit her. She had outgrown it.

"Teodora Terzi," the mayor said. "You and your cohorts have betrayed the trust of Florence."

And then it began. The questioning was relentless. The accusations were many. Teo kept her answers short and to the point and never mentioned any names, although presumably they already knew who the rebels were, until Mr Basile asked her a question and she had to tell him what had happened to his wife. He excused himself and left the room after that.

Mr Terzi lived up to Teo's expectations. The idea of banning the rebels was his all of a sudden. Throwing out the bad elements in the city would be the best, easiest and least expensive solution to the problem. And he spoke well. Father and daughter, for once in political agreement, Teo thought.

Teo was escorted outside the room by one of the sentries to wait while the council discussed and voted. She hoped to get a moment to collect herself, to use the restroom maybe, but barely had the door closed before she found herself face to face with her own mother.

"Teodora!" Valentina Terzi all but screamed. She flung herself at Teo.

"Mom," Teo said, returning the embrace until one of the arbiters keeping watch pulled them apart.

"I'm sorry, Ma'am," the arbiter said, "but this woman is a dangerous criminal."

"Tell me it's all a misunderstanding," Mrs Terzi said to her daughter.

One thing was standing in front of the rulers of Florence. One thing was negotiating with her own father... But Teo felt utterly unprepared to face her mother. She was harder to despise. Teo took a deep breath. "It is not a misunderstanding," she said.

Emotions flickered across Mrs Terzi's face. Confusion, sadness, anger, disbelief. "No," she said, "Teodora. You couldn't possibly have betrayed your own father."

It was a word they all loved to throw in her face. "I belong to the group who worked with Gabriele De Felice," Teo said, clinging to the last shreds of self-control. "I am here to speak for us all."

"I can't believe it," her mother breathed, her face growing white. "How... Why..?"

Teo opened her mouth to reply, but the door opened again and a sentry told her it was time to go back inside.

"Can I have a moment? Please?" Teo asked.

"Miss Terzi," the arbiter who had hovered near them the whole time said in a warning tone.

Teo wanted to tell her mother that they planned on leaving the city. Wanted to offer her to come along, but she knew the answer, and she decided not to put any of them through that. "Mom... I am sorry. I really am," she managed.

And then she was led back inside the room, and somehow she was still able to stand and to listen and to speak although she felt raw and numb at the same time.

"Teodora Terzi," the mayor began, "we have reached a decision."

Teo's gaze met her father's. The movement was subtle, but she thought she saw him nod at her.

41:
Luca

Luca had gotten a few hours of sleep after helping himself to as much hard liquor as he could handle. He'd had a quiet, drunkenly honest chat with Renn before he fell asleep, but he only recalled bits of it afterwards. He was pretty sure he'd gone on about how sorry he was Renn had ended up in this shithole and probably some sappy stuff about Renn being his bestest friend in the whole world.

When Teo returned from the council with the verdict, everybody hugged, some cried with relief, and the next few hours were chaotic for those of the rebels who had families or friends they wanted to write a letter to or who begged to be allowed to go back to their homes and pack a few essentials. Luca, Renn and Mender obviously didn't have that sort of concerns. So Luca kept himself busy with a small task given to him by the doctor and sat drawing simple maps on scraps of paper.

Teo had done an amazing job, first by talking to her father and then by standing up to the whole damn council. Luca was impressed by the sort of badsassery she had shown when push came to shove. Or when quiet, pacifist rebellion came to guns blazing and friends getting killed. He hated to be cynical about it, but he was glad she had come through. Because who else would have become their leader after the old lady had offed herself? Not that Teo was Luca's leader. But he would have to work with her since he'd promised to help the lot of them out. Did she even realize everybody was going to consider her their boss now? Well, she'd figure it out soon enough.

In the afternoon, the rebels were marched through the city. There were twenty-two of them. This included the handful of people who had been apprehended on their way back from the bar the previous night and a few sympathizers or family members who joined the parade when the news reached them. There were even a couple of kids whose parents were affiliated with the rebel group.

It must have been quite a sight to the mob who gathered on street corners to gape at the aspiring exiles. Luca waved and shouted at them until a policeman threatened to punch out his teeth if he didn't shut up.

The people who had returned home only managed to toss what they found in their homes into bags. Clothes, food, bottled water. A few of them had carts loaded with the heaviest items. Those who had children tried to smile and convince their kids that they were moving to a real exciting place outside, but the majority of the rebels were grim and pale and looked like they were on their way to their own executions.

When they first talked about leaving, exhausted and on an adrenaline high and fucked up because of the rebels who'd died, the idea seemed perfect and simple. But in the light of the new day, everybody had to face the facts. It wasn't going to be easy. How did you even found a new society? The rebels were like children. Completely sheltered, without any knowledge of basic skills. Did any of them know how to build a house? How to grow vegetables? How to make a pair of shoes? Or hunt? They were definitely going to need Renn. And Luca. And, even though they had a real doctor, Mender too.

Teo and Arsenio were both carrying the bits of their previous lives they could bring with them, but more clothes and shoes than books and objects of sentimental value. They walked in front. Right behind them, Renn and Mender were carrying whatever they could which, in the case of Mender, was quite a lot. None of their belongings had been returned to them. That was a bit of a dick move since they really had done nothing wrong. Renn had strapped the broom handle to his back, which Luca found sad and hilarious and a little bit flattering.

Luca opted for bringing up the rear of the procession. This was not the liberation of Florence he had imagined. Not the one involving his army of artificials breaking down the wall and all that. Not him overthrowing the rule and taking back his city. Maybe one day that would become reality. But right now, this was as epic as it got. He could think of himself as their saviour, just a little bit, as he was taking the rebels to New Siena. That's what he called their new home in his head. They would probably give it their own name. Teotown or something self-righteous like Freedomville or Pacifist City.

They emerged from the last dome, the one near the gate in the wall, and Luca glanced back over his shoulder, just once. He had half a mind to flip off the audience in the street, but then he decided against it. It might not be a thing anymore, and besides, he didn't want to appear angry that he was being escorted out of the city. The authorities would spin their tale as they liked, pretend that he and the rebels were being kicked out, but he wanted the onlookers to remember him leaving willingly, happily.

The procession went through the gate, and they were at once in that strange conglomerate of old crap and ancient crap that made up the slums. Technically people out here lived under the same rule as the people on the other side of the wall, but from what Luca could tell, they did pretty much what they wanted.

Arsenio had told them that people would gather out here to see what the commotion was about when such a large group suddenly came through the gate. They would hope for work and be curious. He was right. Already the denizens of the slums were drawn to them like kids to an ice cream vendor.

Teo and Arsenio stopped when the guards and policemen were retreating, still watching them to make sure they were really leaving, but not in the mood to follow them all the way out of the slums. The rebels, Renn and Mender gathered around the two. Luca pulled out the folded up sheets of paper from his back pocket, ready to hand them out at Teo's cue.

"People of the outer city!" Teo shouted, drawing even more attention to them. "We are leaving the domes! We are leaving Florence for good!"

The crowd drew closer and denser.

"We are founding a new city," she continued. "One of peace and solidarity, where everyone is equal as long as they follow our simple laws, help building the new city, and do not harm their fellow citizens."

She had their full attention, that was for sure. Luca couldn't help grinning. She also had the attention of the guards still watching them from near the gate, bewildered. Probably unsure if they should intervene, but no one was doing anything, really.

"You may join us now or come to us later if you wish." Teo gestured to Luca at this point, and he held out one of the papers to the audience. "These are maps. They will lead you to our location. It will take around four or five days according to our estimate to walk there. Please spread the word. Thank you!"

One of the people in the crowd took the paper, hesitantly. Then Luca handed another to someone else, moving around the rebels to make sure everybody saw someone who got a map.

"Move it!" one of the guards behind them yelled. "Break it up!"

Teo turned. "What are you afraid of?" she shouted back.

Luca laughed. That was a brilliant last remark.

Around them, the crowd began to disperse. Some ran away from them, sprinting to spread the news maybe. Others stayed near them, discussing amongst themselves. Several people came up to them to ask questions which Teo, Arsenio, Clara or someone else answered to the best of their ability.

Luca heard at least four different people say they would think about it and a couple tell their sob story about part of their home collapsing because of the recent downpour and proclaim they wanted to go to this new place as soon as they had packed. The rebels, of course, couldn't wait.

And so the trek began, slowly and literally uphill on the way out of what had once been Florence.

42:
Renn

Renn studied the dwellers of the outer city as they approached the rebels, searching for faces he knew. But it was out of habit more than hope. He knew he would not find his Covey here and had resigned himself to that.

No... Not resigned. That was not quite right. The bond he had formed with these rebels who believed in equality and appeared to have a fair sense of loyalty to one another, was stronger than he would have imagined after only a few days. They had worked with Luca to rescue him and Mender. And he had fought beside them when it was no longer a matter of principles and beliefs but of sheer survival. Yes, he had lost a Covey, but perhaps, in a way, he had found a new.

"You ready to be their hiking instructor?" a voice cut through his thoughts. Luca had sidled up to him and was wearing a mischievous grin. Clearly, he had recovered from his bout of melancholy the previous night.

"Instructor?" Renn echoed.

"They have lived inside those overgrown snow globes since they were born," Luca said. "I bet they don't know how to walk like you walk."

Renn almost replied that neither did Luca probably, but that would only encourage some kind of rivalry. "They will learn," he said instead.

The inhabited areas of the valley were quickly left behind, and the rebels stopped when they reached the end of the slope. Renn heard gasps and someone's suppressed sobs. The sun was high in the sky, and only few clouds littered the vast blue above them. It was such a quiet day that the dust hardly moved. In front of them was an expanse of barren ground stretching all the way to the horizon with only a little vegetation and outlines of hills and abandoned towns here and there. Renn had seen landscapes like this innumerable times, but he understood the emotional outburst. After all, Luca was right. These people had never been outside their haven of domes.

"It's all right. We need to move on," Arsenio said, falling back on his training as an officer of the law to instill in the others a sense of security.

They had only just begun the trek south when Luca veered off to get a contraption with two wheels that he called a bike. He would leave them for a bit, he explained, to go back to his own home and return with his car so he could bring them useful items and maybe take the things they didn't need immediately to their destination. He donned a helmet and his bike roared to life and took him away from them at an uncanny speed.

It was not more than a few hours before Renn realized how right Luca was about these people's inability to walk. Renn didn't know it would be this bad because he had only traveled with other wanderers and Mender whose efficiency outdid any human being.

The city dwellers complained about blisters and pebbles in their shoes. About aching shoulders and backs. About hunger and thirst. Only Arsenio appeared to match the physical capabilities of a wanderer. Teo and Clara both did well, encouraging others to go on, despite the fact that they too were getting tired.

Mender took on the extra burden of carrying a child on nir shoulders. Renn was surprised the parents let nem. But perhaps they had been jolted so thoroughly out of their daily lives that the addition of a non-human creature was something they could take in their stride.

Renn's primary function, he discovered, was to keep an eye on everyone. Make sure no one got too far behind, pick up things they accidentally dropped. He watched Gabriele closest because the man was injured, and although the doctor hid whatever he felt behind a new pair of glasses, he was pale, and his mouth was drawn in a thin line.

Sooner than he liked, but not as soon as he had feared, Renn had to stride up to Teo. "We will take a break there," he said, pointing to a clump of trees and bushes not fifty paces away.

She nodded.

"Why?" asked Arsenio. "We can push on a little further."

"Yes," Renn agreed, "but the man Mender is walking beside will faint of exhaustion if we go on for much longer, and the doctor is in pain. The rest of them need a break too. It will save us time later if we rest now."

Arsenio seemed disappointed, and Renn thought he was about to argue when Teo cut in.

"Thank you, Renn," she said. "You are our expert. We follow your advice." She turned and raised her voice, "Listen, everybody! We will rest soon. Just a few more minutes. If anyone is having trouble, let the people around you know so they can help."

The break did the fragile stagnants good. As they continued, they were undoubtedly making better progress than they would have by pushing harder.

When they camped for the night and Moon's Road began to appear in the sky and murmurs were heard from groups around him, Renn could almost pretend that these were real wanderers. Teo sat close to him with her knees drawn up and her arms hugging her legs. Her head was tilted back.

"It's beautiful," she murmured.

When he glanced at her, Renn saw she was crying. There was nothing he could say that would comfort her, so he resigned himself to sitting with her until Mender returned from tending to minor injuries and complaints and ushered them both to get some sleep.

The next day, their own actions were beginning to weigh on the minds of the rebels. None of them made any move to turn back, but Renn could tell that the astonishment at the world outside the domes was giving way to hesitation and doubt.

Renn read the wind for signs of approaching storms, but it was remarkably still as though out of respect for these inexperienced travelers. He had to be the eyes and the ears of the group, leading them around areas that could be perilous, telling them to watch out for snakes when they sat down to rest, attempting to teach them the most important rules of survival.

Before noon, he caught sight of someone approaching from behind. It was not Luca, but another group of novice travelers, almost a dozen of the people from the outer city who had struggled to catch up and go with the rebels to their new home. They were greeted with reservation by some, but Teo made sure to welcome them and thank them for believing in the endeavor.

As Renn began to wonder if Luca really would come back, he heard the noise of the car in the distance. True to his word, Luca brought them a lot of water in handy containers and the food he called sandwiches.

Luca gestured for Teo and Renn to follow him a short distance away from the rest. "You know," he said, "I could take some of you in the car and drop you off in Siena. Obviously not all of you at once, but I could come back and pick up a few more. It wouldn't take long to get all of you."

Teo gazed at her people sitting on the ground around the car, drinking and eating. "Thank you," she said, "but no. That's not a good idea."

Luca cocked his head. "Why not? You could go first, get a head start."

Teo smiled. "I don't want special treatment."

"You're going to get that no matter what you want," Luca said. "You have to know that."

It was true. The others saw Teo as their leader. Even her close friend, Arsenio. They perceived Renn and Mender as apart from the majority of the group too, but not in terms of authority in other respects than Renn's expertise on the environment.

"Yes," said Teo. "I realize that. But it would be wrong of me to separate myself from the others. We need to stand together. Or walk together right now. It's hard for all of us, but... I think we need it."

"Okay," Luca said. "Your call. But I can still take stuff you don't need on the way so you don't have to drag it there."

"That would be a great help," Teo said after studying him for a moment, undoubtedly wondering if she could trust him.

"What about you?" Luca asked Renn with a grin. "Wanna go for a ride?"

"I'm a wanderer," Renn told him. "Not a... car rider." Besides, they needed him. Even with a map and a wayfinder, the city dwellers could very well get lost without him.

Luca laughed and shook his head. "Whatever. I'll see you

all later, then."

The trek would have taken Renn only a couple of days. As it were, the rebels took twice that amount of time.

Early in the morning of the fifth day, a jagged shape began to take form on the horizon. There was something about it, even abandoned to the elements for centuries, that stood out as manmade structures rather than whims of nature. Renn did not know what awaited them there. If any buildings were still intact enough to provide shelter. If wild animals had made the ruins their habitat. If it were possible to get to water or grow plants there.

But they had to trust Luca's judgment. And as their path brought the travelers closer to the ruins, Renn could tell the easternmost part of the city looked habitable.

"Renn," Teo said, walking up to him with as much briskness as she could muster, "is that..?"

Renn smiled. "Yes," he replied. "That is Siena."

"Siena," she repeated, then raised her voice to be heard by the others, "Everyone! Look!" She pointed and laughed. "That's our goal. That's Siena!"

Spontaneous applause and laughter broke out. Some hugged one another. Children were lifted up to better see. Gabriele caught Renn's attention and mouthed a silent thank you at him.

And then, in a softer voice again so that only the people around her could hear, Teo added, "That's our new home."

Epilogue:
Renn

"This will sting a bit," said Mender and pressed a wet piece of cloth against Renn's arm. "Are you all right?"

Renn nodded. Under normal circumstances, the old normal circumstances, he would have cleaned the scratch himself with nothing but boiled water. But he knew Mender still considered him nir responsibility, and so he had decided to go to the small infirmary where Mender and Gabriele took care of every injury and illness that befell the inhabitants of Siena.

The infirmary was one of the first things to be implemented in the settlement. It was a rough draft of a hospital, Gabriele said, but he said it with a smile and some pride that they had managed even this already.

Mender took one of the sizable plasters from the supplies provided by Luca and put it on the scratch and told Renn, unnecessarily, not to get any dirt into it.

"Thank you," Renn said, added a goodbye for both Mender and Gabriele and then held the door of the infirmary for one of the Sienans who had lived in the slums before. She was not ill as far as Renn knew, but a small bump was beginning to show on her midsection. Everybody treated her with a special kind of reverence because her baby would be the first child born in the new settlement.

Renn stood in the street for a moment, listening to the bustle of work on the eastern wall. They had barely been in Siena for two weeks, and already the ruins were beginning to look habitable. The first few nights had been spent huddled together, scared and overwhelmed with the enormous task ahead, but plans were laid, priorities were made and counsels were held. And now everybody had a function, combining their talents and efforts to make a town.

Renn turned away from the noise. He helped as much as he could with the practical aspects of rebuilding. He had no experience with being a stagnant or knowledge of the essential components of a settlement, but he could lift and carry and hammer as well as anyone else. Still, his unique ability was to know the land. It meant teaching others how to spot dangers of all kinds and what to do about them.

He went to the watchtower. It was a solid giant whose neighbors had long since fallen. Renn climbed the stairs, faster now that he had tested every single steps and watched for cracks and fractures in the structure and knew they would hold.

He avoided an indention in one step, weaved around a pile of rubble that he had not yet cleared and stepped over a smaller gathering of debris. Renn stepped through a doorless arch on the top floor onto a platform outside. He should really find the time to put a railing or barrier around it. It would be useful to have that safety in case he needed to be up here during nighttime, and if other people were to come up here. But for now, Renn knew this was his place. Not like the room in the house where he slept. There were people on the other side of the wall, people he greeted when leaving and entering the house, people who could at any time knock on the wall and ask permission to go through the opening to see him.

Up here, he was truly alone. Up here, he was an unobserved observer. No one interrupted his thoughts, and he could feel the raw wind on his face and read it, unhindered. He could see the wasteland stretching out on all sides of the settlement, and even far above the wilderness, he felt part of it.

He stepped closer to the edge. Peered over it and saw a group of people pulling and pushing a heavily laden cart full of materials from the ruins. He sat, carefully, with his feet dangling from the edge. The cart was approaching the wall they were building to shield the settlement from dust and sand blowing in from the east.

Renn wondered if his being here meant he had become a stagnant himself. He had never longed for one single place to call home, and he was not certain that was a word he would use to describe Siena.

Down below, the cart reached the place where the small figures were working. It looked effortless from a distance, but Renn knew the slabs being moved around and piled were heavy. He saw Teo on top of the wall, pointing and directing the movements of the others. She tossed a rope down, and someone on the ground, Arsenio, fastened it around the unhandy lump. Then he climbed the uneven wall to stand behind her, and together they pulled the rope to raise the slab.

A glint made Renn look up and beyond the settlement when something metallic caught the sunlight for a moment. There was a cloud moving in from the north, a solid shape at the front spearheading a trail of sand and dust as it sped across the ground. Renn smiled. He knew that sight. It was Luca in his car, coming to visit the settlement. He had kept his word to help out and had already made several trips between his own home and Siena. Teo, being the most knowledgeable of the rebels when it came to masheens, was learning to use various strange tools from him.

They had a well now, deep enough to provide water, but

more would need to be made if they were going to rely on them. A few of the settlers were experimenting with growing plants, and some were learning to hunt. Renn was helping with that. He had made a new staff and taught those who wanted to know how it could be used for multiple purposes. Hunting, fighting... And wandering, of course.

Well, Renn may not be wandering now, but even stagnant for the time being, he was doing what he had always done. He was in a place where he was needed, an essential part of a group. And it felt all right. No, he had a clear purpose here, and it felt more than all right. It felt quite good.

Renn stood up and backed away from the edge. The sky was clear, the air was calm. He began to make his way back down the watchtower. His purpose may change again someday, and when and if it did, he would go where life took him next. His staff was ready. But it could wait.

The Sienans were his Covey now.

Acknowledgements

If this book were a movie, you would now have reached the end credits. You can choose to leave right away or stay out of curiosity or respect of the people behind the work you just sat through. Or to see if there's going to be an Easter egg.

My gratitude to my family and friends for listening to me rant, cheering me on and supporting my writing endeavor. I am grateful to everyone at Spaceboy Books; in particular Nate Ragolia and Shaunn Grulkowski for giving my novel a loving home on board their awesome spaceship. Thank you to my beta-readers for providing valuable feedback and loving my characters; to my fellow writer Aden Ng for alerting me to the existence of e-ink monitors (without which this book may not yet exist); and to the Fish Climbing Trees community. Finally, a special meow-out to my feline gang without whom I would talk a lot more to myself and have a lot less fur on my clothes.

Luca dumped an armful of materials on the workbench. "Just put the rest... where ever," he told Alfredo.

The sentient put down the coils of wire he was carrying, almost pushing Luca's coffee mug off the table in the process. "You seem very excited," he noted.

Luca grinned. "You bet." He had studied the schematics carefully, and now he could practically see where every component would go. "Teo will love this. Renn too if he can wrap his nomad mind around it. This will be real good."

About the Author

Marie Howalt was born and raised in a small North European kingdom called Denmark and started writing stories at the age of 11 after sucking the local library dry of science fiction and fantasy. After graduating from the University of Copenhagen with a master's degree in English studies and religion, Marie worked as a translator between English and Danish for years before sustaining an injury that caused the condition PCS (Post Concussion Syndrome). Now Marie writes as much as physically possible. The stories are a lot longer and quite a bit more complex than the childhood scribbles, but they still take place in the far future, fantasy worlds or alternate realities.

When not writing, Marie enjoys being a cat perch, drawing, reading (it turned out that the suburban library did not have nearly all the books worth reading in the world) and arguing with and bribing imaginary people to tell their stories.

We Lost the Sky is Marie's first traditionally published novel. Several short stories have appeared in venues such as Every Day Fiction and Boned. Say hi on Twitter @mhowalt or drop by www.mhowalt.dk for more stories.

About the Publishing Team

Nate Ragolia was labeled as "weird" early in elementary school, and it stuck. He's a lifelong lover of science fiction, and a nerd/geek. In 2015 his first book, *There You Feel Free,* was published by 1888's Black Hill Press. He's also the author of *The Retroactivist*, published by Spaceboy Books. He founded and edits BONED, an online literary magazine, has created webcomics, and writes whenever he's not playing video games or petting dogs.

Shaunn Grulkowski has been compared to Warren Ellis and Phillip K. Dick and was once described as what a baby conceived by Kurt Vonnegut and Margaret Atwood would turn out to be. He's at least the fifth best Slavic-Latino-American sci-fi writer in the Baltimore metro area. He's the author of *Retcontinuum,* and the editor of *A Stalled Ox* and *The Goldfish,* all for 1888/Black Hill Press.

CPSIA information can be obtained
at www.ICGtesting.com
Printed in the USA
LVHW110839250219
608648LV00005B/107/P